Madman on a Drum

Madman on a Drum

DAVID HOUSEWRIGHT

ST. MARTIN'S MINOTAUR ⚞ NEW YORK

This is a work of fiction. All of the characters, organizations, and events portrayed in this novel are either products of the author's imagination or are used fictitiously.

www.minotaurbooks.com

Library of Congress Cataloging-in-Publication Data

Housewright, David, 1955–
    Madman on a drum / David Housewright—1st ed.
        p.   cm.
    ISBN-13: 978-0-312-37081-7
    ISBN-10: 0-312-37081-4
    1. McKenzie, Mac (Fictitious character)—Fiction.   2. Private investigators—Minnesota—Fiction.   3. Ex-police officers—Fiction.   4. Kidnapping—Fiction.
5. Minneapolis (Minn.)—Fiction.   6. Saint Paul (Minn.)—Fiction.   I. Title.

PS3558.O8668 M33 2008
813'. 54—dc22   2008003303

First Edition: May 2008

10   9   8   7   6   5   4   3   2   1

For Nicholas and Victoria, who wonder
that the "old man" has never dedicated a book to them,
but mostly for their mother, Renée

Acknowledgments

Special thanks to Bob Berkel, Jan Buchholz of the Minnesota Department of Corrections, Special Agent Michael G. Goergen of the Federal Bureau of Investigation (Ret.), Mark Hausauer, Keith Kahla, Douglas M. Mock, CFP, Alison J. Picard, Gary and Pat Shulze of Once Upon A Crime Bookstore in Minneapolis, John Seidel, Ben Sevier, and Renée Valois.

I also would like to express my debt to the crime writers who came before me, specifically Carroll John Daly, Dennis Lehane, and the late, great Mickey Spillane, to whom I pay homage in these pages (you'll know where).

We had no other thing to do,
    Save to wait for the sign to come:
So, like things of stone in a valley lone,
    Quiet we sat and dumb:
But each man's heart beat thick and quick,
    Like a madman on a drum!

With sudden shock the prison-clock
    Smote on the shivering air,
And from all the gaol rose up a wail
    Of impotent despair,
Like the sound that frightened marshes hear
    From some leper in his lair.

And as one sees most fearful things
    In the crystal of a dream,
We saw the greasy hempen rope
    Hooked to the blackened beam,
And heard the prayer the hangman's snare
    Strangled into a scream.

                    —from *The Ballad of Reading Gaol*
                                by Oscar Wilde

Madman on a Drum

I

They kidnapped Bobby Dunston's daughter in the middle of a bright September afternoon off a city street that I had traveled safely maybe a thousand times when I was a kid.

Victoria and her sister, Katie, had been walking the short four blocks from St. Mark's Elementary School to their home. They crossed Marshall Avenue at Prior, even though it took them out of their way, because their mother insisted that they cross at the lights, and followed the street north toward Merriam Park, where their father and I had once played baseball and hockey and where they now played softball, soccer, and basketball. They would have to cut across the park to reach their house on the other side, but they were short of that, just passing Longfellow Public Elementary School. There was a guy, a sixth grader like Victoria at Longfellow, and if Victoria dilly-dallied long enough sometimes she would accidentally be passing the school when it let out and he would come flying out the door and accidentally bump into her. The trick was managing the accident without being too obvious. Katie, after all, might only be in the fourth grade, but she wasn't stupid.

They were strolling past the school, Katie urging her sister to hurry up—"Why are you so slow?"—when a white van came to an abrupt stop behind them and a man dressed in white coveralls and wearing a black ski mask leapt out and grabbed Victoria.

Victoria kicked and squirmed and flailed her arms as the man lifted her off the sidewalk, and she screamed "Fire" as loud as she could and kept screaming it—except when she was screaming at Katie to run—because that was what her father taught her to scream if she was attacked, scream "Fire" because people were more apt to pay attention than if she called for help. Only there was no one to hear Victoria's cries as the man pulled her into the van and the door slammed shut and the van sped off.

Katie paused only long enough to memorize the van's license plate and began running. She ran along Prior until she reached a space in the Cyclone fence where people could enter the baseball field at Merriam Park. She sprinted across the diamond, ran up the hill that bordered left field, then down the other side, crossed Wilder, ran across the lawn and into her house. She ran all that way without pause. I doubt I could have done it.

Katie was screaming when she entered the house, screaming for her mother. Shelby took her by the shoulders attempting to calm her down, all the time trying to make sense of what the child was saying.

"They took her, they took her," Katie repeated.

Shelby told me later that she knew instantly what Katie meant but kept asking, "What, what?" anyway. It was as if her brain froze, she said. This went on until the phone rang.

The man on the other end told Shelby that he had her daughter. He told her that Victoria was safe. He told her not to worry, that he wasn't "some kinda pervert," that this was about money and Victoria would be returned safe and sound as long as Shelby did exactly what she was told. He told Shelby not to call the police. He told her that he had better not see an Amber Alert issued or hear about it on the news. He said he would call back later with additional instructions.

The instant he hung up, Shelby called the police. More specifically, she called Lieutenant Robert Dunston, head of the homicide unit of the St. Paul Police Department.

I was home at the time, finishing up some yard work in the back. Like Bobby Dunston, I was a St. Paul boy, born and bred. Unlike Bobby, I had moved to the suburbs. It had been an accident. I thought I was buying a house in St. Anthony Park, one of the city's tonier neighborhoods, just a short jog from the St. Paul campus of the University of Minnesota. It wasn't until after I made an offer that I discovered I was on the wrong side of Hoyt Avenue, that I had inadvertently moved to the suburbs, Falcon Heights to be precise. I shudder every time I think about it.

Still, there were advantages. Lower property taxes, for one. For another, I had a large, sprawling backyard. At the far end of the yard my father had built a pond complete with fountain amid the fir trees. I was wealthy by then—a tip had led me to an enterprising embezzler named Thomas Teachwell, and I quit the force to collect the substantial reward for his capture and the recovery of the loot. I told Dad we could hire men to build the pond. He wouldn't hear of it. He was that kind of guy. At about the time Dad died, a pair of mallards discovered the pond and took up residence. Soon after, five ducklings appeared. Eventually they all flew south for the winter, yet the following spring a few of them returned and started new nests. They've been coming and going ever since. I used to name the ducks, name them after friends, name them after the Dunstons—Bobby, Shelby, Katie, and Victoria—but over time I lost track of who was who.

While I was cutting grass, my neighbor Margot set up a lawn chair on her side of the pond and stretched out, catching the last of the summer's rays. She was wearing an emerald green one-piece swimsuit that demanded attention. 'Course, Margot dressed in a parka and snow boots would demand attention. She was half a decade older than I was but could pass for ten years younger. Dad had been sweet on her; she was the last woman to kiss him, on the lips, on his deathbed. I had always been grateful to her for that. After I finished with the lawn, I walked a couple of Summit Ales to her chair.

"When do you think the ducks will leave?" she asked.

"What is it? Early September? Probably in a month or so, but with the climate change . . ."

"Don't start that again."

Margot didn't believe in global warming.

"You look good," I said.

"True, so true." She took a sip of beer. "Too bad you never take advantage of it."

Margot had been pursuing me more or less seriously since I moved in, yet every time I thought how much fun it might be to let her catch me I'd see my father's face, see "the look" that he had used to keep me in line when I was a kid.

"I'm afraid I'll just disappoint you like all those husbands of yours," I said.

She gazed up at me, shielding her eyes from the sun with the flat of her hand.

"I've become much better at evaluating men since my third divorce," she said.

Neither of us believed that for a moment.

I left her after a few minutes and went into my house. I had just finished cleaning up when Bobby called and in a perfectly calm voice asked me to hurry over to his place. I thought he was inviting me to an early dinner.

The Dunstons lived in the house where Bobby grew up, a large, pre–World War II Colonial with a wraparound porch. He bought it from his parents when they retired to their lake home in Wisconsin. At first, Shelby wanted nothing to do with it. She told Bobby she was perfectly comfortable in the small six-room love nest in Highland Park that they had found just after they had been married. To me she confided that she was afraid that it would never be "her home," that the Dunstons who grew up there would always think of it as "their home" and her as little more than a caretaker. I thought that was a little over the top, until I learned that during the first few months after she and Bobby took possession, in-laws would come and go pretty much as they pleased, never calling ahead, never bothering to knock. Once Shelby returned from shopping to find her brother-in-law watching her TV, eating a sandwich, and complaining that there was no mustard. A sister-in-law took it upon herself to sort out the garden. This went on even after she forced Bobby to collect all of their keys.

Finally Shelby tore up her mother-in-law's carpet to reveal the hardwood floor beneath, ripped down the wood paneling her father-in-law had installed around the fireplace, tossed out all of the furniture, curtains, and drapes that she had inherited, repainted every room, and replaced the deck in back with a brick patio (actually, Bobby and I did that). Suddenly the Dunston clan was complaining that they didn't recognize the old homestead and over time began referring to it as "Shelby's Place." Even so, she still found it necessary to slap the hands of visitors—mine included—who succumbed to an almost primordial urge to look inside her refrigerator.

I knocked on the front door of Shelby's Place with my right hand. In my left I was holding a bottle of Piesporter; there was a two-liter bottle of orange pop for the girls tucked beneath my elbow. The door opened abruptly. A man I didn't know stared out at me. His arm was stretched across the opening from the door to the frame, blocking my path. There was a tenseness about him, part enthusiasm, part anxiety, that I've seen in guys about to throw a punch in a crowded bar.

"Who are you?" he said.

"I asked first," I told him.

He kept staring, his muscles set. He began to make me nervous.

"I'm McKenzie," I said. "I was invited."

"McKenzie," a voice called from inside.

The man dropped his arm and stepped back, allowing me to pass into the house. His expression did not change.

I cautiously stepped across the threshold. There was a short corridor that led to the dining room on the right and the living room on the left. Special Agent Brian Wilson of the Federal Bureau of Investigation stood at the end of the corridor. I had done favors for him in the past. If we weren't friends, we were at least friendly. He had been to my house, but I had never seen him at Bobby's. Bobby didn't like to bring work home with him.

"How are you doing, McKenzie?" Wilson said.

"I don't know, Harry. You tell me."

A nearly imperceptible smile tugged at Wilson's lips. I was the only person on the planet who called him Harry. I called him that because he reminded me of the character actor Harry Dean Stanton. He let me get away with it because I had once helped him bring down a gang of international gunrunners.

"It's bad," he said.

His words were like a slap in the face.

"How bad?" I said. "Shelby? The girls?"

He gestured with his head. I carefully set the bottles on the floor and followed him deeper into the house. A man was standing directly in front of the fireplace built into the far wall of the living room. He was leaning against the stone mantel with both hands and staring into the pit although there was no fire. He turned toward me as I approached.

"Mr. McKenzie," he said. "It was good of you to come." He extended his hand and I shook it. "I'm Special Agent Damian Honsa of the FBI." He didn't look like an FBI agent. He looked like a guy who had just broken par at the Midland Hills Country Club and decided to stop off for a few to celebrate. "I'm the case agent," he added for emphasis.

"Case agent for what? What's going on?"

I pivoted toward the dining room. Bobby Dunston was sitting at the table with two other men. One of them was the man who met me at the door; he had placed the wine and pop on the buffet behind him. There were four electronic machines on the table. One was a laptop. One was an enhanced radio system. The others were tape recorders. The larger one had several small speakers and was connected to the telephone. The smaller machine was used for playback. Bobby was sitting in front of it. He was wearing a pair of headphones and listening to a tape. The intensity in his eyes—it was like he was trying to melt the tape machine by staring at it. I moved toward him.

Honsa said, "Mr. McKenzie," to my back, and I shrugged it off.

Bobby caught movement in the corner of his eye and glanced up at me. There was an expression on his face—anger, sorrow, hate, fear . . . I couldn't identify the emotion, but I recognized the look. The thing about Bobby, when he's under a great deal of stress, he becomes extremely economical in both words and action. He never speaks ten words when three will do and never three words if a nod of his head or a hand gesture will suffice. Certainly he never raises his voice or indulges in emotional outbursts. It was as if he were hoarding energy to operate that imposing computer in his head.

He slipped off the headphones.

"I need you to listen to this," he said. "The voice is disguised, but I know I've heard it before."

"Tell me what's happening," I said.

Bobby didn't answer. Instead, he rewound the tape and yanked the headphone jack out of the machine. He pressed a button, and the machine's speaker came alive. I heard a phone ringing, and when it stopped ringing I heard Bobby's voice.

"Yes?" he said.

"Dunston?" The voice had an unnatural, robotlike quality.

"Yes."

"Victoria's fine, your daughter's fine, okay? I didn't hurt her. She keeps struggling against the ropes, and I tell her to quit it. Other than that there's not a mark on her. I'm telling you so you shouldn't worry, okay? We're not sexual deviants or anything like that, okay? As long as you do what you're told, as long as you don't call the Feds, the girl'll be fine."

I didn't hear the rest of the tape. There was a noise that blocked it out. I heard it not in my ears but in my head, my heart, my lungs. It hummed through my entire body, a siren then a bell then something else; it changed pitch and tone as it grew louder and louder. It forced me backward until I was hard against the dining room wall. I knocked a Dunston family photograph off its hook, and it slid to the floor between my body and the wall. Harry moved toward me, his arms outstretched like a spotter preparing to catch a gymnast before he falls. Without the wall to lean against, I probably would have fallen.

I didn't know what to think; didn't know how to think. Everything became mumbled and jumbled, and for a moment I felt like that guy on TV who locked himself inside a fishbowl for eight days, breathing out of a tube. Sensory deprivation, they call it. I felt disconnected from the world. Sight, sound, smell, taste, touch, gravity, and heat were lost to me. Even time became distorted. I could have been slumped against the wall for ten seconds or ten minutes.

I had not felt like that before. Not when my parents had died, not when I found dead bodies lying on the floor, not when people were shooting at me. I bent at the waist, my hands on my thighs, and stared at my shoes; my stomach felt hollow. Victoria was mine. I had adopted her the moment I first saw her at Midway Hospital. Bobby was showing her off while Shelby smiled brightly from the hospital bed. "My daughter," he had said. "My daughter." Like it was a benediction. "My daughter, too," I decided. I had no family, had no intention of building one. Bobby and Shelby had been my family. And now Victoria. Before the week was out I had made her my heir. Since I was now worth millions, she was worth millions. And her sister, Katie, too. And Shelby. And Bobby. Everything I had, anything I could borrow or steal was theirs.

"McKenzie."

Bobby's voice was low and firm. He must have been hanging on by his fingernails, only you wouldn't have known it to look at him. I had no idea what emotional strength it took for him to keep it together. The least I could do was make an effort.

"McKenzie."

There are five stages of grief. Somehow I had skipped directly to the fourth stage, depression. I had to get back to stage two—anger. Anger was good. Anger was motivation. You could work with anger.

"We're going to kill that sonuvabitch," I said. I glared at all four law enforcement officers in the room. None of them offered an argument.

I grabbed Harry's forearm and used him as a crutch to straighten up. The nausea was now in my throat. I forced it back down.

"You need to hear the entire tape," Bobby said.

"Tell me what happened first."

He did. When he finished it occurred to me that I hadn't seen any cars parked in front of Bobby's house when I drove up. Or anyone above the age of fourteen loitering at the park across the street.

"We have someone in the back and two agents in the front watching for anyone who might be watching the house," Harry assured me. "All the license plates are being checked, including those in the lot at the park. So far our biggest problem has been keeping the St. Paul Police Department away. Everyone wants to help."

"We're canvassing the neighborhood," Honsa said.

"You're what? You're not supposed to be here," I said.

"We're not," Honsa said. "McKenzie, we don't wear black suits and sunglasses. We don't drive Lincolns with U.S. government license plates. Canvassing around the abduction point is covert. It's discreet. We know what we're doing."

I nodded in agreement, more than a little embarrassed. TV and movies always got it wrong about cops and federal agents. There was very little animosity, jealousy, and distrust between them—probably because there were actually very few FBI agents who were arrogant, imperious, incompetent jerks with my-way-or-the-highway attitudes and even fewer rogue cops who played by their own rules. Especially these days with mutual need—and budget cuts—resulting in so many joint task forces. Maybe things were different in New York or Miami or Washington, D.C. In the Twin Cities everyone got along pretty well. Still, I watched a lot of TV and movies, and sometimes it was hard to shake off the fiction.

"The van was reported stolen two weeks ago," Honsa said in case I required more convincing. "We have a team on the owner. However, we do not consider him a suspect at this time. The description of the van and the license plate number are being circulated using hard messaging systems—MDT screens in squad cars, briefings during shift changes—so it won't be intercepted by someone's police scanner. Our own lines are encrypted, of course."

I nodded some more.

"Young Ms. Katherine did well getting us the plate—all the numbers were correct. Very smart, very brave." That last part was for Bobby.

"She blames herself for leaving Tory," he said.

"Where is she?" I asked.

"Upstairs with Shelby."

"May I see them?"

"Listen to the tape first."

They started it from the top.

"Yes?" Bobby said.

"Dunston?" asked the caller.

"Yes."

"Victoria's fine, your daughter's fine, okay? I didn't hurt her. She keeps struggling against the ropes, and I tell her to quit it. Other than that there's not a mark on her. I'm telling you so you shouldn't worry, okay? We're not sexual deviants or anything like that, okay? As long as you do what you're told, as long as you don't call the Feds, the girl'll be fine."

"I want to talk to her."

"Later."

"I want—"

"Shuddup and listen. Are you listening?"

"I'm listening."

"I don't want no shit from you, Bobby."

He knows Bobby, my inner voice informed me. *They have a relationship.*

"Your girl'll be fine long as you do what I say."

"What do you want?"

"Did you call the cops, call the Feds?"

"You told my wife not to."

"Yeah, your wife. We almost went for her but decided not to. Thought the temptation would be too much, know what I'm saying?"

"We." He said "we."

"No, I don't," Bobby said.

The caller chuckled. There was something about it. Despite the metallic sound, I knew I had heard the laugh before, only I couldn't place it.

"Want me to spell it out?" he asked.

"Go 'head."

More laughter.

"You ain't tryin' to draw this out, are you, Bobby? Tryin' to keep me on the phone longer than I need to be? Maybe you got some people workin' a trace. Feds maybe."

"I didn't call—"

"Yeah, sure. It don't matter none. If 'n you're tryin' for a trace,

know that I'm callin' on a stolen cell phone and I'm drivin' on the freeway in a stolen car and as soon as I'm done talkin' I'm throwin' the cell
out the window and ditchin' the car."

"What do you want?"

"Just so you know you ain't dealin' with no fool, okay?"

"Yes."

"First, you gotta know anything bad happens it's your kid tha's
gonna get hurt, okay?"

"I understand."

"Okay, then. Let's make it simple. You want your kid back, not a
scratch on her, it's gonna cost one million dollars. Simple."

"A million—I don't have a million dollars. I have no way of getting
a million dollars."

"Sure you do."

"How?"

"McKenzie."

"What?"

"Rushmore fuckin' McKenzie."

"McKenzie?"

"You ask 'im. Tight the way you guys are, I bet he gives it to you
without even battin' an eyelash."

"McKenzie isn't going to—"

"Ask 'im. I'll call back later."

The connection was broken. The agent sitting at the table flicked off
the tape machine.

"He's right about the cell phone," the agent said. "It belonged to a
woman who lives in Inver Grove Heights. She thought she had lost the
phone a week and a half ago, she doesn't know where. We were able to
triangulate the suspect's position using the cell provider's communica-
tions towers, but he was moving. He stopped moving the moment the
conversation ended. We found the cell in a ditch off Interstate 694 near
the intersection with Highway 65."

My hand went to my own cell phone attached to my belt. I unclipped it and activated it and searched for the number I wanted using the cell's memory. I found it easily and hit the call button. My financial adviser was named H. B. Sutton. She lived on a houseboat on the Minnesota side of the St. Croix River. Only she didn't answer. I glanced at my watch. It was nearly five. The markets had been closed for two hours. I left a message on her voice mail.

"This is McKenzie. I need cash right away. Call me. Call me right now. I don't care what time it is."

I recited my cell number and collapsed the phone. I wasn't trying to be Joe Cool; wasn't trying to impress anyone. I just didn't want Bobby to have to ask for the money. I wanted him to know that he didn't need to ask.

I slipped the cell into my pocket. Everyone in the room was watching me. I looked at Harry. "What do we do now?" I asked.

"We wait," Honsa said. "Time is on our side." He looked Bobby in the eye. His smile was reassuring. "It's about money."

Bobby nodded.

We were all thinking about Victoria. "We're not sexual deviants," the man had said, and we took him at his word. We had to. The alternative was too terrifying—a freak with a digital camera and a mailing list of pedophiles. We wanted Victoria to be scared when we found her. We wanted her to be angry. We'd even be happy if she was screaming bloody murder. Our greatest fear was that instead she'd have the quiet, vacant-eyed, used-up look of a child who had been drained of her humanity, who was irretrievably lost. I had seen that look in children before. So had Bobby Dunston.

I pointed at the tape machine. "He knows us," I said.

"Which means we know him," Bobby said.

"From where?"

"I don't know. The voice . . ."

"You can get a decent voice changer off the Internet for forty-nine ninety-nine," said the agent sitting at the table. I never did learn his name. "This sounds like an ST-JC-007, but that's just a guess." I was told later that he was a "tech agent." It was he who brought all the additional phone lines into Bobby's dining room. He was also the agent who dealt with the phone companies, setting up traps and traces.

"Even disguised there's something about it," Bobby said.

"The patterns, the way he uses words," I said.

"And the laugh."

"I know that laugh."

"We have people at the St. Paul PD pulling files," Harry said. "We're in the process of reviewing every case you two ever worked on."

"Don't bother," I said.

"We never worked together," Bobby said.

"Never?"

"No."

"Not once?"

"No."

"We were never even in the same district," I said. "When I was working out of Central, Bobby was in the Western District. When he was working Central, I was in the Eastern District. We never worked the same cases. We were never in on the same busts."

"Never?"

Bobby's voice was filled with frustration. "How many times do we have to say it?" he said.

Honsa stepped between Harry and Bobby. He was still smiling his reassuring smile. "The unsub knows you both from somewhere," he said.

The unidentified subject. *Yeah, think about him,* I told myself. *Don't think about Victoria. If you think about her*—everything had happened so fast since I entered the house that I hadn't had time to get my head around it. Not the way Shelby and Bobby had. That was probably for the best. If I thought about it—I was the one who taught Victoria how to keep her hands back while waiting for a pitch, taught her how to stride into the ball as she swung the bat . . .

I looked at the hardwood staircase leading upstairs.

"I'll be right back," I said.

I was surprised at how loudly the steps creaked under my weight. The house, so alive throughout my life, now felt silent and empty. You wouldn't think a four-foot-eleven girl could take up that much space, but she had. In Victoria's absence every sound, every conversation now reverberated like an echo in an abandoned mine.

I peeked into the room at the top of the stairs. Katie and Shelby were lying in Katie's bed. Katie was asleep in her mother's arms. Shelby gave me a head shake, warning me not to speak. I nodded in return. Big, prominent, solemn green eyes stared back at me. If I had not known her, I would never have guessed that those eyes had ever winked at anything, had ever smiled.

I continued down the corridor to Victoria's room. There were posters on the walls. Angelina Jolie as Lady Lara Croft in the Tomb Raider movies and Jennifer Garner as Elektra—both armed to the teeth, both kicking butt. The bed was unmade. Along with the floor, dresser, and chairs, it was littered with clothes, some washed, some unwashed. Books and magazines with the creased, smudged look of the heavily read were scattered among them. At least two dozen stuffed animals— dusty and neglected—were heaped in a mesh hammock stretched high across one corner of the bedroom. Beneath the hammock was a small desk stacked with books. Perched precariously on top of the books were a soccer ball, shin guards, and soccer cleats. Draped over the back of the desk chair was a nylon jersey, number 4. Four had been Bobby's number growing up and playing baseball and hockey. Katie wore number 3. That had been my number.

The room breathed uneasily. The window curtains moved in and flattened against the screen and then billowed out with the breeze. Outside the window, children danced on the hills of Merriam Park. They were probably wondering when Victoria and Katie were coming out to play. I could almost feel the passing of time as I watched the children, could hear the snap, snap, snap it made as each second was stretched to its limit.

"This, believe it or not, is Victoria's idea of clean," a voice said behind me. "I swear, that girl . . ."

Shelby closed her eyes and went far away without moving from where she stood just inside the doorway. When she returned, she smiled slightly and said, "It's always something, isn't it?"

"What is it they say? If you want to make God laugh, tell Him your plans."

She cautioned me with a wave of her finger. "I'm not a big fan of God right now," she said. "I pray and pray and nothing happens."

Shelby slowly sat down, her back against Victoria's dresser. I had often accused her of being the most beautiful woman I knew. Not today. Today she looked like she had been trampled in a stampede.

I found an empty spot on the floor and sat across from her, leaning against the wall beneath Angelina.

"Katie's asleep," Shelby said. "The FBI agent downstairs, what's his name?"

"Honsa?"

"He says that a wave of sleepiness can wash over you in a crisis. I don't know why that is, but I believe it. I'm exhausted."

"Maybe you should try to get some sleep."

"Sleep, perchance to dream. What dreams may come, do you think, McKenzie, if I should sleep?"

"They could give you something . . ."

"Do you think I'm going to take drugs to make me sleep, to make me feel better, when, when my daughter—"

"Shelby—"

"Why is this happening to us?" Her voice was jagged yet clear. "Why did they take my girl?"

"For the money."

"There are a lot of people with more money than we have. Just about everyone has more money than we have. So why us? Is it because of you, McKenzie? Did they kidnap my baby to get back at you, to get back at you through us? At first I thought it was Bobby, because he's a cop. Then I heard the voice on the tape. One million dollars, they asked for. Get it from McKenzie, they said."

"I know."

"I listen to what the kidnappers want and I ask, is it because of you, McKenzie? Because of your money? Because of the things you do, the favors you do for people? Is that why they took my daughter? Tell me."

The idea that I had brought all this down on the Dunston family had occurred to me when I listened to the voice on the tape recording and knew, like Bobby, that I had heard it before. I decided to ignore it. My father and a man named Mr. Mosley—after my mother died, they taught me by their example to keep my emotions to myself. So did eleven and a half years as a St. Paul cop. I was doing that now. Trying to, anyway. Especially the guilt. Only my emotions were dangerously close to the surface and I knew that it wouldn't take much to turn them loose and what good would that do? So *No, it isn't your fault*, my inner voice advised me and I went along with it.

To Shelby, I said, "Someone who knows Bobby and me, someone who knows we're friends—"

"Are you going to give us the money?"

"I'll give you everything I have, you know that."

Shelby gave a small shake of her head, bent over, her hands clasped together in her lap. When her head came up there were tears in her swollen eyes. An odd sound, a fusion of anguish and laughter, escaped her throat, and she placed both hands over her mouth and stared at me.

I wanted to comfort her, hold her in my arms. When I rose from the floor she held up a hand, stopping me.

My cell phone demanded attention.

While I answered it, Shelby left the room.

"H. B. Sutton," I said after reading the name off the caller ID.

"McKenzie."

Sutton's voice was cold and hard and humorless, and hearing it always made me want to turn up the furnace. Once you came to know her, Sutton was actually quite pleasant and interesting to be with, but penetrating the thick walls she built around herself took some effort. I blamed her flower-children parents for the walls. After I had known her for three years, Sutton confided to me what the H. B. stood for.

"Heavenly-love Bambi."

"You're kidding," I said.

"Try growing up with that name, going to school. Try looking for a job."

"Do you even speak to your parents?"

"Only during the summer solstice."

Speaking to her now, listening to her no-nonsense voice, gave me strength.

"What's this about needing money?" Sutton asked.

"I need a million dollars."

"Sure you do."

"I need it right away."

"McKenzie, we've had this discussion before. You have enough invested now where you don't need to spend your own money to buy something. You can borrow—"

"I need it in cash."

"Who the hell deals in cash?"

I explained.

"Wow," Sutton said.

"Will you help me?"

"Of course I will, except it's not as easy as it sounds. We can sell off your holdings right now, right this minute, using after-market networks. Except they have a three-day settlement. It would take three days before you could get your money. We can wait until the markets open tomorrow morning, but they demand a one-day settlement."

"I wouldn't be able to get my money until the day after tomorrow?"

"That's how it works."

"I can't wait that long, H. B. Give me something. Anything."

"We could margin the equity in your accounts and take out a loan. One million against five million in holdings, it shouldn't be a problem. I can start the paperwork right now."

"When would I get the money?"

"We can wire it to your money market or personal checking account by eleven tomorrow morning. Possibly sooner. I'll call you when the transaction is complete."

"Please and thank you," I said. "Put it in checking. Do you have my account number?"

"I do."

"I appreciate this, H. B."

"McKenzie, that little girl . . ."

"I know."

2

Shelby had returned to Katie's room. I watched her for a moment. She refused to acknowledge me. For the first time in my life I felt like an intruder in her home. I continued down the corridor.

The four FBI agents were gathered in a knot at the foot of the stairs. They spoke quietly. There was no laughing, no smiling; nor were there any grimaces or outbursts of anger. They were suppressing all of their emotions out of deference to Bobby and Shelby, and I admired them for it.

When I reached them, Honsa took me by the arm and led me into the kitchen. There was coffee brewing, and he filled two mugs. I took a sip from mine, put it down, and never touched it again. Honsa drank from his as if it were plasma, as if it were keeping him alive. His reassuring smile never left his lips, not for a moment. His eyes, on the other hand, worked me over like a collector appraising an antique armoire.

"You were once a police officer," he said. "You were pretty good. I checked. Agent Wilson, for one, thinks very highly of you. Seems you were helpful on a couple of difficult cases. Unofficially helpful."

I didn't know what to say to that, so I didn't say anything.

"Have you ever been involved in a kidnapping for ransom before?" Honsa asked.

"Not from the inside."

"What we have here"—he waved toward the dining room—"is a crisis negotiation team. We're here to aid in the investigation."

"I don't see much investigating being done."

Honsa regarded me for a moment over the brim of his coffee mug. "You're not supposed to," he said. "We always try to maintain separation from the family. If this were a bigger house, we'd take over a room and operate from there. Instead, we're operating off-site."

"Why?"

"You've been a cop. Do you want the family to hear our conversations? Do you want them to hear our brainstorming or case discussions? Do you want them to hear remarks that could be misinterpreted as disagreements or inexperience or, worse, as indifference?"

"Sorry," I said.

"We're not hiding anything, you know that. We'll keep the family informed about everything that's happening. We'll answer every question."

"Okay."

Honsa refreshed his mug with the coffeepot.

"That's only part of the job," he said. "Investigating. The other part is to work closely with the family of the victim. We establish what we call a NOC, a negotiation operations center. That's in the dining room. We support the family members throughout the ordeal, aid them in negotiating with the suspects, rehearse what they should say, what they shouldn't say, help them respond to threats and demands. We want to immerse ourselves into the family so we can assess family members."

"Assess family members?"

"Part of that is being able to glean information regarding the victim, regarding Victoria." Honsa pointed a finger at me. "You know the girl."

"All her life," I said. "It seems like all of my life, too."

"Tell me about her. Is she brave?"

"She'll take the last shot with the game on the line while playing basketball. Beyond that I don't know. Until now no one has asked her to be brave."

"It might help if we had an idea of how she's holding up."

"Wherever she is, she's afraid. She wants her mother. She wants her father."

"I appreciate that. Tell me how she would do locked in a dark closet. If they put tape over her eyes and mouth and chained her to a radiator."

"As best she can."

Honsa took a deep breath and closed his eyes. For a moment the reassuring smile disappeared, and he said, "I hate this. Lord God, I hate this. A little girl." He opened his eyes. "It could be worse. Much worse. Kidnapping for ransom is traumatic as all hell, but it's not—it's not what it could be. It's survivable. The child, the parents, they'll survive. Things won't be the same. They'll go through a period of transition. Who knows? They may even grow stronger. I've seen it before. But it's like beating cancer. In the back of your mind there's always the fear. Always. It doesn't go away. Still, they should be all right."

"If we get the girl back," I said.

"There is no 'if,'" Honsa said.

Good man, I thought but didn't say.

Honsa poured himself more coffee.

"The family members of a kidnap victim can easily be overwhelmed by it all," he said. "Mrs. Dunston—she's sad, angry, confused, distraught—she's showing every negative emotion you can name."

"Do you blame her?"

"Not even a little bit."

"She'll be all right."

"You think so?"

"When it's time for her to step up, she'll step up."

"You're sure?"

"Yes."

"Are you and Mrs. Dunston close?"

"Yes."

"How close?"

"If Shelby and Bobby should ever have a falling-out, I'd probably take her side."

Honsa raised an eyebrow at that. I didn't know what he was thinking, and I didn't ask.

"What about Lieutenant Dunston?" he said.

"What about him?"

"Some family members—they feel that they need to do something. Lieutenant Dunston is like that. He's acting like a cop. He wants to solve the case. That makes me nervous."

"Why?"

"He's wound so damn tight he could do anything. I have no idea how he's going to behave when we start negotiating with the kidnappers. He could go off."

"Don't worry about it."

"I am worried about it. I wish he would break down, release some of that tension, that anguish."

"Afterward, maybe. When it's all over. For now he'll do what he has to do. He won't make mistakes. He won't screw up."

"Is that a promise?"

"Yes, although when it's over and Victoria is safe and the kidnappers are in custody, you don't want him anywhere near the suspects."

"Or you, either."

"Goes without saying."

It occurred to me then that Agent Honsa was assessing me as he had the others. I wondered what he thought, but I didn't ask.

"How long have you and the Dunstons been friends?" he said.

"I met Shelby in college when she began dating Bobby. Bobby and I have known each other since the beginning of time. I don't think we've ever gone more than a couple of days without speaking to each other. This house—I practically grew up here alongside him. When my mother died, I was about the same age as Victoria, and Bobby's mom kind of adopted me, gave me hell same as Bobby when I behaved like a jerk, used to call my father when I did something she thought he should know about. Bobby and I grew up together, went to school together, played ball together, chased girls together, went to the police academy together. I was best man at his wedding and godfather to his girls."

"That's why you're giving him the money."

"Yep."

"He didn't even need to ask."

"Nope."

"The kidnapper knows that."

"It would seem so."

"How did you come into your money?"

I explained about Teachwell, how I discovered him biding his time in his ex-brother-in-law's cabin on Lower Red Lake in northern Minnesota, waiting for the chance to escape into Canada and eventually to Rio de Janeiro. I explained how I retired from the St. Paul Police Department in order to collect the reward that the insurance company had offered—approximately three million that my financial adviser had since grown to about five million. I didn't explain that I have often regretted my decision.

"I spoke to my money manager a few minutes ago," I said. "The million should be in my checking account by eleven tomorrow morning. Maybe sooner."

"Good," said Honsa. "Very good. We won't tell the kidnappers."

"No?"

"We'll need time to prepare the money. I'll brief Lieutenant Dunston on what to say when they call."

"What do you mean, 'prepare the money'?"

"The kidnappers will ask for old, unmarked bills, tens, twenties, fifties, maybe hundreds, with nonsequential serial numbers. It'll take time to get it together. It'll take even more time to photocopy it."

"You're going to photocopy it?"

"Of course we are. We have two objectives, Mr. McKenzie. First and foremost, we're going to get the girl back, alive and unharmed. Afterward, we're going to get the men who took her. We might be rough about it."

"Agent Honsa," I said, "you're starting to grow on me."

"Do you want to hear the tape again?" the tech agent asked.

"Yes," Bobby said.

"No," I said.

Bobby glared at me.

"I've heard that damn thing fifty times," I said. "Maybe the name will come to us if we stop listening for a while."

Bobby glared some more.

"You need a break," I said.

"I'll decide that."

Bobby readjusted the headphones over his ears. A moment later he pulled off the headphones and tossed them on the table. "I need a break," he said.

We went to the kitchen. Bobby rummaged through his refrigerator. I thought he might be looking for a beer. Instead, he removed a Pepsi, popped the top, and drank greedily.

"Remember Jolt?" he said. "It was pop that they claimed had 'all the sugar and twice the caffeine.'"

"I remember."

"I could use some Jolt right now. I wonder what happened to it."

"You can still get it," I told him. "You can buy it over the Internet in longneck bottles. Although, when you think about it, you can get the same amount of caffeine from regular coffee."

"Never been a coffee drinker."

"Nina likes to eat chocolate-covered coffee beans."

"That's another reason why I question the woman's judgment. That and the fact that she's been seeing you for, what, nearly two years now?"

"I like to think it's a tribute to her good taste."

"You know, sometimes I'll access the Department of Corrections Web site and study the Level Three sex offender information. I find out the exact location of every sex offender who lives within ten miles of here. I make the girls look at the mug shots. I tell them that if they ever see one of those guys . . . Shelby thinks I'm being overprotective."

"Yeah."

"I'm a cop. I carry a gun. I spend my days hunting down murderers and rapists and thieves and every other piece of trash you can think of, but I can't protect my own daughters."

"It's not your fault."

"Who said anything about fault? I know whose fault it is. The bastards who took Victoria, it's their fault. Still, a guy's supposed to protect his family, isn't he?"

"As best he can, yeah."

Bobby finished his soft drink and hammered the empty can against the kitchen counter.

"There are things that I can't do, that I can't get away with because I'm a cop," he said. "Do you know what I mean by things?"

"I know."

"You can do them."

"You mean after we find out who took Victoria. After we make sure she's safe."

"Yeah."

"Yeah," I said.

From the expression on his face, I knew Bobby would hold me to that promise.

Bobby and I returned to the tape recording. A few minutes later, Harry approached us with a handheld radio in his mitt.

"Gentlemen," he said, "we have something." He spoke to the tech agent. "Map."

"City or state?"

"City."

The tech agent spread the map over the table. Bobby and I and all four agents gathered around it.

"St. Paul PD found the van on Jackson Street near East Seventh," Harry said. It took him about ten seconds to locate the spot in the northeast corner of downtown St. Paul.

"That's the Badlands," I said.

Honsa wanted to know, "Badlands?"

"In the twenties and thirties, when St. Paul was a haven for gangsters"—I circled the area immediately east of the state capitol campus casually with my finger—"they called this the Badlands because of the speakeasies and the bootleggers and because it was home to some of the gangsters. Poor Irish, Jews, Mexicans, Italians, blacks—they all lived there, too, and mostly they got along but sometimes they didn't. There's not much left of it now. Mechanic Arts High School is gone, the synagogues—Sons of Moses, Sons of Abraham—the grocery stores, Diamond's Bar. It was carved up in the fifties and sixties when they built the freeways."

"How do you know these things?" Harry asked.

"It's my town."

"The immediate area where the car was found has been recently gentrified." Bobby's voice was low, and he spoke with a measured cadence. He used his finger as a pointer. "Along here they've constructed new condominiums and apartment buildings. On this corner is the Gopher Bar. It's a run-down joint with a lot of upper-class traffic mixing with the lowlifes. It serves the best chili dogs this side of Chicago."

"Why bring Chicago into it?" I asked just to break the tension. It didn't work. I was starting to worry about Bobby as much as Honsa was.

"The van was reported stolen two weeks ago," Bobby said. "We could canvass the bar and condos, asking if anyone had seen the driver, make it sound like a simple GTA. Patrolmen only. No plainclothes, no FBI. That should reduce suspicion if there is anyone to see."

"I agree," said Honsa. "In the meantime, we'll get a city wrecker to tow the van to our facilities and have a forensics team standing by."

"Go," Bobby said.

Honsa turned. He spoke into a handheld as he walked away. Bobby seemed to relax slightly. He was in control.

"Let me hear the tape again," he said.

I was sitting in a maroon wingback chair and staring at the empty fireplace when Shelby descended the stairs. She was carrying a number of large books under her arm. I stood as she crossed the floor. She didn't speak until she was within striking distance.

"I thought you had left," she said. Her voice didn't sound much different than Bobby's. Her fist was clenched, and for a moment I wondered what I would do if she punched me. Nothing, I decided.

"How's Kate?" Bobby asked. Shelby turned her head as he approached. "How's Katie holding up?" He wrapped his arm around Shelby's shoulder.

"Katie—she's asleep. She fell asleep."

"That's good."

"Yes."

"How are you?"

"Me?"

"How are you holding up?"

"I'm not."

Shelby rested her head against Bobby's chest, and he wrapped both of his arms around her and pulled her close.

"Bobby, what if—what if . . ."

"Shhhhh." He stroked her short blond hair. "It'll be all right, you'll see."

I turned away. I would have liked to do that, too, comfort Shelby. Only it wasn't my place. It never would be.

I returned to the dining room table and sat down. A few moments later Shelby and Bobby joined me, Bobby's arm still around her shoulder. Shelby set the books on the table. They were Bobby's—and my— high school and college yearbooks.

"You said before that you might know this—this person," she said. "Maybe these will help."

"Very good thinking," Bobby said and kissed her hair just above the ear.

"I'm going to get some coffee and go back upstairs. I want to be there if Katie wakes up. I don't want her to be frightened."

"Good idea," Bobby said. He kissed Shelby again, this time on the cheek.

Before she left, Shelby rested her hand oh so briefly on the point of my shoulder and gave me a gentle squeeze. I turned to look at her, but she was already walking away. I caught Honsa's eye as she passed him on her way to the kitchen. He was smiling the same reassuring smile he always smiled.

It was 6:05 by my watch when the phone rang. "Wait, wait," Honsa said, and we waited until the tech agent started his tape recorder and contacted the phone company. "All right," the agent said. Bobby answered the phone.

The disguised voice said, "Did you talk to McKenzie?"

"I spoke to him."

"And?"

"And what?"

"You stallin' me, Bobby? You got the Feds there? You tryin' to get a fix on my phone?"

"You said I couldn't trace your phone even if I wanted to."

"That's right. And guess what? I got a new phone, new car, new freeway."

"You're very clever."

"Cleverer than you know, Bobby. Ain't gonna fuck with me this time."

This time, my inner voice repeated.

Harry was standing next to me. He whispered in my ear. "This asshole sure talks a lot."

"He's overconfident," I said.

Harry shook his head. "Just the opposite."

"You got the money?" the kidnapper asked.

"Not yet," Bobby said into the speaker.

"Not yet?"

"It'll take some time."

"Fuckin' McKenzie came through, though, didn't he? Didn't he?"

"Yes."

The kidnapper seemed relieved. "Knew he would," he said. "Knew he would cough it up, McKenzie, fuck. Bet you didn't have to ask 'im twice, neither. Man do anything for a friend. Is he there? Bet he's there. Let me talk to him."

"You're talking to me."

"I talk to who I want. I'm makin' the rules here. You want me to prove it, Bobby? Huh? You want me to do somethin' to prove it?"

"No."

Honsa caught Bobby's eye and gestured with his head toward me. Bobby nodded and gave me the receiver.

"Who's calling, please?" I asked.

A laugh.

"Who's callin', please. Fuck, McKenzie, you are such a comedian."

"A joke a minute," I said.

"Yeah, you're a joke, all right."

"Okay, now you're just being mean."

"You wanna see mean? I'll show you mean on that little girl."

I didn't respond.

"You still there, McKenzie?"

"I'm here."

"Not so funny, now, are ya?"

"No."

"Ain't havin' no fun at all, are ya? You were a big one for havin' fun, too. Used to say it all the time. 'Let's have some fun, guys.'"

Bobby's eyes grew wide and an expression of complete astonishment transfixed his face. *He knows,* my inner voice told me. *He knows!*

"Times have changed," I said.

"Yes, they have. You got the money ready?"

Honsa held up a piece of notepaper on which he had written a single word: *Time.*

"It'll take a while," I said. "I have to wait until the markets open in the morning before I can liquidate my investments and transfer the proceeds into a money market account . . ."

"Liquidate some investments, transfer proceeds—you changed, man."

"Have I?"

"I remember when . . . Ahh, never mind."

"Maybe later," I said.

"Maybe never. I ain't your friend no more, McKenzie. You or Bobby."

"I was thinking that myself," I said aloud, even as my inner voice asked, *Is he daring us to guess who he is?*

"I want the money in cash," the kidnapper said. "Old bills. Nonsequential serial numbers. Twenty-five thousand twenties, ten thousand fifties. Got it?"

"It's going to take—"

"I don't care how long it takes. Only you gotta know, the longer it takes, the longer we keep the girl. Got it?"

"We" again.

"Got it."

He hung up.

I looked at the tech agent. He was holding both hands over the headphones covering his ears.

"We couldn't get a fix this time," he said. He squinted, opened his eyes, and removed the headphones. "He could have been using a Trac-Fone or some other prepaid cell phone that's not traceable."

"No, no, no." Bobby had the Central High School yearbook open and was furiously turning pages until he found the one he wanted in the seniors' gallery. "Yes."

He stabbed a photo hard with his finger.

I looked over his shoulder. First photo from the right, third from the top.

"You got him?" asked Honsa. "You know who he is?"

"Scottie Thomforde," Bobby said. "First we get Victoria back . . ."

"Later, we'll kill him," I said. "Later, we'll kill them all."

3

Agent Honsa pretended he didn't hear the threat. Instead, he propped his forearms on the back of a chair and leaned toward us, studying first me and then Bobby with cool professionalism. I guessed that he had heard threats like mine before and was deciding how seriously to take it.

"Who is Thomforde?" he said. "What is your relationship?"

"Scottie Thomforde is from the neighborhood," Bobby said. "He grew up six, seven blocks from here. Near Aldine. His mother still lives there."

"Aldine is a city park," I said. "Sometimes we had ball games up there. Scottie played with us."

"That's how I connected the dots," Bobby said. "When he said, 'Let's have some fun, guys.' We used to say that just before we went out onto the field. 'Let's have some fun out there.'"

"I used to say it," I said.

"What happened to him?" Honsa asked.

"He quit," I said.

"We were pretty tight for a while," said Bobby. "Except he quit playing sports in high school to take up music."

"He was a madman on the drums," I said. "Used to carry sticks with him and beat out a riff on anything, sidewalk, hood of a car, the tables at Burger Chef—drove the manager crazy. We used to call him 'Sticks' for a while. Scottie got a kick out of that, but the nickname never took."

"After a while, he just drifted away," Bobby said. "Without the game, we had nothing to keep us together, nothing to share, nothing to keep the friendship alive. We'd see him around; we were still friendly, only Scottie began spending most of his time with his musician friends. Some of them formed a band and played small gigs. High school dances. Played across the street once at Merriam Park. They were pretty good. Covered the Stones, Bob Seger, Journey, Elvis Costello."

"Drugs?" Honsa asked. I nearly laughed. Despite everything, he was still the Man. 'Course, I had been the Man once, too.

"Some grass, some hash, plenty of beer," I said. "No more than the rest of us."

"Hey, hey," said Bobby. "Watch it with that 'rest of us' stuff. I have a reputation to protect."

"If you can call it that," I said, and we both smiled.

For a moment he had forgotten about Victoria. For a moment he was the old Bobby. Only for a moment. His heart wrenched him back into the present, and he turned away from us, a pained expression on his face. The family photograph I had nudged off the wall earlier was still resting against the baseboard. He bent to retrieve it. "Tell him the rest," he said and returned the photograph to its hook, making sure it was perfectly straight.

I told Honsa and the other agents that we used to hang out at the Burger Chef on Marshall and Cleveland when we were kids. After we all started driving, it became less of a hangout than a gathering place. One day, during the summer before we started college, Bobby walked to Burger Chef to meet me—it was only a few blocks from here. Along the way he met Scottie and an older guy that Scottie played music with named Dale Fulbright. They were sitting on the curb on Marshall Avenue directly across the street from a mom-and-pop convenience store—it's not even there anymore. Bobby said, "Hi, guys. What's going on?" Scottie said, "Nothing." Fulbright said, "Leave us alone." So Bobby continued on to Burger Chef, bought a cherry cola, and sat in a corner booth waiting for me. I drove up a few minutes later in my father's car. "What do you want to do?" "I don't know, what do you want to do?" That was pretty much how we began all of our conversations back then. I saw Scottie and Fulbright on the curb, and I asked what that was all about. Bobby said, "Who knows?" We drove off. I don't remember where we went. It must not have been much fun, though, because we returned about an hour later to find cops all over the place, especially in front of the store. We wandered over, asked what was going on. We were told that a couple of guys armed with a .45 just robbed the place. A plainclothes cop asked, "Did you see anyone hanging around the store?" Bobby answered, "I saw Scottie Thomforde and Dale Fulbright sitting on the curb about an hour ago." The cops drove to Scottie's house and knocked on the door. Mrs. Thomforde answered. The cops said, "We would like to speak with your son." That was all it took. Scottie broke down, started crying, said he was sorry, said he had never done anything like that before, said it was all Fulbright's fault and asked to be forgiven. Fulbright, on the other hand—no one ever confused him with a scholar—answered his door with the .45 in his hand. He shot a cop. The cops shot him. They killed him. The cop he shot had only a flesh wound, but now everyone was angry and they couldn't take it out on Fulbright. So even though Scottie was two months shy of his eighteenth birthday, had no previous record, and had nothing to do with the shooting, the county attorney went for the max, aggravated robbery in the first, forty-eight months. Scottie served thirty-two. Ruined his life. Scottie blamed—

"Lieutenant Dunston," Honsa said.

"It never occurred to me that I was ratting out a friend," Bobby said. "Never entered my mind."

"It's what got us thinking about becoming cops," I said.

"You said Thomforde served thirty-two months," Honsa reminded me.

"Yes. Except that was just the beginning. He's been in and out of prison ever since."

"Why now? Why wait all these years to get revenge on Lieutenant Dunston?"

"I don't know."

"Why is he angry at you?"

"Up until now, I didn't know he was."

"McKenzie did him a favor once," Bobby said. "Before that first jolt in Stillwater, Scottie got into trouble and McKenzie helped him out."

"Something changed," Honsa said.

"Something," I said.

"I have his record," the tech agent said. All this time he had been working his laptop and I hadn't noticed.

Honsa peered at the computer screen. "Last crime—he did a short stretch in Stillwater for check forgery, been out for about six months, released to a halfway house . . ." Honsa's head came up from the laptop and fixed me with his eyes. His reassuring smile had been replaced with something hard. "It's in the Badlands."

"Let's go get him," Bobby said. He had his Glock out of its holster, and he was checking the load.

"Go where?" Harry said. "I doubt he's calling from the halfway house—"

"Let's go," Bobby insisted.

"Don't even think about it," Honsa said.

"I'm going to get my daughter back."

"You're not leaving this house."

"Don't try to stop me."

Honsa put himself between Bobby and the front door. "Think, Lieutenant Dunston, about what you're going to do," he said.

"I'm thinking about my daughter."

"So am I."

"Boys, boys, boys," chanted Harry.

"Shut the hell up, Wilson," Bobby said. He waved the Glock at him. *Bobby doesn't wave guns,* I told myself. Only this was a different Bobby than the one I knew. I wondered what I was going to do about it when Bobby reached for the doorknob and Honsa moved to intercept him.

Shelby called from the staircase. "Bobby." She was sitting on the steps and peering through the posts that supported the banister, holding one in each hand like the bars of a prison.

Bobby turned toward her.

"Listen to what he has to say," she said.

Honsa took his cue. "Scottie Thomforde isn't holding all the cards anymore," he said, "but he still holds the most important one. He has Victoria. That's what we have to think about now."

"I am thinking about her," Bobby said.

"No, you're not, Lieutenant Dunston. You're thinking about what you want to do to Thomforde."

Bobby stared hard at Honsa for a few beats, then dropped his eyes to the Glock in his hand. He slowly holstered it.

"Victoria comes first," Honsa said. "Thomforde, now that we know who he is, we can pick him up anytime. He's not going anywhere. Until we get Victoria back safe and sound, we want to give him the illusion of space. We want him to think that he's in control, that he has options. The last thing we want—the very last thing—is for him to panic, and if he sees us coming, he might do just that. Lieutenant Dunston, if Thomforde feels trapped, if he feels that his plans are shit and that everything is going against him, he's not going to blame us. Or himself. He's going to blame the girl."

"I understand," Bobby said.

"Do you?"

"Yes. But . . ."

"But what?"

"So many things can go wrong. You know that. My fault, your fault, his fault, nobody's fault—so many things can go wrong that we can't allow this opportunity to go by. If we can find him . . ."

"What about his partner?" Honsa asked. "We know Thomforde has at least one. He keeps saying 'we' and 'we're,' and then there's Katie's story. She said a man grabbed your daughter and carried her back to the van. Who was driving the van?"

"So Scottie has a partner—"

"What is he going to do if we arrest Thomforde?"

"We don't have to arrest him. We can surveil Scottie until he leads us to Victoria."

"How do we find him without tipping our hand?"

We all took a few moments to think about it. Harry supplied the answer. "Thomforde's parole officer."

4

Karen Studder had the face of a woman whose prettiness was five years behind her. She was built large on top, with a narrow waist and hips and tennis-player legs. Her skin was burnished bronze beneath her dark blue shirt and khaki skirt; apparently she was one of those women who are convinced they look better with a tan despite evidence that it's the sun that turns grapes into raisins. She would still be pretty if not for the sun.

"No," she said. "I don't know where Scott Thomforde is. I know where he's supposed to be."

"You don't keep track of your people?" Bobby said.

We were all standing in the space between Bobby's living room and dining room. Karen was on one side; we were all on the other. She must have felt outnumbered.

"I supervise about a hundred offenders," Karen said. "I don't follow each and every one of them around. I don't know the exact moment that they're in violation. When an offender is paroled to me, I'll look in on him twice a week, maybe three times if I want to see more. Later it's once every two weeks, sometimes once a month. I usually arrange for employers to contact me if an offender doesn't show up for work, but they're under no obligation. Thomforde is in a halfway house. If he doesn't come back from work, the supervisor will let me know. It's still early, though." Karen looked at her watch. "Not even six thirty."

"They don't have to be back in their hole by a specific time?" Bobby asked.

"They don't live in holes," Karen said. "They live in a limbo between prison and real life, and we cut them slack when there's slack to cut them. Scottie has been in compliance all the time I've had him. Never a problem. That earns him some leeway. We don't freak out if he's not back immediately after work. Maybe he stopped for coffee with his co-workers, maybe he's visiting his mother, maybe he's with a girl . . ."

Bobby took a photograph off the wall and thrust it into Karen's hands. "Maybe he's with a twelve-year-old girl," he said.

Karen studied Victoria's photograph and stole a quick look at Shelby, who was watching intently from her spot on the staircase. She shook her head. "No," she said. "No. There's nothing in his jacket that indicates sexual crimes."

"We don't think it's a sex crime," Honsa said. "It's a kidnapping for ransom."

Karen said she didn't believe it. Bobby told her she had better.

"What do you want from me?" she said.

"You're an officer of the court," Honsa reminded her.

"You want me to take Scottie into custody? I don't do that. If you want a warrant, I can call a judge. If we can't find a judge, I'll issue an apprehension and detention order myself. But I don't arrest people. I work for the Minnesota Department of Corrections. We have rules."

"Bend them," said Bobby.

"Bend them?"

"What do you do when an offender is in violation?" I asked.

"I call the police and have them execute the warrant."

"Ms. Studder," Honsa said. When he had her full attention, he said, "Calm yourself."

"I am calm."

"Ms. Studder, we do not wish to arrest Thomforde at this time. We merely wish, if possible, to learn his current location."

"You want me to find him?"

"Yes, Ms. Studder. After that, we'll take over."

"Just find him?"

"You do do that, don't you?" Bobby said. "You do look in on your parolees?"

"Yes," said Karen. "We call them home visits. Kind of like a pop in-spection. We look in on them at home, at work, find out who they're hanging with. I've done it twice with Scottie already."

"Then he won't be suspicious if you do it again," Bobby said. "I'll go with you."

"No," said Honsa. His voice was combative, his reassuring smile gone. "We've discussed this before. Just the sight of you might cause Thomforde to panic. We'll send one of my agents."

"You don't think seeing the FBI won't make Scottie freak?" Bobby said.

"I'm not going alone," said Karen.

This went on for about thirty seconds until Bobby conceded in a loud voice. "All right, send McKenzie."

Honsa shook his head.

"McKenzie knows the neighborhood," Bobby said. "He knows more people than Larry King. He'll know where to go when she"—he gestured with his thumb toward Karen—"runs out of ideas."

Honsa shook his head some more. "I don't think that's a good idea," he said. His voice was suddenly neutral. "The man who took your daughter knows McKenzie as well as he knows you. I am deeply con-cerned about what might happen if Thomforde saw him."

"Thomforde will be suspicious if anyone goes looking for him," Harry said. "But McKenzie"—Harry waved a finger—"isn't the cops. He isn't us. If Thomforde discovers that McKenzie is looking for him, he'll think it's just McKenzie and not law enforcement. He'll still believe that he has the upper hand. He'll still think he's in charge. He won't panic."

Honsa stared at Harry as if he were looking at a traitor. "No," he said.

"We need to send somebody," Harry said.

"I'm not going alone," Karen repeated.

"No," Honsa said.

"Yes," Shelby said. "Victoria is my daughter. I say yes."

We all turned toward her. She was still sitting on the staircase, still peering through the posts. I had forgotten that she was there.

"Mrs. Dunston, it's against my better judgment," Honsa said. "If Thomforde sees McKenzie coming . . ."

I felt the weight of Shelby's eyes fall on me.

"Hey, Scottie," I said.

Honsa pivoted toward me. I walked up to him, slipped my arm around his shoulder, hugged him close. "Scottie. Man, you gotta help me. For old time's sake. I know you don't like Bobby Dunston cuz of what happened. I don't blame you. But someone just took his kid. Someone kidnapped his little girl, man, and we can't tell the cops. You gotta help me. You've been around. You know people. You can ask questions, okay? You gotta help me find her. Will you help?"

Honsa stared at me for a moment as if I were drunk, dangling car keys in his face.

"I don't like this," he said.

You think I do? my inner voice replied.

"Be careful," Honsa said.

5

It was nearly 7:00 P.M. when we walked out of Shelby's Place, but daylight savings promised us at least another half hour of sun.

"I'll drive," I said and led Karen Studder to my Audi 225 TT coupe parked on the far side of Wilder. She circled the light silver sports car, examining it carefully before speaking to me across the roof while shielding her eyes against the setting sun.

"You're not a cop, are you?" she said.

"No."

"I didn't think so. This car—if you're a cop and you drive up to 367 Grove Street in this, Internal Affairs would be all over your ass."

I let the comment slide, although she was right. You don't see many luxury sports cars in the parking lot of the St. Paul Police Department. I thumbed my key chain to unlock the doors. When we were both safely inside the Audi, Karen said, "I wish I had a car like this. How much does a car like this cost?"

"Fifty thousand dollars."

"Well, maybe someday."

I snapped my seat belt into place, and Karen did the same.

"Where to?" I asked.

"You know, we could make this a lot easier on ourselves. Just make some phone calls, call the house, call Scottie's employers, call his mom . . ."

"Where to?"

Karen sighed significantly. "His job first," she said. "See if he's been in today. Then the halfway house."

I fired up the engine.

"Do you have a gun?" Karen asked.

"I can get one."

"No."

"Are you sure?"

"No guns."

"What if . . . ?"

"No guns," she repeated.

"You're the boss," I said.

"Since when?"

I pulled away from the curb. Bobby and Shelby were watching from the window as I drove off.

Karen directed me to I-94 and told me to take the Dale Street exit and hang a left. As I drove, she said, "If you're not a cop, what are you doing here? Why are you doing this?"

"Call it a favor for a friend."

"A favor?"

"Uh-huh."

"You do a lot of favors like this, McKenzie?"

"Depends on how you define 'a lot.'"

"Don't go all Bill Clinton on me," she said.

"Yes, I do a lot of favors for friends. Usually it's no big deal. Sometimes it involves an element of, ahh . . ."

"Danger?"

"Uncertainty."

"Why?"

"Because they can't do it for themselves and I can."

"They can't call the cops? They can't call——"

"An officer of the court?"

Karen hesitated for a beat and said, "I guess I had that coming."

"No, you didn't," I told her. "You're just trying to do your job, and your job has rules."

"I'm guessing that you're the guy who bends them."

"Something like that."

"Why?"

"I told you."

"You told me why people call you for favors. You didn't tell me why you do them."

"I used to be a cop. I quit when I became independently wealthy. Only the thing is, I liked being a cop. I liked helping people. I saw a lot of terrible things when I was in harness; I was forced to do some of those terrible things myself, yet I always slept well at night. When my head hit the pillow and I looked back on the day, no matter how crummy the day was, I could always say, 'The world's a little bit better place because of what I did.' It made me feel good; made me feel useful. I used to tell people that I liked being a cop so much that I would have done it even if they didn't pay me. Now they don't have to."

"So you help friends, even at the risk of your own life, because you think you're making the world a better place?"

"Sounds pretentious as all hell, doesn't it?"

"Depends on how you define 'as all hell.' "

I am embarrassed to admit I was glad to finally leave Shelby's home. It was as if a heavy, wet canvas tarp had been lifted from my shoulders. I felt like I could move again; I felt like I could breathe. When we hit the freeway, I powered down all the car windows and let the warm autumn air slap my face and ruffle my hair. Karen put her hand on the top of her head to keep her own hair from blowing about and gave me an impatient look. I ignored her. I understood Bobby's frustration at sitting helplessly in his home. Only I was out and about, now. I was being useful.

We took the Dale Street exit and turned north toward University Avenue. In the old days, this had been one of the most notorious intersections in St. Paul. When I first broke in with the cops, it embodied 20 percent of the city's adult businesses, including all of its sexually oriented bookstores and movie theaters. It also accounted for over 70 percent of its prostitution arrests. That made it a political issue. To appease voters, the city bought out the X-rated Faust Theater for $1.8 million, and it eventually was transformed into the Rondo Community Outreach Library. The gay-oriented Flick Theater was replaced by a shopping mall. R&R Books was bought for $600,000 to make room for a commercial development, and a strip joint called the Belmont Club became the Western District headquarters of the St. Paul Police Department. Now neighbors don't find as many condoms on their lawns and sidewalks as they used to, there are fewer sex acts performed by prostitutes and their johns on the street and in alleys, and girls going to school and young women coming from work aren't as likely to be propositioned. Still, I kind of miss the old neighborhood. It had color, and St. Paul was becoming less and less colorful as we went along.

I followed Karen's directions and pulled into the parking lot of a store that sold and mounted brand-name tires under the banner of a well-advertised national chain. Before we left the car, Karen told me that she would do all the talking. I told her to be careful not to use my name.

A bell chimed when we stepped into the store, and a black man dressed in a blue work shirt looked up at us from the paperwork he was reviewing. He set down a pen and put both hands on the chest-high counter in front of him. Years ago, I took a course that taught officers how to identify drug couriers by observing their facial expressions and body and eye movements. The man smiled when he first saw Karen. Then he raised his upper eyelids showing fear, thrust his jaw forward displaying anger, wrinkled his nose in a sign of disgust, and let the corners of his lips drop down portraying sadness—I've known very few people who could burn through so many emotions so quickly.

"Karen," he said and extended his hand.

"Mr. Cousin," she answered and shook the hand.

"Did one of my boys go astray?" he asked. The sadness in his voice matched his expression.

"One of your boys?" I said.

"Who are you?"

"He's with me," Karen told him. To me she said, "Mr. Cousin has been very good to us. He's given work to a lot of parolees over the years. A good man."

Cousin shrugged off the compliment. "Just trying to help them make it," he said.

"Why?" I asked.

Cousin studied me hard. "You're a cop," he said.

I didn't answer—if he wanted to believe that, it was fine with me.

Karen flicked her thumb in my direction. "He's observing," she said.

"Is he now?" Cousin wasn't satisfied with the answer, but he didn't press it.

"How many boys do you have?" I asked.

"Eight. All of my employees are on parole. I try to . . . Listen. A man, any man, who's been in the system, I don't care if he's guilty or not guilty, I don't care if he's been acquitted or exonerated or pardoned or what, I don't care if he's just a kid who screwed up or a repeat offender, if you've been in the system, you'll never be considered innocent again. You'll never be given the benefit of a doubt. People look at you; to them you'll always be a thief."

I had a feeling he was talking about himself, so I asked, "How long have you been out?"

"Twenty-three years, seven months, eighteen days." Cousin recited the numbers like a recovering alcoholic who knows the exact moment when he had his last drink. "It took me so long to get a decent job. I started applying when I was in stir. Back then you had to have a job or be assured of getting a job before you got parole. I only responded to the want ads that had a post office box. You don't make collect calls from Stillwater. I'd tell them they'd never have an employee who would work harder. 'So what?' they'd say. 'We'll be getting a thief.'

"The jobs I did get, they treated me like a leper, like I had a communicable disease. Or worse. One employer tried to blackmail me, said he was going to accuse me of stealing from the company unless I boosted some TVs for him. I turned him in. Nothing happened except that I had to get another job. When I became manager here, I figured I might be able to help some guys who were like me, guys who did stupid things when they were young and paid the price and now were trying to live it down. The owners, they didn't care as long as sales were solid, as long as there were no complaints about service. Now I am the owner."

"Good for you," I said, and I meant it, although I doubt it sounded that way.

"Why are you here?" Cousin asked.

"Scottie Thomforde," Karen said.

"What about him?"

"I want to talk to him."

"He's gone. His shift ended a couple hours ago."

"Was he here?"

"Yeah, he was here."

"For his entire shift?" I asked.

Cousin pressed his lips together, a sign of determination. Or anger. Or both. "What did Scottie do?" he asked.

"I don't know that he did anything," Karen said. Her voice was carefully neutral, as if she wanted Cousin to know her presence in his store wasn't personal. "I was conducting a home visit. He wasn't where he was supposed to be. You know how that makes me nervous."

"Karen, how many guys have gone through here over the years, excons looking for a chance? Got to be forty or fifty. I should add it up someday. Of those guys"—he held up four fingers—"that's how many violated. That's how many couldn't stay away from the bad thing."

"You're a shrewd judge of character," I said. Again, I was trying to be complimentary. Again, he took it differently.

"If I pull your tail off, will it grow back?" he asked.

Karen stepped between us. "About Scottie," she said.

Cousin was staring at me when he answered. "I gave Scottie the afternoon. He left at about one. You can check his time card if you want. He said he had some personal matters to deal with."

"What personal matters?" Karen said.

"I didn't ask. He didn't tell."

"Mr. Cousin, you know better than that."

"He's a good kid."

"Would any of your other employees know where he went?"

"You could ask."

We went through sound-resistant glass doors into the back. Three men were working on two cars. They were reluctant to help us for fear of jamming up their co-worker, or because they just didn't like us, or both. I doubt they would have spoken to us at all if not for the encouragement of Cousin. We didn't learn much except that Scottie tended to keep to himself—which was a lot different than the Scottie I used to know—and that he had the name "Sticks" stitched to the pocket of his work clothes. In between screeches from the air wrenches, a man with far too many tattoos that had nothing to do with art told us, "I saw him at Lehane's a couple weeks ago. It was a Saturday."

The name alone was enough to send a ripple of fear coursing through both Cousin and me. Lehane's was a bucket of blood on the East Side that the city had been threatening to close for years. More murders and assaults with deadly weapons have occurred in and around there than in any other one place in the Twin Cities.

"What the hell were you doing at Lehane's?" Cousin wanted to know.

"Do we need to spend more time discussing the terms of your release?" Karen asked.

The man shrugged and smiled the way some people do when they're caught doing something they shouldn't.

"I take it you're not the head of the local Mensa chapter," I said.

"What's Mensa?"

"Never mind."

"Shut up," Cousin told me.

I shut up.

"Scottie at Lehane's—was he with someone?" Karen asked.

The man grinned. "It's not the kind of place you go into alone," he said.

"Who was he with?"

"I don't know. White dude. Had some size to him, like he did a lot of weight lifting, body building."

"Did you get a name?"

"Not then, but the next day I said, 'Hey, Scottie, who was that woman I saw you with last night?' You know, tryin' to be funny. Scottie said, 'That was no woman. That was T-Man.'"

Cousin winced at the name.

"Something," I said.

Turned out that around the same time, Cousin had invited Scottie to lunch only Scottie begged off. "I have to see the T-Man," Scottie told him.

"T-Man?" Karen asked.

"Yes," Cousin said.

"Do you have any idea who that is?"

"No, but . . ."

"What?"

Cousin said, "Back in the old days, when Elliot Ness was chasing Al Capone, that's what they used to call agents of the Treasury Department. T-men."

"That went well," Karen said when we were back in the Audi. "Do you think you could have been any more condescending?"

"I thought I was the soul of restraint," I said.

"Is that what you call it. God, once a cop, always a cop."

"What's that supposed to mean?"

"You know, McKenzie, there's a big difference between being on parole and being on probation."

"Is there?"

"If a man is out on parole, it's because he did his time. He paid the price for his mistakes, and now he's trying to make the transition from prison life to real life. But you cops refuse to give him a break. You confuse him with offenders who are serving probation, offenders who were convicted of crimes but instead of being sent to prison or jail are slapped on the wrist and told to 'be good.' I don't blame you if you're pissed off at them.

"There are twenty times more criminals on probation than in prison. That's because ninety-six percent of the felony convictions in Minnesota are achieved through guilty pleas and seventy-eight percent of those convictions result in probation—so, yeah, I can understand why you might get frustrated, you and the cops. Especially since thirty percent of the criminals are going to keep on offending and not much bad is going to happen to them. They'll commit one offense and get probation and then commit another offense and get probation and then another and another. Seven out of ten offenders are going to go straight; they're going to learn their lesson. But that thirty percent—I knew one offender who was serving twenty-two probations simultaneously, all of them theft related. The judges who sentenced him just didn't believe the nature of his new offenses warranted time.

"That's just the way it is. In Minnesota only the most nefarious offenders go to prison. The state legislators set it up that way. Maybe they did it because it costs over forty thousand dollars to send an offender to prison for a year and only eighteen hundred to monitor an offender who's on probation. Maybe they're just too cheap to spend the money to build more prisons to make room for all those offenders. I don't know. I only know it's not my fault and it isn't the fault of my parolees, so cut it out. Okay?"

"Okay," I said, but only to maintain peace in the car, only to secure Karen's future cooperation. See, it wasn't an offender out on probation that kidnapped Victoria Dunston. It was one of her parolees. Besides, two out of five ex-cons return to prison for one reason or another, I don't care how well they behave while on parole, so what difference did it make?

At Karen's direction I hung a right on University and headed east. On the way I called Harry on my cell. Probably I should have called Special Agent Honsa since he was in charge, but I didn't know him. I told Harry that we hadn't learned much so far, only that Scottie Thomforde had had the entire afternoon free to kidnap Victoria.

"Something else," I said. "He has a friend called T-Man. I don't have anything more on him except that he apparently showed up a couple of weeks ago."

"About the time the white van was stolen," Harry said.

"He's big from weight lifting."

"Big enough to carry a squirming eighty-pound girl to a waiting van, I bet."

"Maybe he did his body building in prison."

"He wouldn't be the first."

6

As we drove toward the state capitol campus at the far end of University Avenue, it occurred to me that St. Paul was fast becoming the most boring city in America. Take the name. The city was originally called Pig's Eye Landing after its founder, Pierre "Pig's Eye" Parrant, a notorious and thoroughly likable fur trader turned moonshiner, until a French priest came along and decided it wasn't PC enough. That was just the beginning. St. Paul had always been a city of neighborhoods, and those neighborhoods used to have names with character: Beanville, Bohemian Flats, Frogtown, Swede's Hollow, Cornbread Valley, Oatmeal Hill, Shadow Falls. Sure, some people still use those names, old-timers mostly, only you'll rarely see them in official documents. That's because in 1975, St. Paul formed community councils in seventeen districts and charged them with creating new "neighborhoods" whose boundaries were influenced more by streets and traffic flow than by shared identity and communal history. These districts were given politically acceptable names like Como, Midway, Summit Hill, and Battle Creek. Take "the Bad-lands." That's a name now known to only a few people who actually grew up there and a handful of researchers at the Minnesota Historical Society. Yet at one time, the Badlands was as prosperous a neighborhood as any in St. Paul. 'Course, that was before Interstates 94 and 35E carved it into pieces and scattered them among the conservatively named Thomas-Dale, Downtown, and Dayton's Bluff districts.

Karen directed me northeast from the capitol to a residential street near the Gillette Children's Hospital, where we found a sprawling two-story building shaped like a horseshoe with a courtyard at the center. It had once been a hotel, considered quite swank, that was rumored to have been the last hideout of Dillinger accomplice Homer Van Meter before he was gunned down by cops at University and Marion Street, about half a mile away.

That's another thing. We used to have celebrity gangsters living in our midst. Now it's just punks. And politicians.

The hotel was old and worn, with crumbling sidewalks and a facade in dire need of paint. There was a low Cyclone fence surrounding it, and I wondered if the people living nearby and sending their kids to the Franklin Elementary School knew what it was used for.

We parked in back on broken asphalt and hard-packed earth, found an opening in the fence, and followed it around the outside of the building to the top of the horseshoe. There was a balcony that ran the length of the second floor, and we walked beneath it toward the office. An old man sat in a frayed lawn chair at the base of the horseshoe. He was staring at the courtyard beyond. It was overgrown with weeds and uncut grass that grew between the broken stones. In the center was an unused fountain. The floor of the fountain was cracked, and I doubted it could hold water. It was an altogether depressing sight, yet the old man found something there that made him smile nonetheless.

We stepped inside two glass doors and were greeted by a long, high, battle-scarred desk that was once the center of the hotel. It now served a lone receptionist. Karen greeted her as Agnes and asked if Roger Colfax was in. Agnes smiled as if they were old friends, and I wondered if Karen spent a lot of time here.

"Yeah, sure, you betcha," Agnes said, and I winced. Ever since the Coen brothers film came out, I am quick to tell outsiders that no one in Minnesota actually speaks with the vocabulary and accents of the characters in *Fargo*. Only to my embarrassment, I am reminded from time to time that some of us do.

Agnes led us to an office just off the reception area with badly chipped wood paneling, a threadbare carpet, and furniture that should have been replaced a decade ago. Cardboard boxes, used as file cabinets, were stacked on both sides of the desk. There was an ancient air conditioner sitting precariously on a windowsill; a stiff wind could probably topple it from its perch.

Agnes said, "Wouldja lookit who came for a visit, now."

Roger rose quickly from the desk. "Karen, it's always a pleasure to see you," he said, and from the way he said it, and the way his eyes swept over her body, I believed he was telling the truth. He took her hand and said, "You look wonderful, as usual."

Karen said, "Thank you, Roger."

Agnes smiled brightly, said "Okay, then," and left the office.

"You've done something to your hair," Roger said.

Karen glanced at me. "No. I just let it blow around in the wind a bit."

"Very becoming."

"You're too kind."

Roger led her to a chair without releasing her hand until she was safely seated. He went to his own chair and tucked himself behind his desk. His grin reminded me of one of those middle-aged guys who won something in high school and still display the trophy.

"You're not here on a social call, are you?" he said.

"I'm looking for Scottie Thomforde," she said. "Is he here?"

Roger shouted, "Agnes." Agnes poked her head into the office. "Has Scottie reported in yet?"

"Not yet," she said. She smiled benignly as though she expected him at any moment.

"Let me know when he does."

"You betcha."

"Tight ship you run here, pal," I said.

Roger looked at me like he was seeing me for the first time. "Do I know you?" he asked.

"He's with me," Karen said.

"Are you going to violate Scottie?" he said. "Why?" He was staring at me when he spoke, giving me the impression that he thought I was a cop serving a warrant. Neither Karen nor I corrected him.

"I don't know that I'm going to do that," Karen said.

"I've had no problems with him," Roger said. "He's gone to all the meetings. He's never missed a counseling session. He hasn't broken a rule."

"I did a spot check this afternoon. He left his job around one and hasn't been seen since. Do you know where he is?"

Roger leaned back in his chair; his left hand beat a monotonous rhythm on the desktop.

"Is that a yes or a no?" I said.

"He's on Huber," Roger said.

"What's that mean?"

"Work release program. It allows offenders to leave the house to go to work as long as they return to the house immediately afterward. Scottie's not supposed to leave his place of business, but you have to understand"—he was lecturing me now—"it's our job to help prepare offenders for the outside world. We can't do that solely within these walls. You can't teach offenders how to behave in a free society unless you give them some freedom."

Yeah, sure, my inner voice replied.

"I give Scottie thirty minutes' travel time by bus," Roger said, "plus an additional hour's grace in case he has to work overtime and doesn't have a chance to call in, before I become unduly anxious."

"When does Scottie get off work?"

"Five thirty."

"Add ninety minutes in case he wants to get his ashes hauled or score some blow—"

"That's unfair," said Karen.

"And Scottie should be under your personal supervision no later than 7:00 P.M. Right?"

"That is correct."

"What time is it now?"

Roger glanced at the clock on the wall behind me. "Seven forty-five," he said.

"Are you anxious yet?"

Roger slouched in his chair, disappointment etched across his face. He turned his head reluctantly and looked at Karen. "What do you want to do?" he asked.

"Nothing, for now," she said. "We don't know that he's in the wind. Maybe he was hit by a truck. You men"—she was looking at me now—"if you expect the worst, you'll usually find it."

Roger shrugged. "He could be at his mother's home. I've given him furloughs so he could spend the weekend there twice."

"When was the last time?" I asked.

"Two weeks ago."

I almost told him that Scottie was sighted at Lehane's two weeks ago, but let it slide.

"Could be at his mom's," Karen said. "We'll take a look."

"Do you want the address?" Roger asked.

"I know her," Karen said.

I almost said, "So do I," but caught myself.

I wanted to interview the other parolees in the house, find out who Scottie's friends were. I let that slide, too. I could hear Special Agent Honsa's voice in my ear telling me not to tip our hand, not to alert anyone that we were searching for Scottie who wouldn't normally learn about it through Karen's employment. Besides, there was plenty of time for interrogations once Victoria was returned and the FBI launched a full-scale investigation.

Karen and Roger walked side by side to the door. He had his hands clasped behind his back and she was gripping her bag, and they moved carefully as if they were afraid to bump into each other. When they reached the door, Karen rested her hand on Roger's arm and said, "This probably isn't as big a deal as it seems. As far as we know, Scottie hasn't done anything to cause any trouble for anyone, except for being tardy. We can't let that go unpunished."

"Of course not."

"It doesn't mean we have to violate him."

"No."

"When he returns, call me. Don't tell him that I was here. Just call me."

"I will."

"You have my cell number?"

"It's on speed dial," Roger said.

The warm smiles they flashed at each other were so fleeting that you had to be an unlicensed, semiprofessional private investigator with years of experience to notice them. It occurred to me then that Roger and Karen had once been lovers, perhaps still were, and didn't want anyone to know.

"One more thing," I said.

"What?" I could tell that Roger wanted me out the door and down the street.

"Do you have any offenders housed here that they call T-Man, or who might be referred to as T-Man?" I asked.

Roger thought about it for a few moments, then shook his head and said, "No."

I almost believed him.

.

It took about fifteen minutes to work our way through St. Paul back to the Merriam Park neighborhood. Karen spoke only twice during the trip. The first time was when we left the parking lot and she offered directions to Scottie Thomforde's mother's home. I told her I knew the way. She seemed surprised by that. The second time was ten minutes later when I hung a right off Snelling Avenue onto Marshall, heading west. "How do you know where Scottie Thomforde's mother lives?" she asked. She had been nursing the question all that time.

"I grew up with him," I said.

"You were friends?"

"Yeah."

"You were friends with Scottie?"

"Yeah."

Karen seemed to have a difficult time wrapping her head around the idea. "Were you good friends?" she asked.

"For a while we were."

"Why aren't you friends anymore?"

"He kidnapped Victoria Dunston."

"We don't know that for sure."

"If you say so." I wasn't in the mood to argue with her.

"I don't believe you and Scottie were good friends," she said.

"Good enough that I testified on his behalf when he killed a guy."

"Scottie never killed anyone."

"Yes, he did. Right"—I pulled the Audi to the curb between Herschel and Wheeler and pointed across the street—"there."

Karen looked at the spot I had indicated and back at me. "I don't believe it," she said.

"We were sixteen. I was driving my father's car, and he was driving his mother's car. We had driven to the Wabasha Caves down by the river one night and had drunk some beer, me and Scottie and Bobby Dunston and six or seven others. When we were driving home, Scottie took a hard right turn off Fairview onto Marshall. An old man dressed all in black was crossing the street in front of us. Scottie didn't see him until he hit him. Guy flew over his hood, over his car. I was driving behind Scottie. I almost hit the man myself. We stopped. Someone, Bobby, I think, ran to one of the houses"—I gestured toward the homes on the far side of the street—"and called the police.

"This was before Mothers Against Drunk Driving, before driving while intoxicated was considered such a horrendous crime. This was before the term 'designated driver' even entered our collective vocabulary. So when they came to investigate, the cops didn't bother asking Scottie to blow into a PBT to see if his breath could change the color of the crystals. There was no blood test. Instead, they asked him to touch his nose and walk in a straight line, and Scottie did. Then they measured his skid marks and decided that he hadn't been speeding. The next day an investigator from the county attorney's office questioned me because I had been driving the other car, because I had seen everything. He asked if Scottie had been drinking. I said no. I said the other kids had been drinking but Scottie and I hadn't because our parents would have killed us if they caught us drinking and driving. That was good enough for the investigator. They let Scottie go. No charges were ever filed."

"You lied," Karen said.

"Yes, I did."

"To protect Scottie."

"To protect myself. My father was sitting there when the investigator questioned me. If I had said Scottie was drinking, I would have had to admit that I had been drinking, too, and I was far too frightened of my father to do it. It was an act of cowardice that's haunted me on and off ever since. But at the time, Scottie thanked me profusely. So did his mother. Now he's kidnapped a young girl that I love from her mother and father that I love and has demanded one million dollars of my money for her safe return."

"That's why you're so angry?"

"That's it."

"I understand," she said. I doubted that she did.

I checked the traffic, pulled onto Marshall, and hung a right at the next intersection. A couple of turns later I was parked in front of the house where Scottie Thomforde had once lived.

"I forgive you, McKenzie," Karen said.

"Forgive me? For what?"

"For being rude to my friends, Mr. Cousin and Roger. For being rude to me."

That slowed me down. There was no question, I had been rude, even insulting. Still, I figured I had just cause. Besides, who asked her?

"Gee, thanks a lot," I said.

"I forgive you for being sarcastic, too."

We never reached the entrance. Tommy Thomforde intercepted us before we were halfway up the walk, bursting through the front door, crossing his arms over his chest, and demanding to know, "What did Scottie do now?"

"Good evening, Mr. Thomforde," Karen said.

They had recognized each other by the light of the streetlamps.

"You wouldn't be here if Scottie wasn't in trouble," Tommy insisted.

"What?" I said. "No polite greeting? No chitchat?"

Tommy glared over Karen's shoulder. His expression quickly changed to surprise and then to genuine pleasure.

"McKenzie?" he said. "Rushmore McKenzie? It is you. How are you, man?"

Tommy brushed past Karen, took my hand, and we hugged, our hands clasped between us so onlookers wouldn't think we were gay. I could feel hard muscles through his shirt. "Man, it's been years. How you doin'?"

"Pretty fair, Tom. Pretty fair. How 'bout yourself."

"Same old, same old."

"How's your mom?"

"Feisty, as usual. What are you doin' here, McKenzie?"

I flung a glance at Karen. "We're looking for your brother," I said.

"I am right. He is in trouble, again."

"Not necessarily," Karen said. "It's just that we don't know where he is. We were hoping he was here."

Tommy shook his head. "He's not here. Hasn't been here since— the last time I saw Scottie was two weeks ago when he spent the weekend. Mom invited the entire family over. Made a big dinner. Except Scottie was hungover; he was sick from going out and drinking the night before. So much for the family reunion. I probably shouldn't have told you that."

"Has he spoken to your mom recently?" I asked.

"He calls her a couple times a week. Always has, even when he was in prison. Scottie was always a mama's boy."

"Can we talk to your mom?"

"She's not here. She went over to the Silver Bucket for the meat raffle."

"Meat raffle?" Karen said.

"Yeah. She goes there at least once a month. Meets her old friends, drinks some beer, buys raffle tickets to win steaks, chops, chicken. Last time she won ten pounds of hamburger." Tommy smiled at me. "What can I say? You can take the girl out of the East Side, but you can't take the East Side out of the girl."

"I've always liked your mom," I said.

"She's always liked you, McKenzie." Tommy looked up and down and around, everywhere but my face, as if he were afraid of his own question. "I know why Studder is here. This isn't the first time she's checked up on Scottie. Man, why are you here? What did Scottie do that makes you come here?"

"No, no," I said and gave his shoulder a playful shake. "It's nothing like that. I was looking for Scottie because I need to ask him for a favor. I just ran into her"—I gestured toward Karen—"and we decided to look together."

"A favor? What kind of favor?"

Be careful, my inner voice said.

"I'd rather not say," I answered. "But your brother, he knows people, people who might be able to help me with a problem I have. It involves—well, if you hear from him, just say I need a favor and ask him to call me."

"I'll do that," Tommy said.

"Are you expecting to hear from Scottie?" Karen asked.

"No," Tommy said.

"Mind if we take a look around?"

Tommy's eyes flashed at the insult. "I said he's not here. I said I haven't seen my brother in two weeks. Do you think I'm lying?"

"I'm required—"

"Hey, you do what think you have to." Tommy pivoted toward me. "If you want to search the house, go 'head."

I gave him my best, most sincere shrug. "I'm good," I said.

"I need to look," said Karen.

I gave my head a little shake and spoke quietly to Tommy. "Officer of the court. What can you do?"

"Nothing," Tommy said. He waved at Karen. "Go 'head. Knock yourself out. I'll wait here."

While we waited, Tommy told me that he moved back home a few months ago after his divorce. "Bitch took my kids, my house, my car, all my savings, and now I have to pay alimony and child support on top of it."

"That sucks," I said just to be friendly.

"Tell me about it. You ever get married?"

"No."

"Well, don't. Not unless you're absolutely, positively, rock-solid sure about the girl because, man, the only thing worse than a bad marriage is a bad divorce, I'm here to tell you."

"Good advice. I'll keep that in mind."

A few moments later, Karen emerged from the house and joined us on the sidewalk. "I'm sorry about that, Mr. Thomforde," she said. "It's just something I have to do."

"It's okay," Tommy said.

"I noticed the drum kit set up in one of the bedrooms."

"My mom's idea," Tommy said. "She set it up for when Scottie came to visit. Said it would make him feel more at home. One thing about my brother, all the other shit aside"—he was looking at me again—"the sonuvabitch sure can play the drums."

We thanked him and were making our way back to the Audi when Tommy called to us. "Hey, McKenzie? Did you try Joley?"

"Are they back together?"

"I don't know. Scottie called her when he was here. They were on the phone for hours."

"You're kidding me."

"Talk about your bad relationships."

We were pulling away from the curb before Karen asked, "Who's Joley?"

"A woman Scottie was once involved with," I said. "I'm surprised you weren't informed about her."

"Why would I be?"

"She had to take out a restraining order to keep him from stalking her."

Her mouth hung open for a moment, and then she closed it with a snap. I could hear her teeth grinding behind her lips. After a moment, she said, "I should have been told that." Later she hissed, "Bureaucracies," as if the word were an obscenity.

Who was I to disagree?

7

Jolene Waddell was one of those girls who peaked at age seventeen, going from high school midwinter queen to dowdy middle-age in about a summer. Back in school, she was perky with a long-jumper's body and legs. But the legs were the first to go, then the waist, then the rest of her. Only her voice remained unchanged. You'd hear that hot and humid voice over the phone and you knew—knew!—that she had the goods.

We met her under the porch light of her small bungalow in Highland Park, not far from where the Ford plant used to be. It had been a long time since I'd seen her, and when I hugged her my arms easily made it around her torso.

"You've lost weight," I said.

"Thirty-five pounds since New Year's," she said. "Another thirty to go."

"You're lookin' good."

She smiled like a woman who hadn't received a compliment in a long while, yet still remembered how it felt.

"No, I'm not," Joley said. "I will be, though. I'm trying to get to my high school weight plus ten. That's fair, isn't it, McKenzie? Weighing ten pounds more than you did in high school."

"More than fair," I said.

"Our high school reunion is coming up, you know."

"Is it?"

Joley nodded and smiled. "Still, a girl can't hope to look like she did in high school."

"I don't know, Joley. You look pretty damn good to me."

She smiled some more. She had a lot of lines around her mouth and wrinkles at her brow, and her hair had gone through so many dye jobs it had forgotten its original color and had settled on crayon brown. Her eyes—I had known her when they sparkled with blue. They had since deepened to gray, yet they remained clear and luminous.

"Oh, McKenzie. You were always so sweet." Looking over my shoulder, she asked, "Who are you?"

"I apologize," I said. "I should have introduced you. Jolene Waddell, this is Karen Studder."

"Ms. Waddell," said Karen and extended her hand. Joley shook it carefully.

"Karen is Scottie Thomforde's parole officer."

"Oh," said Joley. She released Karen's hand as if it were suddenly radioactive.

"Have you seen Scottie?" Karen asked.

"Seen him? No."

"You've heard from him," I said.

Joley hesitated for a moment, then said, "Come in." She held the door open for us. I could almost feel her thinking as I moved past her into the house.

I was surprised by how clean her home was. Her living room was furnished with matching sofa and chairs that looked as if they had never been used and a rich blue carpet that looked as if it had never been trod upon. The prints on all four walls were enclosed in identical silver frames and mounted at the exact same height. The novels in her bookcase were arranged in alphabetical order, and so were the CDs on the shelf next to the CD player. There was no dust, no dirt anywhere, and it made me feel uncomfortable, made me feel like I was soiling her house just by being there. 'Course, I've lived like a bachelor since I was twelve years old. My idea of cleanliness is stacking plates in the dishwasher.

The only thing that seemed unplanned was the well-used blue three-ring binder bustling with ruffled white paper that lay opened on the gleaming coffee table and the cell phone that was next to it. The phone rang while Joley was suggesting that we take a seat. She picked up the phone, wrote down a number that she read off the display onto one of the pages in the binder, and returned the phone to the table.

"We're not interrupting, are we?" I said.

"No," Joley replied. "He'll call back."

"Who?" said Karen. I was sure she thought the call came from Scottie.

"A client," Joley answered.

"Joley's a telemarketer," I said.

She smiled at me and said, "That's a diplomatic way to put it."

Karen seemed confused, and I would have been happy to let her stay that way. Joley wasn't.

"I'm a phone-sex operator," she said.

Joley had acted in a few plays in high school—played Marian the Librarian in *The Music Man* and Emily in *Our Town*. Afterward, she did some voice work in radio spots and videos, only not enough to pay her bills until she met a woman who put her to work selling a variety of products over the phone. Joley discovered that she had a knack for it, that she was particularly good at drawing men out in conversation. Her employer noticed, too, and asked Joley if she would be interested in a different kind of telemarketing, something that would utilize her acting skills.

Now the phone rings and she answers, "I'm blond, and I have big brown eyes, and I'm about a thirty-six double D." The men who call believe her, too. Listening to that sweltering voice, they believe her to the tune of about two-ninety-eight a minute, not counting the forty-dollar panties that she has never worn or the twenty-five-dollar photographs of a blond brown-eyed woman she has never met that she also sells. On a good day, for five hours' work she'll gross as much as eight hundred bucks that she splits with her employer. Add that to what she makes for her legitimate voice work and Joley does very well for herself.

"It's not like it's prostitution," she told Karen. "It's not unsafe sex. It's not stripping. It's just words, just talking dirty on the phone. A lot of the men who call, they're lonely. They're calling cuz they need someone to talk to. What my callers are really buying—it isn't sex. What they're really buying is a few minutes of human contact."

I wondered if that wasn't the reason Joley had agreed to work the job in the first place, why she kept going back to it even though she had quit at least three times that I knew of. For the human contact. I wondered if that wasn't the same reason she continued to involve herself with Scottie Thomforde. Joley had been as popular as hell in high school—pretty can do that for you. Only she wasn't pretty anymore, and losing another thirty pounds wasn't going to change that.

Karen nodded her head when Joley finished her story. She said, "I can see where the job rewards your creativity and imagination," and nodded some more.

"I'm not educated," Joley said. "Unlike the big guy here"—she waved her hand at me—"I wasn't what you call college material. I doubt there's another job anywhere that they would let me do that pays as well as this."

Karen nodded again. She had the gift of empathy. She understood other people's emotions and knew how to make you feel good about having them. Either that or she was one of the most duplicitous women I have ever met.

"Tell me about your relationship with Scottie," Karen said.

Joley gave me a quick glance and settled on the sofa next to Karen.

"The summer after we graduated from high school, we started to spend time together," she said. "I suppose mostly it was out of self-defense. Neither of us was going on to college, and a lot of our friends, like McKenzie here, that was all they could talk about. It was fun, being with him. I'd go to his gigs and listen to him play. And then—you know about the robbery."

"I know," Karen said.

"Scottie says that to this day he doesn't know why he let Fulbright talk him into it. It was just so dumb."

"Is that what you spoke about on the phone?"

Joley's eyes grew cautious.

"Scottie's brother, Tommy, said you talked for hours a couple of weeks ago," Karen added.

"Yes, when he spent the weekend with his mother."

"Have you spoken to him since?" I asked.

"A few times."

"Did he ever mention any of his friends?"

"Sometimes. Sometimes we'll talk about the people we grew up with and went to school with, you know, Peter, Steve, Mary, Milo, Zap, Bev, John, Mary Beth—those people."

"Bobby Dunston?"

"Bobby? No, I don't think so. Why?"

"No one from prison? A guy called T-Man, maybe? Or Mr. T? Anyone like that?"

"No."

"Do you have any idea where he might be now?"

"No." Joley's eyes swept up to her ceiling and back to me. "How much trouble is he in?"

"We don't know that he is in trouble," Karen said. "We're just trying to find him."

Joley was staring at me when she said, "Why can't people just leave him alone? He's not a terrorist. He's not a drug dealer. He didn't abuse schoolchildren—"

"Jolene," Karen said.

"If people would leave him alone—"

"Jolene." Karen snapped off the name, forcing Joley to face her. I was convinced she did it to keep me from saying or doing something foolish at the mention of schoolchildren. Like I said, empathy.

"Jolene, I'm trying to keep Scottie from going back to prison," Karen said. "Can you help me?"

"I don't know where he is. He said—"

"What did he say?"

"When we were talking, he said he would never go back to prison."

"Why were you talking to him at all?" I asked. "I thought you were through with him."

"The last time—the last time, he was mean to me. This time, though, he was kind and funny, and he was up, you know, up, like he had plans, like he had a future. And he seemed a little sad, too, like he needed a friend."

"What about the restraining order?"

"I didn't think about that. I forgot about that."

"Why did you take out a restraining order in the first place?" Karen asked.

"That was because of when he got out of prison the first time. When he went to prison—it was so awful what happened to him, and we would talk about it all the time. I would visit him while he was waiting for his trial, and afterward he would call me from prison and write, and I would write back and sometimes I would visit him there. I was eighteen years old, though. Eighteen. My life was just beginning. Was I going to spend years waiting for Scottie?"

"You met a man," Karen said.

"I met a guy, yes, and I told Scottie about it and asked him not to call anymore and not to write. He kept at it anyway. He said we were meant to be together. I guess he thought that way because I was his first, and I guess I was his last, too, because now he was in prison. I said no, no, no, only he kept calling and writing until I called the prison and they restricted his phone use and wouldn't let him send me letters anymore. Then he got out, and he began coming over and calling and following me, and finally I got the restraining order, and the judge told him that if he didn't leave me alone they would put him back in prison to finish the rest of his sentence. And then he stopped."

"How did you get back together?" Karen asked.

"Well, we didn't *really* get back together. At least, not yet. I mean, I didn't hear from him again until he went back to prison the last time for check fraud. He wrote me a letter. It was a beautiful letter, a beautiful thing. In the letter he told me how sorry he was for frightening me. He said that he finally realized, now that he was back in prison again, how much pain and anguish he's been causing others, causing his family and me and people, and how he had finally seen the light and was going to change his life. He wrote that he didn't expect me to answer the letter and that was okay. He wrote that he only wanted to apologize to me for what he did and wish me well. He said I should have a long and happy life. That is what he wished for. So I answered the letter. It was such a beautiful letter. Did I already say that? I told him that I wished that he had a long and happy life, too. And then he wrote me back. And I wrote him back. Anyway, we've been in touch ever since, just writing and talking. Talking on the phone."

Imagine what a voice like hers might mean to a man in prison, my inner voice told me.

"You haven't seen him?" I said aloud.

"No. He can't have visitors at the halfway house except family. He invited me to visit when he stayed at his mother's house, but I didn't think that would be right cuz I'm not family."

"So you haven't actually seen him at all since he got out?"

"No."

Imagine what Scottie is going to think when he sees where that voice came from, my inner voice added. I silently told my inner voice that it was a jerk. It wasn't listening, as usual.

"Jolene?" Karen said. "If you see him, if you hear from Scottie, will you call me?"

"Is Scottie in trouble?"

"He will be if I don't hear from him soon."

"Then I'll call you."

Joley was staring at me when she took Karen's card. *That's your cue,* my inner voice said.

I gave Joley pretty much the same story I told Tommy: I ran into Karen while I was looking for Scottie; I was hoping Scottie might do a favor for me. I didn't explain why, and Joley didn't ask for more.

She was escorting us to the door when her cell phone rang.

"No rest for the wicked," Joley said.

My own cell phone rang while I was pulling away from the curb. I don't often use the phone while I'm driving, but the display told me that Nina Truhler was calling. For her I make exceptions.

"Hi, sweetie," I said.

"Hello, honey," she said.

After two years, we've reached a point in our relationship where we call each other names.

"What's going on?" I asked.

"Business sucks."

"Does it really?" Nina owns Rickie's, a jazz club named after her daughter, Erica, located in the Summit Hill neighborhood of St. Paul.

"Actually, it's a pretty good crowd for a Wednesday," she said. "Except there's this spot at the bar where a man I know usually sits, and since he's not here tonight, I figure the bar must be losing a fortune."

"Since you usually comp the man his dinners and drinks no matter how often he demands a bill . . ."

"I like that you always ask for a bill."

"So, business isn't off."

"Tips, McKenzie. Tips. The man nearly always leaves a tip that covers the cost of his meal and beverages. Do you know what that means to the waitstaff, especially considering how poorly their employer pays them?"

"I hadn't given it that much thought."

"You didn't honestly believe Jenness and the others were extra nice just to suck up to me, did you?"

"And they say money can't buy love."

"Besides, I distinctly remember you telling me this morning that you were dropping by."

"I meant to. Something came up."

"Oh, really? Another one of your crusades? Pity you couldn't be bothered to tell me about it."

"Nina . . ."

"McKenzie, you can be so inconsiderate sometimes."

"Nina, don't say any more," I said. "You'll only feel worse later when I explain everything."

Nina paused before asking, "What is it?"

"I'm on the road. I really can't talk about it now."

"Is it serious?"

"As serious as it gets."

She paused again. "Shelby and the girls," she said.

"What makes you say that?"

"If it's that serious, it has to be someone you love. Who do you love besides Shelby and the girls? And Bobby?"

"You."

"Well, it's not me and it's not Rickie. That leaves Shelby and the girls. Should I call? Should I go over there?"

"No, no, it's . . . it's still . . . Later, maybe. Later would be better."

"Can you tell me what's going on?"

"Not now."

"You will tell me."

"Of course."

"Promise?"

"I'll call first chance I get."

"Thank you."

I deactivated the phone. We were already on I-94 and heading toward the East Side of St. Paul when Karen said, "Was that your wife?"

"I'm not married."

"Girlfriend?"

"Yes."

"What's her name?"

"Nina Truhler."

"Do you love her?"

"She'll do until the real thing comes along," I said. It was a pat and stupid remark, but I didn't want to discuss Nina with a stranger.

"You called her sweetie," Karen said.

"Stop asking so many questions and I'll call you sweetie."

8

For decades, when you thought about the blue-collar East Side of St. Paul, you thought about the Payne Reliever, an infamous rock 'n' roll club and strip joint located on Payne Avenue. With its catchy name and wicked reputation, the Payne Reliever pretty much defined the rough-and-tumble neighborhood to the outside world, so much so that once when I told a guy in Florida where I lived, he asked if that was anywhere near the club. And did I go there? And how many shootings and knife fights had I seen? It's gone now, just like the Faust and Flick adult theaters, replaced, I swear, by an Embers family restaurant. Yet the reputation for mayhem it embodied persists. As a result, people seldom go to the East Side unless they actually live there, and many of those are cagey about it, telling outsiders they reside in Hazel Park, Prosperity Heights, or Lake Phalen. Still, most East Siders are fiercely loyal to their neighborhood. I played hockey with one guy, you could insult him, insult his politics, his religion, even his mother, but say something nasty about the East Side and he'd drop his gloves. Boom.

Mrs. Thomforde was loyal like that. Her husband might have moved her to Merriam Park, yet once a month she'd faithfully return to gossip with her East Side friends. As kids we used to think that she was tremendously courageous—or just plain crazy.

Usually the friends would gather at the Silver Bucket, located not too far from where the Payne Reliever once stood. The Silver Bucket is a family joint that's been thriving since the turn of the last century, when they actually served beer in small buckets. It had been built long before people decided it was okay to put windows in bars, and as a consequence it always looked like the inside of an old movie theater. There was no smoking—the result of a recent City of St. Paul ordinance—yet the odor of a million cigarettes could be smelled in the carpet, booths, and chairs.

There were at least one hundred people in the Silver Bucket when we arrived, and by the way they cheered you would have thought it was a sports bar and the Vikings had just put six on the board. Instead, a middle-aged woman dressed in a business suit was collecting her prize of a combo pack of chicken breasts and cheesy hash browns. Like a running back following a touchdown, she accepted about a dozen high-fives as she gamboled her way back to her table. Meanwhile, the manager held a plastic-wrapped package high above his head and called for order.

"Next up, a five-pound package of pork-chops-on-a-stick," he announced. That brought more cheers. "Don't forget, all proceeds go to the Johnson High School Hockey Association," he added as two waitresses fanned out through the bar, each carrying a round tray. On the tray were little tents of paper, a number written on each, the tents arranged in a circle along the edge of the tray. People dropped dollar bills into the middle of the tray and snatched paper tents at random, or according to some secret betting system.

"Should we buy a chance?" I asked Karen. "Pork-chops-on-a-stick. I love pork chops."

"Do you see Mrs. Thomforde?"

"We'll have a barbecue. The last barbecue of the season."

"Is that her?"

Karen pointed at a woman with white hair cut short sitting at a large table with seven other women. I had known Mrs. Thomforde for nearly three decades. During those years, along with the usual wear and tear of life, she had lost a husband just as he reached retirement age and had seen her favorite child sent to prison—more than once. Yet somehow her face had managed to retain a youthful contempt for the passing of time, for mortality itself. Looking at her, I decided that the old aphorism was true: *That which does not destroy us only makes us stronger.*

I came up from behind her and set a hand on her shoulder. She turned toward me. Curiosity, then recognition flashed across her face. She did not even say my name, simply stood and hugged me and said, "Oh, my, I haven't seen you since your father's funeral." She hadn't actually been a friend of my father's, but she came from that generation that went to funerals when someone in the neighborhood died.

Mrs. Thomforde touched my face and said, "You turned out so handsome." She turned to her friends sitting around the table. There was at least a case of longneck beer bottles, most of them empty, scattered in front of them, as well as the remains of several appetizer platters. "Isn't McKenzie handsome, girls?"

The girls agreed with Mrs. Thomforde. The one called Ruth thought I was handsome enough to take home and lock in the basement.

"You're just being polite," I told her.

"Are you kidding?" said a friend. "Compared to the ground chuck she's been chopping, you're Grade A sirloin."

Instead of being offended, Ruth said, "A body needs a nice fillet every once in a while, if you know what I mean."

The women all laughed like they knew exactly what she meant and I was reminded of yet another aphorism, this one more recent: *Girls just wanna have fun.*

Mrs. Thomforde pulled out an empty chair and said, "So what brings a nice boy like you to the East Side?"

"Isn't this where all the good-looking women hang out?"

The girls liked that answer, and it occurred to me that if I were into sexagenarian romance, I could have made out like a bandit.

I sat in the chair and asked, "So, did anybody win any meat?"

Turned out that Ruth won a five-pound package of New York strips that she expected her husband to ruin. "He's awful. Burns everything. I say, 'Let me cook the steaks.' Oh, no, grilling's a *man's* job. He'll turn these steaks into charcoal, wait and see."

The girls all nodded in understanding. They had known each other for decades, knew each other's families as well as they knew their own. The general consensus was that Ruth's husband could screw up a ham sandwich.

While they were telling me this, Mrs. Thomforde rested a hand on my forearm. "You brought a friend," she said.

"Actually, she brought me."

"Good evening, Mrs. Thomforde," Karen said.

"What do you want?" Mrs. Thomforde asked. I noticed she didn't offer Karen a chair.

"I'm looking for your son."

"Why? Is he lost?"

The girls all thought that was a pretty witty reply until Karen said, "Yes, he's lost, and if I don't find him soon, he's going back to prison."

"Oh, Jeezus," said Ruth.

"May we speak privately?" Karen asked.

"What is it?" Mrs. Thomforde gestured at the other women. "You can speak in front of my friends."

Karen said, "Scottie is late reporting back to the halfway house. Several hours late."

"You're going to send him back to prison for that? Scottie is a good boy."

"Mrs. Thomforde, everyone in a halfway house program is treated as if they're incarcerated in jail. If they're not where they're supposed to be when they're supposed to be there—"

"You saying that Scottie broke out of jail? That he's a fugitive?"

"If I don't find him soon, he'll be treated that way."

"Why can't you people just leave him alone?"

It was the same question Joley had asked, and it made me angry. I tried not to let it show.

"Mrs. Thomforde," said Karen. "The way the system works—"

"The system, the system. I hate the system. The system put a seventeen-year-old child in prison for a crime he didn't even commit. He didn't shoot that cop. That other boy shot him. The cop wasn't even hurt that bad. Only they punished Scottie for it, and see what's happened? Do you see? His life was ruined, that's what happened. The system—"

"Mrs. Thomforde," said Karen.

"—is terrible. The system doesn't work. Now you say that Scottie's run away—"

"I didn't say that."

"Wouldn't you run away, too, from such a system?" Mrs. Thomforde glared at Karen; her mouth was twisted with fury. "He wouldn't be running away if he was living at my house. None of this would happen if you let him stay with me. I thought you were going to let him stay with me?"

"That's what I thought, too," Ruth said. The girls were listening intently.

"I don't see how that's going to happen now," Karen said. Her frustration was palpable; whatever empathy she felt for Mrs. Thomforde had been left at the curb. "After this incident . . ." Karen shook a finger at the older woman. "When he was furloughed to your home the last time, he didn't stay there the entire weekend like he was supposed to. Did he?"

"He certainly did. He was in the house the whole time." I noticed that Mrs. Thomforde was looking upward and to her left when she spoke. "He helped me do some chores around the house, helped me move furniture and clean. He played the drums. He's such a fine musician."

"He was seen in a bar, Mrs. Thomforde. That's a terrible violation of the terms of his parole."

"I don't know where you're getting your information, but you better go back and get some more. Anyone saying Scottie wasn't at my house is lying. Scottie wasn't anywhere else but at my house for the entire weekend. We had a family reunion. The entire family came over and we had dinner together. Scottie played the drums for us."

"Mrs. Thomforde—"

"Are you saying she's a liar?" one of the East Siders asked. "We don't lie."

I liked the collective "We," but didn't say so.

"What's important is where Scottie is now," Karen said. "Do you know, Mrs. Thomforde?"

"No, I don't. You're the one who's supposed to be watching him."

Karen was this close to losing it. She clenched her fists and stepped forward. Something was about to come out of her mouth, and my inner voice warned, *It ain't gonna be pretty.*

"Miss." I spoke loudly and gestured. Both women turned toward me, as I had hoped they would. I purposely looked past them. "Miss," I called again. A waitress pivoted and stepped between Karen and Mrs. Thomforde to reach my chair. "How many tickets do you have left?"

She did a quick count of the remaining tents on her tray and said, "Ten."

"I'll buy them all." I dipped into my pocket for cash. "Ladies, pick a ticket, my treat." I dropped a ten on the tray and leaned back while each woman made a selection. Ruth said that I certainly knew the way to a girl's heart. Her friends suggested that Ruth was a cheap date.

"Take a ticket," I told Mrs. Thomforde. "You, too, Karen. Pork chops, yum."

Mrs. Thomforde selected hers, and Karen followed, leaving one ticket on the tray for me. I pulled a four. Victoria's number. Suddenly I wasn't having any fun. Suddenly I was angry again. I kept it to myself.

The waitress thanked us, scooped up the cash, and made her way to the front of the bar where the manager stood next to a spinning wheel. They both scanned the crowd for the other waitress, catching her eye. The waitress held up four fingers.

"Four tickets left for a chance at winning five pounds of pork-chops-on-a-stick," the manager announced.

"You and Scottie talk a lot, don't you, Mrs. Thomforde?" I said.

"Of course we do," she said. "I'm his mother. He calls me all the time. He's a good boy."

"Did he ever mention any friends to you? People he spends time with?"

"You mean from prison?" She was looking at Karen when she said, "He doesn't spend time with that trash."

"Did he ever mention anyone called T-Man, for instance? Mr. T?"

Mrs. Thomforde looked up and to her right. "I don't think so," she said. "No. No, I'm sure he hasn't. Why are you doing this, McKenzie?" She flung a look at Karen. "Why are you helping her?"

I patted Mrs. Thomforde's hand. "I'm not," I said. "I'm trying to help Scottie. When I found out Karen was looking for him—I was looking for him because I was hoping he might know some people who can help me out with something, but then she told me"—I flicked a thumb in Karen's direction—"that Scottie was missing . . ."

"Yes, yes," Mrs. Thomforde said. "You were always a good friend to Scottie. I remember what you did that one time. I won't ever forget it." She sighed dramatically. "Back when you were kids—everything seemed simple back when you were kids. Scottie was so full of fun and love and . . ." She was looking up to her right again. "If only . . ."

The manager spoke loudly from the front of the bar. "Here we go, ladies and gentlemen. For five pounds of pork-chops-on-a-stick." He spun the wheel. It completed several revolutions before slowing and eventually settling on number sixteen. The woman who had won the chicken and hash browns gave out a squeal from a table behind us.

"Did she win again?" asked Ruth.

"It's so unfair," said Mrs. Thomforde.

I thanked Mrs. Thomforde for her time and said good-bye to the girls and led Karen out of the bar. I stopped her just outside the door and studied my watch, counting the seconds as they ticked by.

"What are you doing?" Karen asked.

"I think Mrs. Thomforde was lying about knowing where Scottie is," I said.

"What makes you say that?"

"Did you notice that while she was speaking to you she was looking upward to her left, but when she was speaking to me, she was looking upward to the right?"

"No, I didn't. What difference does it make?"

"Right brain, left brain. When you glance up to the right, you're pulling your thoughts from your memory. If you glance up to the left, you're pulling thoughts from your creative side. Often, that means the person is lying. When Mrs. Thomforde told us she didn't know where Scottie was, she was looking to her left."

"That doesn't tell me what you're doing."

"I'm giving Mrs. Thomforde a ninety-second head start."

"To do what?"

At ninety seconds, I opened the bar door and both Karen and I stepped inside, standing close to the entrance. From where we stood we were able to see Mrs. Thomforde's back. She was speaking on a cell phone.

I asked Karen if she was hungry. She said she was, so I drove to a vacant lot lit up by the streetlights on the corner of Arcade and East Seventh Street. There was a food trailer like the kind you see at state and county fairs anchored against a wooden fence. It was rigged with tiny yellow lightbulbs and covered with hand-painted scenes of a pastoral Mexico.

"You're kidding, right?" said Karen.

"It has authentic Mexican food," I said. "The best in town. Unless you prefer Taco Bell."

I had the impression that she did. Just the same, I parked in the lot next to a Lexus SUV, which was parked next to a Ford minivan, and joined the line. Karen followed reluctantly. The owner, a man named José, stood behind a white folding table loaded with pastel-colored coolers containing soft drinks. He scribbled orders on a pad and handed them through a window into the kitchen inside the trailer. There was a large chalkboard to his right. The trailer served a full menu, yet I recommended the tacos. The tortillas were warmed on a griddle and piled high with chopped onions, fresh cilantro, hot sauce, and your choice of fifteen different kinds of meat, including cow brains. I ordered chicken. Karen requested shrimp. I didn't say anything at the time, but shrimp tacos? Really? That's so Southern California.

There were a few picnic tables with huge umbrellas scattered around the lot, only they were all full, so we ate with the Audi between us, using the hood for a table.

"This is amazing," Karen said after her second bite.

"What did I tell you?"

"The sauce, though. It's so hot."

"I like it that way."

We continued eating in silence until Karen asked, "How do they get away with this, selling food in a vacant lot?"

"The owners get away with it because no one has complained yet. I mean, look. Their customers love them." The lot was filled with every ethnic group you can find on the East Side: Hispanics, Somalis, Hmong, Native Americans, blacks, and whites, some with money, some obviously without—a true melting pot. " 'Course, it's only a matter of time."

"What do you mean?"

"Sooner or later someone will complain, and the city will step in with their ordinances and permit requirements and zoning regulations and shut it all down. The owners and their customers will protest, yet in the end the city council will explain how it's making St. Paul a better place to live, and that will be that."

"You're a cynical man, McKenzie."

"No, I'm not. I'm just having a very bad day."

Not as bad as the Dunstons, my inner voice reminded me.

"Do you think Mrs. Thomforde was calling Scottie?" Karen asked.

"Who else would she call? All her friends were sitting at the table."

Karen took her last bite of taco and washed it down with bottled water. "What do we do now?" she asked.

"If you're up to it, we could visit Lehane's and ask around, see if any of the regulars can give us a handle on this T-Man."

"What do you mean, if I'm up to it?"

"It's a dangerous place. More Minnesotans have been killed in and around Lehane's than in Iraq."

"It's not that bad."

"How would you know?"

"I've been there."

"Alone?"

"No, I was—all right, I was with police officers looking to serve an apprehension and detention warrant on an offender."

"Yeah, well, it's different when you have guns. We should get guns."

"No guns."

"Karen."

"No."

"Fine."

"They're not going to talk to you anyway, McKenzie. You start asking questions of that crowd and they're going to kick your ass."

"That's debatable."

"They might talk to me, though."

"What makes you so popular?"

Karen's blue shirt was open at the collar. She reached up, undid the next two buttons, and batted her eyelashes at me. "I'm a babe," she said.

I hadn't thought so when I first met her, but I was beginning to reconsider.

"Oh, this should be fun," I said.

Lehane's was three blocks away from the taco trailer, yet it might as well have been on the far side of the moon for all the similarities. For one thing, there were no minorities. Lehane's was whites only, and you didn't need a sign in the window to figure it out. The place reeked of bigotry and hate. Men didn't go there to relax or watch the ball game. They went to Lehane's to nurse their grudges against mankind and to plot their revenge. They went there to rage against the world and their place in it.

Fights were commonplace. When I worked the Eastern District for the St. Paul cops, the very last call you wanted to take was to quell a disturbance at Lehane's. Sometimes you found guys going at it with fists, sometimes with knives, sometimes with guns. That's how Patrick Lehane got his. A slug from a nine-millimeter fired by a customer who refused to take last call for an answer. That was back in the mid-eighties. Since then the bar had changed hands at least a half-dozen times while retaining its name, rowdy reputation, and white-trash clientele.

It was specifically because of Lehane's that the St. Paul City Council adopted what it labeled "a nuisance ordinance." The statute allowed them to shutter any business they wanted if they could prove "by a preponderance of evidence that the property owners operated in a manner that maintained and permitted conditions that unreasonably annoyed a substantial number of people and endangered the safety, health, morals, comfort, or repose of considerable numbers of the public." Yet, while the ordinance had been used to threaten and shut down several other less notorious bars over the years, including a pretty decent African American–owned blues joint, Lehane's remained in business. Go figure.

I opened the door and was slapped in the face by the smell of cigarettes and beer and the sour odor of industrial disinfectant. I tried not to react to it. The bartender glanced at me when I stepped inside. His eyes worked me over, wondering if I was trouble, how much, and whether or not he could handle it. From the way he smirked and turned his head, I doubt I impressed him much.

There were six other men in Lehane's. At first glance you would have pegged them as working class, except I doubted any of them actually had a job or filed a tax return. More likely, they all made their living in the so-called underground economy. I would have bet my Audi that each of them had a criminal record.

The men were divided into pairs. One pair sat at the bar near the door, and another sat at the opposite end, as far away from the first pair as possible. The two other men sat at a table in the corner, their heads close together, speaking intently—at least until I somehow interrupted their conversation by moving to the center of the bar. When they spotted me, they both leaned away from each other and frowned. The others looked at me with an expression of casual indifference before returning their attention to the TV above the bar—I could live or die or go to Iowa for all they cared. Maybe it was my clothes. I was overdressed because I was wearing a clean shirt and jeans. Maybe if I went outside and rolled around in the gutter.

Instead of a legitimate sport, they had ultimate fighting on—think professional wrestling with real malice, real violence, and real injuries. The customers didn't seem to be rooting for anyone in particular, just watching the mayhem, maybe taking mental notes on how to hurt and disable. "Wooooo," one of them hummed when a fighter head-butted his opponent, hurled him down on the mat, and proceeded to pound his face with a forefist. "I bet that hurts."

"He's a pussy," his companion said without indicating which fighter he meant.

The bartender seemed annoyed that I distracted him from the program. He needed a shave and a haircut, his eyes were unsteady, and his belly strained the buttons of his shirt. I set a ten on the bar in front of him and said, "Shot of rye and a bottle of beer. And quarters for the pool table."

"No bottles," he said. "Only cans." A good policy, I decided. Having been attacked with both over the years, I could testify that aluminum cans were definitely less lethal than broken glass.

While the bartender's back was turned, I fished a pack of Marlboros and a brand-new Bic lighter from my pocket. I had bought both at a SuperAmerica store down the street. When Karen asked why, I said, "Props. An actor needs his props."

I was lighting the cigarette when the bartender set the shot glass and beer in front of me. "Law says you can't smoke in here," he said.

"What the fuck do I care?"

The bartender gave me a small squat glass to use as an ashtray. "I don't want to see no butts on the floor," he said, even though the black rubber tiles were already littered with cigarette butts as well as crushed pretzels, peanut shells, and kernels of buttered popcorn. There weren't any baskets on the bar, so I figured the debris must have been what remained of Lehane's happy hour spread.

The bartender took the ten and returned a moment later with my change, including seven quarters. I used four of them to buy a round of pool at the table in the back. I racked the balls and carefully selected a cue from the half-dozen sticks collected in a busted wooden frame screwed to the wall. I found only one that was reasonably straight and still had the tip attached. I was chalking the cue when she walked in.

The men had merely glanced at me, found me uninteresting, and looked away. Karen they studied with the intensity of an astronomer encountering a new celestial body. An unescorted woman in Lehane's? I doubted they could believe their luck. "Hey," said the guys nearest the door as she passed. One of them patted his pocket, no doubt mentally counting his money, wondering if he had enough to pay her fee.

Karen spoke first to the bartender. The volume on the TV was up, and I couldn't hear the conversation. They spoke for a long time. Or maybe it was just me counting the seconds. More and more I began to feel that visiting Lehane's wasn't the best notion I ever had. If it hadn't been for Victoria, for my dismal failure at learning anything more about where she was and who took her, I would never have done it. Desperation makes fools of us all.

Karen made the rounds after she finished with the bartender, speaking first with the pair of jokers at the door, then the pair at the opposite end of the bar, and finally the men at the small table in the corner. I watched her the way a parent watches a small child at a crowded park while pretending not to, giving the kid her freedom, yet ready to pounce at the slightest provocation.

None of the men blew her off—I wouldn't have, either. They all smiled when she approached, all sat up straighter when she asked her questions, and none of them seemed remotely hostile. Yet all of them looked her up and down and licked their lips as if she were an ice cream cone and it was a hot day. The men nearest the door in particular—they stared at her breasts when she spoke to them, not her eyes, and when she left they tilted their heads so they could get a good look at her ass as she walked away. Instead of smiling, they leered. They called to her when she settled in with the bartender a second time.

"Hey. Hey, honey."

Karen glanced over.

"What you doin' lookin' for this Mr. T asshole when you could have a real man?"

Karen averted her eyes.

"Seriously, me and Marky can help you out if you're lookin' for a good time."

"I'll go first," Marky said. He nudged his pal in the shoulder. "Joey here, he likes sloppy seconds."

"Fuck you, man," said Joey.

The bartender chuckled loud enough to be heard over the TV. He said something and laughed some more. Karen smiled weakly. The boys at the end of the bar kept at it. The one called Marky told a joke about the difference between a good girl and a nice girl that cracked up his pal and the bartender. Karen draped the strap of her purse over her shoulder as if she were about to leave.

"No, no, don't go," said Joey. "How 'bout you let me buy you a drink?"

At the same time, Marky slid off his stool and casually moved to the door.

The bartender backed away from Karen, as if giving his customers plenty of room.

"No, thank you," Karen said. Her voice was steady and clear.

"What? I ain't good enough for you to drink with?"

"No, thank you," Karen repeated. She slid her hand inside her bag.

"You fuckin' look at me when I'm talkin' to you."

Karen didn't look. If she had, she would have seen Marky sliding the bolts at the top and bottom of the door into place.

"Who do you think you're dealin' with, bitch, treatin' me like that? Like I ain't even worth lookin' at?" Joey said. He came off his stool and approached Karen from the edge of the bar. "You ain't friendly at all."

Marky swung wide so that he could come up on her from behind. The other four men watched from their seats. None of them were looking to get involved in the action, yet I knew that none of them would turn it down when their turn came. As for the bartender, he seemed bored, his arms folded across his chest, his eyes half closed, as if this sort of thing happened all the time.

Marky was about three steps behind Karen, who kept looking straight ahead. Joey was an equal distance to her left. They were closing in.

"You know what you need?" Marky said. "You need a good fuck."

"Hey, pal," I said.

Marky turned. I was behind him. He had forgotten about me. Everyone had.

He said, "Wha—"

That's all he said.

The pool cue was in my hands. I had rotated it so I was gripping the thin end. When Marky turned I swung it like a baseball bat. It made a loud whoosh as it cut through the still barroom air and then a cracking sound as it exploded against his face, catching him across the upper lip. I felt the contact rippling through my hands and arms and deep into my shoulders as I followed through. Marky's head snapped back and his legs came out from under him and he splashed against the dirty rubber floor, bounced once, and settled among the cigarette butts, pretzels, and popcorn.

I glanced at Joey. He didn't seem to understand what was happening until I moved toward him, gripping the stick like a batter walking to the plate. He drifted backward until his spine was hard against the bar. His arms were spread wide in a pose of surrender, and his eyes were locked on mine as if I were a bad traffic accident and he couldn't make himself look away. I halted, rested the pool cue on my shoulder, and smiled. Joey just stared, his mouth open, like a man whose brain synapses were too far apart. I walked slowly past him to the door. I opened the bolt at the bottom, then the top, and moved back into the bar. None of the men spoke a word to me, so I didn't speak to them. I carefully stepped over Marky's body. He was moaning softly now; blood dribbled from his nose and from both corners of his mouth. I still had three balls on the pool table, and I sank them one at a time without a miss. Afterward, I returned the pool stick to the rack.

"I'm ready to leave. How 'bout you?" I said.

Karen nodded and slipped off her stool. "Gentlemen," she said and walked briskly to the door. I followed. Nobody would meet my eyes; no one spoke until I moved past Joey. He said, "Asshole," so I stomped on his kneecap with the outer edge of my shoe. I don't know if I smashed it, but Joey went down screaming just the same. I caught his hair as he fell and held him up while I punched his face until my knuckles became sore.

I was breathing hard when I left the bar; sweat had pooled under my arms and at the small of my back.

"Are you happy now?" Karen asked. I had unlocked the Audi with my key-chain remote, and we were talking to each other over the roof of the car. "You've been wanting to hit somebody all night. Now you've had your chance. Does it make you feel better?"

"Am I missing something?" I said. "Did you not know what was going on back there? Did you not see Marky locking the door?"

"I saw."

"What the hell do you think that was about?"

"I know what it was about."

"They were going to rape you, Karen. They were going to hold you down on the bar and spread your legs and rape you. Every man in that place—"

"I know."

"They were going to rape you and abuse you and degrade you

simply because you were there and they're all pissed off at the world and why should you be happy if they're not—and do you know what would have happened afterward? Nothing. I doubt that they would have celebrated. I doubt that they would have even given each other a high-five."

"McKenzie, that wasn't going to happen."

"That's because I was there. I can't believe you're giving me attitude over this. I was helping you."

"I didn't need help. I had it under control."

"What were you going to do, Karen, when they put their hands on you? Kill 'em with kindness?"

Karen's hand was in her bag. When it came out, she was holding a .380 Colt Mustang pocket gun. She slapped the semiautomatic on the roof of my Audi, and my first thought was *Hey, lady, that's a fifty-thousand-dollar car.* My second thought I spoke aloud. "You had a gun?" That's why she had draped her purse over her shoulder and why her hand was inside it. "What are you doing with a gun? You said no guns."

"I said no guns for you. Lucky I did, from what I saw in there. You would have shot those men."

"Hell, yes," I said.

"So instead you beat on them. That should make you happy."

"Karen—"

"Tell me, McKenzie. Do you think either of them will be any less of a jerk tomorrow because you beat on them?"

"Karen, I was concerned for your safety."

"No. You were upset that you haven't been able to do anything for Victoria Dunston, and you took it out on them."

"Get in the car."

Once we were both inside the Audi and she had put her gun away, I said, "Karen, I have a lot to apologize for." She turned in her seat and looked at me as if she suddenly thought I was interesting. "For the way I've treated you, the way I spoke to your friends."

"I've already forgiven you for that," Karen said.

"I know. I just wanted you to know that I was sorry. I have no reason to get down on you and your pals. You're true believers. You're honestly concerned about helping people."

"We sure don't do it for the money," she said.

"Only I am not going to apologize for what I did in Lehane's. I didn't know you had a gun, and even if I had, I still would have stepped in."

"I wish you hadn't."

"Tell me, Karen. If those men had laid hands on you, would you have used the gun?"

"I would have pulled it."

"Yes, but if they weren't afraid, if they didn't back off, would you have squeezed the trigger?"

She didn't answer. I don't think she had an answer. She turned in her seat and gazed out of the passenger window looking for it. After a few moments, she said, "You think I'm naive, don't you?"

"A little bit."

"I'm not. Truly, I'm not. I know these people. I know what they're capable of. I had one offender, he wanted to show his girl a good time, so he ordered a pizza and then shot the delivery boy in the back of the head for the money he had in his pockets. Another offender, a woman, she was angry that her boyfriend discarded her for someone else, so she burned down the boyfriend's apartment building, killed seven people. The boyfriend wasn't even home."

Another offender kidnapped a twelve-year-old girl and terrorized and traumatized her and the people who loved her for a little bit of money, and maybe some payback for an imagined offense that occurred over two decades ago, my inner voice added. *What madness is that?*

"None of it makes sense to me," Karen said. "I understand why they do the things they do. I understand their motives. Yet the motives so often pale in comparison with the enormity of their crimes." She shook her head sadly. "I don't forgive them, McKenzie. Who am I to forgive them for the terrible things they do? Except this is the difference between you and me—I want to help them. I want to change them. I want to make sure they don't do terrible things again. I mean, what's the alternative if we don't help these people, if we don't try to change them? What else would you do with these people?"

"I don't know."

"Neither do I."

"Karen, what's a nice girl like you doing in a place like this, anyway?"

"You mean sitting in an expensive car outside a sleazy bar after being nearly assaulted by a half-dozen degenerates?"

"Exactly."

"After I earned my criminal justice degree, I worked at Lino Lakes as a jailer. I had taken a lot of psychology courses, and my plan was to work as a juvenile probation officer. I wanted to get a sense of what prison for kids was all about first, so I went to work for the juvenile detention center in Lino Lakes." Karen stared out the window of the Audi some more. "Prison is a terrible, terrible place," she said. "A bad place."

It's supposed to be, my inner voice said.

"It chews people up in a way that's . . . that's hard to explain unless you've seen it firsthand. I saw kids, I don't care what they did to get there, they were kids, but after a few months—what is it the philosophers say? 'If you live where they live and are taught what they are taught, you'll believe what they believe.' For these kids, prison became their teacher. Most of what they knew about life they learned behind bars. I suspect that's what happened to your friend Scottie. Anyway, I decided I would work to keep people out of prison. I know it's not a popular goal. Yet"—she turned and looked hard at me—"when my head hits the pillow and I look back on the day, no matter how crummy the day is, I can always say 'The world's a little bit better place because of what I did.' "

"Where have I heard that before?" I asked.

I started the car, and we drove off. After a few blocks I said, "Did you learn anything? Back at Lehane's, did anyone say anything interesting?"

"The bartender didn't recognize any names, but he said he remembered .serving two men who fit the descriptions of Scottie and the T-Man. He said they reminded him of one of those ads for a health club, the kind with a before and after photo, Scottie looking wimpy and the other looking muscular."

"Did he remember anything else?"

"No."

We managed to negotiate Spaghetti Junction, the confluence of Interstates 94 and 35E and Highway 52, without getting wrecked and were heading west when Karen's cell phone rang. I could hear only her end of the conversation.

"Yes . . . When . . . ? What did he say . . . ? You're kidding . . . No, tell him nothing. I'm on my way."

Karen folded her cell and slipped it back into her bag.

"What?" I said.

"Take me back to the halfway house."

"Why?"

"Scottie Thomforde just rolled in."

9

Special Agent Damian Honsa worked hard to keep his reassuring smile in place. He paced the length of Shelby's dining room and back again, his hands clasped behind him, while we all watched from chairs around the table. "What do we know?" he said.

"We don't know squat," Bobby said.

Bobby had been in favor of arresting Scottie immediately. Honsa had talked him out of it. "We have two teams on him," Honsa said. "He's not going anywhere." Again, he used the threat to Victoria's safety to keep Bobby in his place.

"We know that Scottie is lying," I said.

"You don't know," Karen insisted. "You weren't there. You didn't see his face. You were waiting in the car when I spoke to him. He could be telling the truth."

"Why are you still here?" Bobby asked.

"He was contrite, he was apologetic," Karen said. "I believe he was legitimately afraid that I would violate him. When I told him I'd give him one last chance, he nearly cried."

Wouldn't you? my inner voice asked even as I wondered how it was possible that a woman who did what Karen did for a living could retain such a rosy outlook. "You said that Scottie told you he went to his girlfriend's for a quick visit after work," I reminded her. "He said he fell asleep. He said that when he woke up he first called the halfway house and then reported there as soon as he could."

"That's right."

"He said the girlfriend was Joley Waddell. Did you see Scottie when we were at her place?"

"Maybe he was sleeping in the bedroom. Maybe Joley didn't say anything for fear that he'd get into trouble. Or maybe she was embarrassed that we caught them together."

"Maybe you've lost touch with reality," Bobby said. "Ninety minutes' leeway before he has to report in—I never heard of anything so ridiculous. Parolees in halfway houses are supposed to be treated like they are incarcerated. No leeway at all."

"Those are the rules—"

"Then why weren't you following the rules?"

"Because they're men, not animals," Karen said. "Besides, you don't even know for sure that Scottie had anything to do with the kidnapping. You heard a voice on the phone. A voice that was disguised. You're just guessing."

"Ms. Studder," Honsa said. His voice, as always, was in neutral. "Did you contact Ms. Waddell to confirm Thomforde's story?"

"I didn't. Roger did."

"He's the facility's administrator?"

"Roger Colfax, yes."

"Did Ms. Waddell confirm Thomforde's story?"

"Yes."

"She said that Thomforde had been with her?"

"Yes."

"All evening?"

"I know it looks bad, but there could be a perfectly reasonable explanation."

"Jeezus," Bobby said.

"Did Mr. Colfax believe Ms. Waddell?" Honsa asked.

"Yes."

"Did you contradict her story?"

"No. You said—you said before that you wanted to give Scottie the illusion of space. You wanted him to think he was still in control. So I told him I was satisfied for now, but that we'd discuss the matter again, later."

Honsa smiled his reassuring smile at her. "That was excellent work, Ms. Studder. Thank you." To the rest of us, he said, "If McKenzie is correct, and Mrs. Thomforde managed to contact her son, managed to tell Scottie that McKenzie and Ms. Studder were searching for him, Thomforde has to believe that McKenzie suspects him. But he must also believe that the police and the FBI aren't involved. If he thought we were, I think he would run. What other choice would he have? But he hasn't. Which means he thinks he's safe. So now we can watch, just as we had hoped."

"It's possible," Harry said, "that Mrs. Thomforde didn't contact her son. That this is all part of the plan. Thomforde kidnaps Victoria, makes sure she's secure for the evening, and then returns to the halfway house to avoid being violated, to avoid having anyone look for him."

"Then why not return at seven when he was expected?" asked the tech agent. "He already had the girl. His partner could have made sure she was secured for the evening."

"We don't know the partner's situation," Honsa said. He was doing what he said he wouldn't—brainstorming in front of the victim's family. Yet I doubted either Bobby or Shelby would have had it any other way. "Perhaps he's on parole as well. Perhaps the conditions of his parole are more stringent and carefully monitored."

If Karen felt a jab at that last remark, she didn't show it.

"They left Victoria alone, didn't they?" Shelby said. "They chained her up and locked her up and left her alone. She's all alone."

She didn't have a reason to make that assumption, but who was going to argue with her? Not me.

"They won't do anything to endanger her," said Honsa. "They need Victoria . . ." He nearly added "alive and unharmed," yet edited himself. The words hung in the air just the same.

"She's alone," Shelby said. She gripped Bobby's hand so tightly that his fingers turned white. He didn't so much as grimace.

"Did you check the prison records?" I asked.

"Yes," Harry said. He slid a computer printout across the table to me. "The staff at Stillwater has no recollection of a prisoner called T-Man or Mr. T. This is a list of everyone with a first or last name starting with the letter *T* who's been released in the past twelve months. Lieutenant Dunston checked the names that he recognized."

I studied the list. Bobby had checked eight names with a red pen. I could add nothing. It had been a while since I arrested anyone.

"One thing, though," I said. "I think you should tap the phones at the halfway house, Mrs. Thomforde's house, and Joley Waddell's house."

"Already taken care of," said the tech agent.

"I think you should put Tommy Thomforde under surveillance as well," I added.

Bobby leaned forward. "Why?" he said.

"He just went through a messy divorce. He needs money. Plus, he's been working out, and, well, his name does begin with a T."

Bobby leaned back and Honsa and Harry glanced at each other as if they had all simultaneously flashed on the same idea that I had had—maybe it was Tommy's voice on the phone, not Scottie's. I didn't believe it. Yet it was possible.

Honsa passed a look to the tech agent. The tech agent grabbed a handheld and left the room.

"What happens now?" Bobby asked.

"The hardest part," said Honsa. "We wait."

"Oh, God," moaned Shelby.

"I'm optimistic," Honsa said.

No one agreed or disagreed with him out loud, yet we all understood the possibility: Scottie learned we had been looking for him, panicked, killed Victoria, and returned to the halfway house to avoid detection. It was a fear too great to speak aloud.

"We'll wait for the kidnappers to call," Honsa said. He looked first at Shelby and then at Bobby as he spoke. "They will call. They will call tomorrow. As soon as it's humanly possible, we will arrange to exchange the money for your daughter. Once your daughter is safely home, we will make sure these men pay for their crimes."

"I don't care if they pay or not," Shelby said. "As long, as long . . ."

"I understand," Honsa said.

"Do you have children, Agent Honsa?"

"Yes, ma'am. That's one of the reasons I do this job."

I don't know if she found comfort in that or not. She slowly rose from the table and, without speaking, left the room. After a few moments, Bobby followed her.

Karen and I left Shelby's Place at the same time.

"I pray that the girl comes home safely," she said. "I pray that no one gets hurt."

"Me, too."

My car was parked on the far side of Wilder, facing north. Her car was on the near side, facing south. As I passed her car, Karen said, "I am so wired, there's no way I could possibly fall asleep. I really don't want to be alone, anyway. McKenzie, will you have a drink with me? Or . . ." The "or" is what made me stop in the middle of the street. "The way I feel right now, I could be talked into anything."

"Anything?" I said.

"The way I feel—if you feel the same way . . ."

I thought about it. I gave it all of five seconds before I said, "I have to make a phone call."

"Nina?"

"Yes."

"I'll wait."

"No."

Karen nodded as if a great truth had been revealed to her. "Before, you said that Nina would do until the real thing came along. She is the real thing, isn't she?"

"As real as it gets."

"Why didn't you say so? Were you embarrassed?"

Good question. Nina and I had discussed the M-word on several occasions, only she had been there, done that, and had nothing to show for it except some extra bad memories and a lovely daughter, so marriage wasn't on the agenda. Still, in essence we had pretty much vowed to forsake all others. Why I had a difficult time admitting that aloud was as much a mystery to me as it was to everyone else.

"I'm told I don't express my feelings well," I said.

"You should work on it."

"I've been told that, too."

Karen took several tentative steps toward me, paused. Her hand dipped inside her bag. For a moment, I had the irrational fear that she was reaching for her gun. Her hand came out with her wallet instead. "I'd really like to know what happens with that little girl," she said. She took a card from her wallet. "Will you call me? Will you tell me what happens?" I took the card and put it in my pocket. "Or I could call you."

There was that "or" again.

"I'll call you," I said.

I was on I-94, heading west toward the Highway 280 exit, driving with one hand while holding my cell phone to my ear with the other. Nina Truhler was asking questions and I was trying to answer as best I could. "Ohmigod," she kept saying. "Oh. My. God!" As if saying it often and loud enough would convince him to intervene on Victoria's behalf. Personally, I thought she was taking the Lord's name in vain. God never intervenes. He leaves that to us mere mortals.

I had hoped that Nina would invite herself over to my house. Like Karen Studder, I felt the need for some TLC. Instead, Nina announced that she was going home early to check on her own daughter, Erica. I didn't blame her a bit and told her so.

It wasn't until we finished our conversation that my hands began to shake. To avoid a wreck, I took the Larpenteur Avenue exit off 280 and pulled into the rutted lot of the abandoned service station at the top of the ramp. I had Stacey Kent in the CD player; she was wrapping her cool, hip, girlish voice around some jazz standards. It took a half-dozen songs before I stopped trembling and another half dozen before I felt up to driving home. I might have broken down altogether except what good would that do?

10

It should have been cold and gray with a hard, wet wind that plucked at the heart—a morning to match my mood. Instead, it was one of those golden days that remind Minnesotans why they live here. The air was warm and clear, the sky a rich blue, and a light breeze made the leaves tremble with the promise of autumn.

I was in my backyard, drinking coffee, watching the ducks, trying to remember which one I had named Victoria. My muscles ached from lack of rest, and my stomach murmured uncomfortably. For some reason, when I don't get a full night's sleep, I feel nauseous until I've had something to eat. I didn't feel up to facing a plate of eggs, so I drank my breakfast. Coffee and Jim Beam.

Several times I checked to make sure my cell phone was fully charged, several times I scrutinized my watch, several times I debated calling H. B. Sutton, all within a few minutes. I could have gone to Shelby and Bobby's place, only I didn't want to intrude. I might have claimed them as family, but their pain, their anguish, belonged to them alone. It was fueled by blood and couldn't be shared.

I would have called Nina. Despite the late hours she keeps, she always rises early to help Erica get off to school. I could have caught her before she returned to bed. Only I was afraid of tying up the phone.

Eleven, H. B. had said. She'd transfer the money and call by 11 A.M. I studied my watch yet again. Three and a half hours to go. Two hundred and ten minutes. Twelve thousand, six hundred seconds. Sonuvabitch.

I convinced myself that the Dunstons would be anxious to hear from me—or at least the Feds would—so I drove over there. I parked in front of the house. It looked exactly as it had the day before. So did the park across the street, and I wondered briefly how that was possible. The kidnapping of Victoria was beyond terrible, yet the world had not changed because of it. Only Shelby's world and Bobby's world and my world had changed. I flashed on the lyrics of an old country-western ballad. Like Skeeter Davis, I couldn't figure out why the sun kept on shining. It didn't make a lot of sense to me.

I met Harry on the porch. He had changed clothes, so he must have gone home. For how long I couldn't say.

"Anything?" he asked.

My cell phone was in my hand, and I held it up for him to see. "Any minute now," I said. "Have you heard from the kidnappers?"

"No."

"What about Scottie?"

"He left the halfway house at seven forty, walked to University, took the bus to Dale, walked the rest of the way to work, arrived ten minutes before it opened. He's been there ever since. Our agents don't believe he's used a phone."

"Terrific."

Harry was holding a mug emblazoned with the logo of the Girl Scouts of America. "Fresh coffee inside," he said. "Shelby made it."

"How's she holding up?"

"She's . . ." Harry sighed as if he were disappointed he couldn't find the right adjective to describe her. "Yesterday there were a couple of times when I thought we might lose her. Today . . . today she seems to be gathering strength. Bobby's the one I'm worried about now. He's burning so much fuel trying to keep it together, to maintain control. I have to think the tanks are getting close to empty."

"What can I do?"

"A couple hours of sleep would make a big difference. He hasn't been to bed yet."

"I'll talk to him," I said.

I stepped inside the house and looked for Bobby. I couldn't locate him, but I found Katie standing on the staircase. Damian Honsa and the tech agent both said, "Good morning," from the dining room table. I blew them off when she waved me over.

"They kept me out of school," Katie said.

"Probably a good idea," I told her.

"I don't mind missing school, only we have soccer practice afterward. I hate to miss that."

"I understand."

"Victoria won't mind missing practice. She's getting bored with soccer, I think. She'll miss going to school, though. She likes school, I don't know why. They gave her an award, you know."

"I know."

"Student of the quarter. Nobody had better grades. Nobody in the entire school. Even the eighth graders. I think it's because Victoria likes to read. McKenzie?"

I brushed the hair out of her eyes.

"They keep telling me not to be afraid," Katie said. "They say I should stay in my room as much as I can and keep out of the way and not be afraid because they're going to get Victoria back and she's going to be okay and I shouldn't be afraid. McKenzie, are you afraid?"

"Yes."

"I'm afraid, too."

"I know."

"Do I have to go back to my room?"

"Not if you don't want to."

"It's just that I don't want to wake Daddy."

"Is your dad in your room?"

"He came in a little while ago to talk to me and he fell asleep."

"Don't wake him," I said.

"Where should I go?"

"Have you had breakfast?"

Katie nodded. "I wasn't hungry, but Mom made me eat a bunch of waffles. Not the ones you put in the toaster. The real kind. Mom made waffles and eggs and sausage. I only ate the waffles. Do you think it would be all right if I went into Victoria's room? I won't touch anything. I just like sitting in there."

"I'm sure she won't mind."

"I don't know. Victoria got real mad the last time."

"Times change."

"I'm glad you're afraid," Katie said. "I tried hard not to be afraid, but I couldn't help it. I thought maybe there was something wrong with me."

"There's nothing wrong with you," I said.

I found Shelby in the kitchen. She was washing a platter that she normally would have placed in the dishwasher.

"Hey," I said.

"Good morning." I rested my hands on her shoulders, and she lifted her cheek for me. I kissed it, and she said, "So, how are you holding up, McKenzie?

"As best I can."

"Good. I need all my men to be strong today."

All my men, my inner voice repeated.

"I expected you over an hour ago," Shelby said.

"I didn't want to get in the way."

She stopped washing the plate and looked at me as if I were a tourist attraction, something odd and improbable that she had never seen before. "In the way?" she said. "You're family, McKenzie. You were family long before you agreed to give us a million dollars."

"Yeah, well, once we bring Victoria home I expect to get the money back."

"Amen," Shelby said. She finished washing her plate and set it on a rack to dry.

"You okay?" I asked.

"No."

"You look better."

"That's because I'm holding it in. Like Bobby. If I start to let it out again, I'll never stop."

"Katie said you made waffles."

"I made breakfast for everybody, including the FBI. It was the least I could do. Besides, it helped me keep my mind off of things. Are you hungry? I could make you an egg sandwich. With shredded cheese. And a couple slices of tomato. I know that's one of your favorites."

"If it's no trouble," I said.

Shelby began making preparations, pulling out a carton of eggs and a block of cheddar from her refrigerator and the remains of a loaf of bread that she had baked using a machine that I had given her for Christmas. She stopped after she retrieved a skillet from her drying rack and turned toward me. "You're not just trying to humor me, are you?" she said.

"I swear I haven't had a bite to eat all morning. Just coffee."

"With a slug of bourbon in it, I bet."

"Shelby. We're going to get Victoria back. I promise."

She didn't say if she believed me or not.

The Feds were listening in on Scottie's, Tommy's, and Joley's phone conversations. Agents watched Scottie and Tommy from afar. Nothing happened. Bobby and Shelby's phone didn't ring.

"The kidnappers know it'll take time to assemble the money," Honsa said. "They're not going to call every five minutes to check on it. I wouldn't be surprised if we didn't hear from them until later this afternoon."

"In the meantime," I said.

"In the meantime we try to keep the lid on. It seems every cop in the St. Paul PD knows what's happening. It won't be long before the media finds out, too. The daughter of a top cop is kidnapped—do you think there's a TV station in town that wouldn't broadcast the news, even though we ask them not to, even though it might jeopardize the girl's life?"

"I'd like to think so."

"So would I. But I don't. The networks are launching their new fall schedules, and they'll do anything to attract eyeballs."

I studied Honsa over the remains of my egg sandwich. His eyes were heavy, his face unshaven, and his reassuring smile seemed wilted. His clothes were wrinkled—he was wearing the same shirt and slacks as the day before. He reminded me of an unmade bed.

"Maybe you should take a break," I said.

He shot me a look that could have flash-frozen ice cream. "Have you been speaking to Wilson?" he said. "I'm the case agent. I'm in charge here. I'm fine." The tech agent rose from his chair at the dining room table and excused himself. Honsa called after him as he disappeared into the kitchen. "I'm fine."

"Tired people make mistakes," I said.

"I'm not tired."

"I am."

"We'll have to keep an eye on you, then, won't we?"

I was contemplating my reply—it involved several four-letter verbs and an equal number of seven-letter nouns—when my cell finally rang. "Talk to me, H. B.," I said after reading the name on the display.

"The money has just now been deposited into your checking account."

"You're early," I said.

"So I am."

"You really are a heavenly love."

"Let's keep that to ourselves, shall we?"

"Thank you, H. B." I folded my phone and dropped it into the pocket of my black sports jacket.

"And?" Honsa asked.

"We're good to go."

"Agent Wilson," he called. A moment later, Harry was standing next to me in the dining room. "You know what to do," Honsa said. "Use as many people as you need."

Harry set a hand on my shoulder. "Have you ever seen a million dollars in cash in one place, McKenzie?"

"Can't say that I have."

"It's a sight to behold."

"Well, then, let's go behold it."

Harry pulled a nine-millimeter SIG Sauer from the holster on his belt and checked the load. Lately the FBI had been encouraging its personnel to switch over to .40 Glocks. Harry was an old-timer, though, and he preferred to carry the gun he broke in with. He returned the SIG-Sauer to his holster and buttoned his jacket over it. "I'll drive," he said.

A young woman with a full chest and a tight shirt staffed the reception desk at the main branch of my bank. Her eyes looked startled behind her glasses and didn't change during our entire conversation; it was as if life were a continuous surprise to her. Certainly she seemed surprised when Harry flashed his photo ID and announced, "FBI," like it was the most fun he'd had in days. She stammered and hemmed and hawed and wrung her hands and abruptly stood and said she would fetch help without once asking what we wanted or why we were there. While she scurried away in search of a supervisor, I glanced at Harry.

"You big bully," I told him.

"I pick on hostesses in crowded restaurants, too. 'FBI. I need a table by the window.' Never fails."

"To serve and to protect."

"That's the cops. I work for the federal government."

The senior vice president of branch administration was a tall woman who wore a matching pinstripe jacket and trousers over a body that looked like it spent a great deal of time in a gym. Her cotton-blond hair was artfully disheveled, and her face, although not pretty, was animated with the rosy glow of excitement. She stood in front of the reception desk while her assistant reclaimed the chair.

"FBI," she said. "Wow. To what do we owe the pleasure?" She was speaking to me, I presume, because I was better-looking.

Harry got her attention by flashing his ID again. "Special Agent Brian Wilson," he said. "This is McKenzie."

She shook his hand first and then mine. "Lauren Onberg. Please come with me."

Lauren led us to an office with glass walls. There were chairs in front of a large, cluttered desk and a single chair behind it. After everyone was made comfortable, she asked, "How may I help you?"

"I need a million dollars in cash," I said. "Five hundred thousand in fifties, the rest in twenties."

She smiled the way a woman might smile at another woman's child that is misbehaving. "You're kidding, right?" she said.

"Do we look like we're kidding?" Harry said.

"Gentlemen, we don't have a million dollars on-site. Not in twenties, not in fifties, not in any denominations."

"It's a bank," I reminded her, and she smiled some more.

"You guys watch too many movies, too many television shows where characters withdraw huge sums of money from a cashier and then carry it around in a black attaché case. It doesn't work that way. This is the real world."

"Ms. Onberg, this isn't my first rodeo," Harry said. "I know how the real world works. Let's get the process moving."

"If you want a million dollars in cash, you'll need to get it from the Federal Reserve Bank in Minneapolis. Now, I can help you with that, but it'll take three days—assuming, of course, that one of you has an account with our bank. Otherwise . . ." She spread her hands wide in a gesture of unconcerned helplessness.

"Ms. Onberg," Harry said.

"No, let me," I said.

Lauren was still smiling when I leaned across the desk. I slowly and carefully explained the situation to her, making sure to emphasize exactly how old Victoria was and exactly how long she had been missing. I did not raise my voice; I did not threaten her. Yet when I was finished, the smile had left her face and she was on her phone.

"Mr. Starr, this is Lauren. I need your help." She paused for the reply and said, "Yes, sir, it's an emergency."

Neil Edward Starr was smiling when he entered Lauren's office, and he kept smiling while Lauren introduced Harry and me and he shook our hands. I wondered if everyone smiled who worked in a bank and why they would—was it really that much fun? Starr said, "What's the emergency?" Although it faded somewhat while we explained the situation, the smile was still there when we finished.

"Well, gentlemen, Lauren was correct," he said. "It's doubtful that we have that much cash on-site, especially in the denominations you require. As for the Federal Reserve Bank, those guys are fanatics. Worse than fanatics. They're bureaucrats who rely on technology. If we placed your order right now, you still wouldn't receive delivery of the bills until late tomorrow afternoon at the earliest. There is simply no way to expedite it."

"So you see," Lauren said from the chair behind her desk, "there's nothing we can do to help you."

For the first and only time, Neil Edward Starr stopped smiling. He turned slowly and glared down at Lauren. His eyes were as hard as agates and so was his voice. "What did you say?" The color in Lauren's face drained away until it resembled her cottonlike hair. "Do you have a daughter, Lauren?" Starr tapped his chest. "I have a daughter." Starr turned away from his vice president and faced me. His smile returned to his face.

"We have a remote vault where we process our largest transactions with our most cash-intensive customers—casinos, grocery chains, check-cashing stores, other banks," he said. "Our armored trucks will collect their cash deposits and begin rolling to the vault as early as two thirty this afternoon and continue through the evening. What we'll do, we'll camp out, and when the deposits start coming in we will retain the twenties and fifties that we require."

I liked the way Starr kept saying "we."

"I don't know how long it will take to collect twenty-five thousand twenties and ten thousand fifties," he said, "but the process will certainly be a lot quicker than waiting on the Federal Reserve. At any rate, it's the best I can do for you."

"Your best is pretty damn good," I said and shook Starr's hand.

"Yes, well." Starr seemed embarrassed. "We have a reputation here for being very customer friendly. You are a customer, right?"

I assured him that I was.

"We'll have to shuffle a lot of money around to make this work," Lauren said.

"We're bankers. That's what we do," Starr said. "All right, I have to take off for a second. McKenzie, give Lauren your account number. I'll be right back."

While Starr was absent, Lauren ran my account number on her desktop PC to make sure I actually had one million dollars in checking. She then called the bank's wire transfer department to verify that the number was correct. A moment later, Starr returned.

"Are we good?" he asked.

"Yes, sir," Lauren said.

"Okay." Starr was smiling when he handed me a small sheet of paper. "Here. Fill this out."

"What is it?"

"Why, McKenzie, it's a withdrawal slip."

While I filled out the slip, Harry called Honsa on his cell phone. According to the surveillance teams, Scottie Thomforde had walked to the fast-food joint just a few doors down and ordered lunch. He bought a couple of burgers, fries, and a fountain drink and sat at a table next to the front window. He ate alone. The phone at the Dunston house did not ring.

Harry and I followed Starr to a small, unobtrusive business park located in a residential neighborhood not too far from the main branch where we found a large, white, windowless, one-story cinder-block building that reminded me of a warehouse. There were no signs identifying it. To get inside, we had to pass through a series of rooms known as bandit traps—it was impossible to open a door to one room without first locking the door from the other. Digital cameras covered each of the traps. If a door was left open for more than twenty seconds, ear-splitting alarms would be activated.

Once inside, we were greeted by a security team that did an excellent job of searching us without actually searching us. Even Starr was put through the drill. No purses or briefcases were allowed. They even asked Harry to place his SIG Sauer into a locker. There was a number of security guards—it was hard to count them. They weren't stationed in any one place, but rather moved seemingly at random through the vault so you couldn't pin them down. None of the guards was smiling. Nor were any other employees, for that matter. It might have been fun and games at the bank; this was different.

The main processing room was huge. It contained about a dozen rows of five-foot-wide, twenty-foot-long tables. They had metal legs and smooth, easy-to-clean Formica tops and reminded me of fifties-style kitchen tables. Only about a third of them were active when we arrived. Three employees stood at each table busily stuffing currency into cassettes that would later be installed into ATMs.

Starr studied his watch. "The first trucks won't start rolling in for about an hour yet," he said.

He gave us coffee. We didn't drink much. It was just something to hold in our hands. The three of us soon ran out of conversation, and I began to meander through the room, pacing between the tables with my hands in my pockets. I let my mind wander—always a bad thing to do. I wondered why we hadn't heard from the kidnappers, if Scottie knew we were on to him, if I had blown it by scouring the neighborhood for him with Karen Studder, if I had endangered Victoria's life. I wondered if Shelby had been right, if somehow the situation was entirely my fault, and if it was, what I could possibly do to make it good. I wondered about Bobby and Shelby, about the pain they were enduring, about how all this would affect their marriage. *Who knows? They may even grow stronger. I've seen it before.* That's what Honsa had said. God, how I hoped he was right. I wondered about Victoria, what she must be going through, if she was chained to a radiator as Honsa had suggested, what she must have been thinking. Did she still have hope, or was she filled with despair? I wondered if she had been beaten, if she had been abused. I wondered if she was still alive. All the while my heart felt like it was being twisted into the shape of various balloon animals.

Where are those goddamn trucks? my inner voice wanted to know.

This time Honsa called Harry. Harry made no attempt to hide his frustration at whatever Honsa was telling him. "No, I don't know when we'll be finished," he growled into his cell phone. "We haven't actually started yet."

Harry listened for a few moments. He said, "No, we don't need more agents. We're being well taken care of here . . . We're waiting for the trucks . . . Look, it's too complicated to explain right now . . . Damian, you're starting to piss me off . . . I do understand . . . Yes, of course. Of course . . . What's happening on your end?" After a long pause, Harry said, "I agree with you. We need to wait . . . That's the father speaking, not the cop . . . I'll report in as soon as I have something to report . . . You, too."

Harry returned the cell to his pocket. He answered my questions without waiting for me to ask them. "We haven't heard from the kidnappers, and everyone is starting to get anxious. Meanwhile, Thomforde is taking a cigarette break. Bobby Dunston is lobbying hard to arrest him. Honsa wants to wait, and I agree. Honsa is afraid that Bobby will pull an end-around, get his detectives to make an arrest."

"He won't do that," I said.

"Can you guarantee it?"

I shook my head.

"I didn't think so."

The first armored truck backed into a bandit trap. After it was secured, canvas bags of currency were hefted from the rear of the truck onto large carts. The carts were rolled through the remaining traps one at a time and finally wheeled into the main processing room. Bank employees began to appear as if by magic. They were all wearing old shirts and jeans, dressed as if they were cleaning out a garage. There were several containers of baby wipes on each table so they could clean off the black, waxy film that soon covered their fingers.

"It's dirty work handling money," Starr said. He was smiling when he said it, but then Starr was always smiling. I began to think that he was one of those rare people who never forget just how good they have it.

The bags were emptied; currency spilled out on the tables in front of the employees. Tens of thousands, then hundreds of thousands of dollars. Harry had been correct. It was a sight to behold.

According to Special Agent Damian Honsa, Scottie left his job at five thirty and walked to the bus stop on the corner of University and Dale. He waited seven minutes before an MTC bus picked him up. The surveillance team followed the bus to his stop near the state capitol building. From there he walked to the halfway house. He did nothing suspicious. Nor did his brother, Tommy, who was now eating dinner at his mother's house. There were no phone calls to or from either man.

"How are Bobby and Shelby taking it?" I asked.

"About what you'd expect," Harry said.

"That bad, huh?"

The money was starting to pile up. Deposits from a couple of casinos nearly took care of our need for twenties by themselves. Gathering ten thousand fifties was taking more time, but Starr assured me that it wouldn't be a problem. "A couple of out-state bank branches have yet to make their nightly deposits," he said. "That'll put us over the top." Of course, he was smiling when he said it.

My cell phone rang. I read the name off of the digital display. Karen Studder.

"Hey," I said.

"Hi, McKenzie. I'm not interrupting, am I?"

"No. We're just sitting around counting money."

"The ransom money?"

"Yes. It'll be ready soon."

"So the girl, Victoria, she's . . . she hasn't come home yet."

"Not yet."

"I was hoping."

"So was I."

"I don't want to bother you. I just called—"

"I understand."

"—to find out if there was any news."

"Sure."

"I'll just hang up, then, and—"

"Karen?"

"—call some other time."

"Karen? We haven't heard from the kidnappers today."

"Not at all?"

"Meanwhile, Scottie Thomforde is going about his life as if nothing has happened."

There was a long pause on the other end, and for a moment I thought she might have hung up. Finally Karen said, "If you want to ask me, go 'head."

"When we went to the halfway house last night, I stayed in the car so Scottie wouldn't freak out. I wasn't there to hear your conversation. I don't know what was said."

"You can ask. I won't mind."

"Did you tip Scottie off?"

"No, McKenzie. I didn't."

I believed her. I needed to.

The twenties and fifties that we culled from the night deposits were funneled through two Canon CR-180 scanners featuring optical character recognition software. When the process was complete, Harry would have two DVDs containing the images—front and back—and serial numbers of thirty-five thousand bills. This, I was told, is what they mean by "marking money."

"What?" Harry told me. "Did you think we put a little blue dot on the top right-hand corner of each bill?"

I wondered aloud how the banks would be able to read the serial numbers off the bills when the kidnappers started to spend them. Harry rolled his eyes at me.

"They can't," he said. "Tracking actual bills is nearly impossible. Remember the Piper kidnapping in '72?"

I told Harry that I was still eating Crayons in 1972.

"Virginia Piper was kidnapped from her stately manor in Orono," Harry said. "When her husband came home, he found a tied-up housekeeper and a note demanding one million dollars."

"It's nice to see inflation hasn't hit the kidnapping industry," I said.

"Her husband was a retired investment banker. He dropped the ransom—all in twenties—behind a North Minneapolis bar. Those bills were marked, too. The next day they found Virginia Piper chained to a tree in Jay Cooke State Park up north."

"Alive?"

"Yes, alive. But in all the years since the kidnapping, we've been able to recover only four thousand dollars of the ransom."

I gestured at the machines. "What's the point of all this, then?"

"The point is, when we do catch the kidnappers and find the ransom money on them, we can point and go, 'Ahh-haa!'"

Which seemed like a reasonable plan to me. Except the scanners could only record 180 bills per minute. Our progress slowed to a crawl.

Neil Edward Starr read the time aloud. "Ten twenty-two P.M. You might not believe this," he said, "but putting all this together in less than eight hours is kind of amazing."

The currency had been divided among three Star Case 306 aluminum cases with combination locks. The cases were about eighteen inches long, twelve inches high, and six inches deep and were just big enough to contain all the bills: ten thousand fifties in one case and twelve thousand five hundred twenties in each of the other two. I figured the cases must have retailed for about a hundred bucks each, and I offered to pay for them. Starr wouldn't think of it.

"All part of the service," he said. "If you had opened a personal savings account, I would have thrown in a free toaster, too."

I signed a receipt for the money and lifted one of the aluminum cases. As impressed as I had been by the actual bulk of the money, the weight caught me by surprise.

"Each bill weighs about one gram," Starr said. "There are four hundred and fifty-four grams to a pound. You have thirty-five thousand bills. Do the math."

"Seventy-seven pounds," Harry said. He reached down and grasped the handle of the case containing the fifties. "I'll take the light one."

"We can lend you an armored truck to take you wherever you want to go," Starr said.

"That might be just a little conspicuous," Harry said.

"An armed escort, then."

"Thank you, sir. We can take it from here."

We loaded the aluminum cases into the trunk of Harry's car while Harry retrieved his SIG Sauer.

"Will you let me know what happens with that little girl?" Starr said.

I told him I would.

"I don't know if I told you, McKenzie, but I have a daughter, too."

Harry and I lugged the aluminum cases into Bobby Dunston's house. Bobby met us at the door, and I gave him one of the cases. He seemed as surprised by the weight as I had been. We carried them to the dining room table, set them on top.

"Open it," I said.

"What's the combination?"

"I set it for your wife's birthday."

I quickly opened my case and stepped back. Bobby was having trouble with his. "Zero six twenty-seven?" he asked.

"Zero six twenty-*eight*," I said.

"Shelby was born on June twenty-seventh," he told me.

"Honestly, McKenzie," Shelby said. She was behind me and moving toward the table. "How long have we known each other?"

"At least I got the month right."

All three cases were open, and Bobby, Honsa, and the tech agent joined Harry and me in admiring all that cash. Only Shelby seemed unimpressed.

"I thought there would be more," she said. "I thought it would be bigger. It should be bigger."

11

Once I delivered the money, I figured that my part in all of this would be over, that I'd be like Karen and H. B. and the president of my bank, all waiting for the final curtain, hoping someone would tell us how the play finally ended. Except Bobby asked me to stay close. And while Shelby didn't actually say anything, the way she looked at me prompted my inner voice to repeat the words she spoke earlier—*I need all my men to be strong.* Honsa thought it was a good idea, too. "It's possible that the kidnappers want more from you than just money," he said. That's why I was in the Dunston home early the next morning when Honsa's cell phone rang.

"Godammit!" Honsa said. His reassuring smile disappeared. "Godammit. Where the hell did you get your training? The goddamned CIA?"

His outburst caused both Shelby and Bobby to rise from their chairs at the dining room table. They reached for each other the way a tired swimmer reaches for the ladder at the end of a pool.

"I apologize," Honsa said. "That was inappropriate."

"What happened?" Bobby asked.

"It's not as bad as it sounds."

"What happened?"

"Our agents lost Scottie Thomforde."

"Butterfingers," I said.

"Our agents had watched Thomforde catch the bus on University Avenue and head for work," Honsa said. "When he didn't get off at his regular stop, the agents followed the bus all the way into Minneapolis. When he still didn't disembark, the agents boarded the bus. Thomforde wasn't on it."

"Which means he got off the bus and your agents didn't see him," Bobby said. "Which means your agents are incompetent or somehow Scottie managed a disguise." Honsa nodded helplessly. "Which means he knew we were watching."

"Not necessarily."

Bobby cut loose with a long list of profanities interspersed with several personal epithets that he never, ever would have allowed his daughters to use. Honsa, to his credit, just stood there and took it. While Bobby vented, Shelby's entire body sagged. She closed her eyes and gripped the edge of the dining room table as if she were trying to keep from falling. Harry interrupted Bobby's tirade.

"Mrs. Dunston?" he said. "Shelby?"

She opened her eyes and searched his face, looking for something, anything, that she might hold on to besides the furniture.

"This is a good thing," Harry said.

Bobby wanted to know, "How do you figure?"

"He'll call us now."

You wouldn't think that hearing from the man that kidnapped your twelve-year-old daughter would be a cause for celebration, but from the expression on Bobby's face when the phone rang, I was sure he was ready to break out the champagne. Shelby not only stopped trembling, she began looking around her as if she were thinking she should pick up the house, maybe display the good china. I felt relieved myself, although the feeling didn't last long.

"Yes," Bobby said into the phone.

"You got the money," the electronically altered voice said. It wasn't a question. He spoke as if it were a confirmed fact.

"I have it."

"See, that didn't take long, did it? Now listen carefully. What I want you to do—"

"I'm not going to do anything until I have proof that Victoria is alive."

Bobby and Honsa had discussed this moment at length, even engaged in some role-playing to make sure Bobby was comfortable with what he was demanding. Only it was apparent that the kidnapper had not planned that far ahead. He hemmed and hawed and tripped over his tongue.

"Proof of life," Bobby said. "I need to know my daughter's alive." Not want, *need.* "I want to hear her voice." Not need, *want.* Bobby and Honsa had agreed they would negotiate this point, maybe have the kidnappers ask Victoria a question only she could answer. The voice on the phone didn't recognize the nuances.

"I'm giving the orders here," it said.

"You want the money. I want to hear my daughter's voice. I want proof that she's alive. You don't get dollar one until I know that she's alive."

"I'm giving the orders," the voice repeated.

"You want the money. It's sitting right here waiting for you. Three nice, shiny suitcases full of cash. But first I'm going to speak to my daughter."

"Fuck you. Bobby. You're gonna—"

Bobby hung up the phone. We all stood motionless, watching him. No one spoke. I couldn't testify that any of us were even breathing. I had never heard silence so loud. A few moments passed. It could have been hours. Finally the phone rang again. Bobby waited until the third ring before answering. "Yes?"

"Who the fuck do you—?"

Bobby hung up again.

Honsa winced and turned his back so no one could see his expression. I don't think he and Bobby had rehearsed this part.

Bobby sank slowly into a chair. He gripped the arms tightly and lowered his head until his chin was touching his chest. "Oh God, oh God," he muttered. "What have I done?" Shelby knelt next to the chair. She wrapped one arm around Bobby's legs and lowered her head into his lap. Bobby released the chair and draped his arms around her.

"He'll call back," I said to no one in particular. Maybe I was talking to myself.

"Of course he will," Honsa said.

Einstein once said that an hour spent holding a pretty girl's hand at a party might seem like only a moment, while a moment spent touching a hot stove might seem like an hour—that's relativity. For the next ten minutes, we were all sitting on a stove. It was very hot and it was very painful and I, for one, wondered how we got there and how we would get off.

And then the phone rang.

And Bobby answered it.

And Victoria Dunston's voice said, "Daddy?"

Bobby lost it for the first time. "Oh, Vic, Vic," he said, his voice choking on the words.

"I'm not afraid," Victoria said. "I told them I'm not afraid. I told them that they're the ones should be afraid when you come for them."

We could hear the kidnapper wresting the phone from Victoria's hand. "Yada yada, yada. Is McKenzie there?"

"No," Bobby said.

"Get 'im."

"Why?"

"Cuz we don't want no fuckin' irate father playin' Superman for his kid, that's why. You got ten minutes."

Honsa turned to the tech agent. "Anything?" he asked.

"We only have a general location. It looks like the Badlands again."

Honsa nodded, and the tech agent was quickly on his feet. "What should I do?" he asked.

"McKenzie," Honsa said. "Do you have an onboard navigation system in your car?"

"Yes, but I never use it."

"Give me your keys," the tech agent said.

"My keys?"

"Hurry."

I tossed him my car keys and asked, "What's going on?" as he hurried out the front door.

"The navigation system has a GPS component," Honsa said. "If it's sensitive enough, we can use it to track your whereabouts to within fifteen to twenty meters."

"My whereabouts?"

"It looks like you'll be delivering the ransom."

"I'll deliver the ransom," Bobby declared.

"You heard him on the phone. There's a good possibility that the kidnapper won't allow it," Honsa told him. "He's afraid of you."

"He should be."

"We don't want him afraid, Lieutenant. We want him as calm as he can be. If he asks for McKenzie, we're going to give him McKenzie."

"It's my daughter."

"It's not our decision to make," Honsa said. "It's Thomforde's."

"It's my daughter."

"I know."

I knew, too. This was Bobby's job, Bobby's place. He must have thought I was usurping his position in his own family. Only it wasn't my idea. None of this was my idea.

"It's all right with me if you deliver the money," I said. "You can use my car."

"Your car," said Honsa. "That's another thing. Your navigation system has a dashboard microphone that allows you to talk to your computer, that allows you to contact emergency personnel in case of an accident. It works like a cell phone."

"So?"

"We're going to activate the microphone and reroute the signal to our own receivers so we can hear everything that's said in the car."

"Talk to us, McKenzie," Harry said. "You won't hear us, but we'll hear you."

"It's my daughter," Bobby repeated. "It's my job."

"I don't know what to tell you, Lieutenant," Honsa said. "Thomforde is calling the tune now."

"And we're all going to dance to it?"

"Yes." Honsa nodded his head emphatically. "Yes, we are. Until it's time for us to call the tune. Then we'll make him dance."

A moment later, the tech agent returned. He was carrying a soft-sided toolbox. "The car's ready," he said. He hefted the box onto the dining room table. He was looking at Honsa when he asked, "Who gets it?"

Honsa was staring directly into Bobby's eyes when he said, "McKenzie," and then, "I'm sorry."

Bobby nodded.

"Take off your shirt," the tech agent told me.

"Why?"

The tech agent held up an audio transmitter that was about the size of a wallet with a small whip antenna. "It's a five-watt body wire. Has a line-of-sight range of about three miles."

"Thomforde will be looking for a tail," Harry said. "This will allow us to run surveillance teams parallel to your location. Just tell us where you're going. We'll be close enough to intervene if necessary, yet far enough away to avoid detection."

"I thought you rigged my car for that."

"We are big believers in redundancy at the FBI," the tech agent said.

"Besides, there's no guarantee that Thomforde will let you stay with your car," Harry said.

The tech agent fixed the transmitter to my chest using white surgical tape.

"This is going to hurt coming off," I said.

"Let's step into the bathroom," he said.

That's something a guy has never said to me before. "I'm not sure I know you that well, Agent," I said.

The tech agent held up a sturdy plastic box about the size of a pack of cigarettes. "Real-time GPS transmitter, in case you leave your car, like we said. This one we'll put between your legs."

"Is that wise?" I asked.

"Don't worry, McKenzie," Harry told me. "It's waterproof."

When I returned, Harry was hiding a second GPS transmitter under packets of twenty-dollar bills in one of the aluminum cases. "You never know," he said.

"We'll also be able to track you using your cell," Honsa said. As he said it, the tech agent motioned for my phone. I gave it to him.

"Looks like you've thought of everything," I said.

"We'll have several teams of agents following you," Honsa said. "Don't look for them. They'll know where you are. Also, our SWAT team, as well as the St. Paul Police Department's SWAT team, has been alerted. Listen to me, McKenzie. Are you listening?"

I took my cell from the tech agent and dropped it into the pocket of my sports coat. "I'm listening," I said.

"Don't screw around. Don't be a hero. You get Victoria. You get out. Bring her back here. We'll take care of the rest."

"What if they pull something like they did with Virginia Piper? What if they demand that we drop the ransom behind a bar somewhere in exchange for telling us what tree she's chained to?"

Honsa and Bobby traded glances. Apparently they had already made a decision concerning that possibility.

"We'll deal with that when they call back," Honsa said.

"Anything else?" I said.

"I don't know how to say it but to say it."

"Go 'head."

"The girl is everything. Her safety is paramount. It's essential. You must not do anything that jeopardizes it."

"I won't."

"Whatever Thomforde tells you to do, you do. No arguments. No discussion. If he tells you to jump in a lake, you jump. Understand?"

"Yes."

"The money is expendable, and so, I'm afraid, are you."

"Yes."

"It's a lousy situation."

"Tell me about it."

The phone rang. Bobby waited until the FBI was ready before answering it. "Yes," he said.

"Is McKenzie there?" the mechanically disguised voice said.

"Yes, but you need to understand something first."

"*I* need to understand something? You need to understand, I ain't takin' no more fucking orders from you."

Bobby continued speaking in a flat voice as if the kidnapper had never said a word. "This is going to be a straight-up exchange. Victoria for the money."

"You put the money where I tell ya to put it. Then I'll—"

"That's unacceptable."

"Unacceptable?"

"You want the money. One million dollars in untraceable twenties and fifties. It's waiting here for you. All of it. Give me Victoria and I'll give you the money. One million dollars."

"That ain't gonna be the way it works. I'll tell you where—"

"One million dollars. You'll be a wealthy man. You could live anywhere you want. Do whatever you want. Give me my daughter and you can have the money."

There was a long pause. For a moment I thought that this time it was the kidnapper that had hung up. Finally he said, "No, no. That ain't the way we're gonna deal."

"Then we don't have a deal," Bobby said. I was astonished by how quiet his voice was.

There was a blustering sound, as if the kidnapper couldn't believe what he was hearing, followed by a shout. "You want your daughter back or don'tcha?"

"I want her back alive and unharmed."

"Then do what I say."

"How do I know that after I pay the ransom you won't kill her?"

"You'll just have to trust me."

"Why should I?"

"You got a choice?"

"Yes, I do."

"Let me talk to McKenzie."

"No. Not until you agree to my terms."

"Put McKenzie on the phone."

"We'll give you the money at the same time as you give us Victoria. One million dollars. It's sitting here waiting for you. You can have it right now. Right this minute. One million dollars. Just tell us where you're holding Victoria and I'll bring it to you."

"McKenzie will bring it to me. I don't trust you, Bobby. Not for a second."

"Then McKenzie will bring it to you. If you give him Victoria, he'll give you the money. One million dollars."

"I know how much it is." The kidnapper paused again, then said, "I'll call back."

After he hung up, Bobby sought Honsa's face. "What do you think?" he said.

"He and his partner are discussing it."

"If they are," the tech agent said, "they're doing it on Interstate 94 heading east, toward Woodbury."

"I'll bet you a nickel they're holding Victoria somewhere near the Badlands," I said. "Maybe Dayton's Bluff. Maybe the East Side."

Honsa nodded.

"Will they agree to our terms?" Bobby said.

"Question is, what are we going to do if they don't?" Honsa said.

It wasn't for me to say, but I said it anyway. "Pay the money."

Bobby nodded. "Any chance is better than no chance."

"No." Shelby was speaking from the step on the staircase where she had sat two days before, again holding the posts of the banister and peering through them. "We talked about this before, Bobby. We are not going to reward these people for hurting our child."

"Shelby," Bobby said. He moved to the foot of the staircase and looked up at her. She slowly shook her head. Her expression was something I had never seen before. Ever. It was determined yet frightened, perfectly calm yet also crazed. It was the expression of a woman who had never bet on anything in her life, who had suddenly, inexplicably wagered everything in her life on the turn of a single card.

"Shelby." Bobby repeated the name like a prayer.

In that moment I recognized just how fragile they had become since

Victoria had been taken. The wrong word spoken at the wrong time could have shattered both their lives. Yet the wrong word was not spoken; no words were exchanged. For at that moment, when all bad things were possible, the phone rang. Bobby answered it. The voice of the kidnapper said, "All right, we'll do it the hard way. See if you like that better. Put McKenzie on the phone."

He handed me the receiver and I said, "This is McKenzie."

"I want you delivering the ransom," the voice said. "That Bobby, he's liable to do anything. But you—you ain't gonna fuck around with the life of someone else's kid, are you, McKenzie? You ain't gonna try nothin' heroic, are you?"

"Not me."

"Fuckin' right, not you. You got a cell phone, McKenzie?"

"Yes."

"Give me the number." I did. "Your phone better be charged, cuz if I lose you, McKenzie, I ain't gonna be responsible for what happens next."

"It's charged."

"You do what I say, McKenzie. You go where I say. If I see anyone following you, if I see a helicopter in the sky—I had better not see no fuckin' helicopters."

"I'm not an air traffic controller. I can't control what's in the air."

"Just so you know. Anything goes wrong, bad things are gonna happen."

"I understand."

"I want you to get into your car and start drivin', okay? Take the money and go for a ride."

"Where?"

"Just drive. I'll call later when I'm ready and tell you where I want you to go. Remember, I'll be watching you."

After he hung up, Honsa patted my shoulder. He didn't say anything, just patted.

Harry was standing near the front door. He was holding two of the aluminum cases. I picked up the third and moved to join him.

"McKenzie," Bobby said. He took hold of my arm and led me toward the door. "I haven't even asked if you wanted to do this."

"Are you asking now? Cuz I don't, you know. I really don't."

"It should be me."

"Yes, it should."

"You're the only one I trust to do this. Anyone else . . ."

"Don't worry about it, Bobby. I'll bring Victoria home."

"I know you will."

I glanced up at Shelby. She was standing on the staircase and looking down at me. "See you in a little bit," I said.

She opened her mouth, but words did not come out. Instead, she nodded at me. I nodded back.

Harry helped carry the cases to my car and load them into the trunk. "Are you ready?" he said.

"Ready as I'll ever be."

"We'll be with you every step of the way."

"Harry, if it all goes bad . . ."

"It won't."

"If it does, make sure I get the blame. Don't let Bobby and Shelby . . . Don't let them blame themselves. Don't let them blame each other."

"Nothing will go wrong."

"I hope you're right," I said. "As I live and die, I hope you're right."

12

I took Marshall Avenue west toward Minneapolis, turned off at Mississippi River Boulevard on the St. Paul side of the river, and drove south.
With no particular place to go, I reverted back to the time just after I
first earned my license and drove simply for the sake of driving. The
boulevard was a popular track in those days, especially when we managed to lure girls into the car. Somehow we got it into our heads that following the meandering Mississippi was a romantic drive. Toward the
end of the road we'd hit a series of sharp curves. My friends and I used
to call them the SOBs—the Slide Over Babies. The idea was that if you
took the curves fast enough, the girl would be compelled to slide across
the seat and end up next to you, which we always assumed was where
she wanted to be anyway. I can't honestly remember a single instance
when this maneuver was successful, but I had friends who swore that it
had worked for them. At least that's how I explained it to the FBI agents
who I assumed were hanging on my every word. I could see Bobby in
my mind's eye turning to Shelby and saying, "I would never do anything

so crass," and Shelby giving him her famous I-can't-believe-I-married-this-guy smile and telling him, "No, of course not."

I was coming out of the SOBs when my cell rang. I picked it off the seat next to me. The digital display said the call was coming from someone called Gazelle. I could only assume that Gazelle was a woman and Scottie had stolen her phone, but what did I know—Gazelle could have been a bartender at the Gay Nineties.

"Where are you?" his mechanically altered voice said.

"Mississippi Boulevard, near the Ford Bridge."

"You got a ways to go, then. You know where Parade Stadium is?"

"Parade Stadium," I said for the benefit of all those listening. "Yeah, I know where it is."

"Park in the lot."

After he hung up I said, "Gentlemen, we're going to Minneapolis." I spoke loudly, hoping both the body wire and the microphone on my altered navigational system picked it up. I remembered that Honsa cautioned me not to look for his agents. *They'll be around,* he said. It didn't fill me with confidence. After a few anxious moments I added, "If you can hear me, someone beep a horn." No one did. "God, I hope this works," I said to no one in particular.

Parade Stadium was little more than a few bleachers wrapped around a baseball diamond. It had been considered state-of-the-art when it was built in the 1950s. Not so much now. Still, from the parking lot I had a spectacular skyline view of downtown Minneapolis and was within strolling distance of both the Walker Art Center and the Minneapolis Sculpture Garden. There were three cars in the lot—two near the entrance and a pale blue Toyota Corolla hatchback near the center. I parked between them, turned off my Audi, and waited.

And waited.

And waited some more.

I kept twisting in my seat, looking for someone, anyone. There were no pedestrians, not even a neighbor walking a dog, and the only vehicles I spied were zooming along I-394 just north of the stadium. At first I kept a running commentary for the agents I dearly hoped were listening on the other end of the wire. As the minutes ticked by and I became more apprehensive, I stopped talking altogether. I knew Scottie was out there somewhere watching, and I slowly became convinced that he had spotted the tails.

At least twenty minutes had passed by my watch before my cell phone rang. The sound of it startled me. I spoke into it too quickly.

"Yeah," I said.

"What's the matter, McKenzie? Nervous?"

"I thought it was Cities 97 and I had just won tickets to see Prince."

"Talkin' like that, what, do you think this is a game?" Scottie said. It occurred to me then that he was as nervous as I was.

"No."

"You do what I tell you to do and keep your mouth shut."

Yeah, why don't you? my inner voice agreed.

"Yes," I said.

"See the Toyota?" Scottie asked.

"I see it."

"Park behind it."

I set the cell on the seat without shutting it down, started the Audi, and drove to the rear of the Corolla. I retrieved the cell and said, "Now what?" My head swiveled from the elegant homes on Kenwood Parkway to the Walker to the Sculpture Garden to I-394. I saw no one.

"Get out of your car."

I shut off the Audi, opened the door, and slid out. "Now what?" I repeated.

"Take the money out of your car and put it in the backseat of the Toyota. The door is unlocked. Do not get back into your car. I'm watching you, McKenzie."

I did what I was told. The kidnapper must have been close, because he saw me handling the aluminum cases. "Why three cases, McKenzie?" he said.

"It wouldn't fit into just one," I said. "The money weighs seventy-seven pounds."

The way he inhaled made me think that he was as surprised by that as I had been. "Okay," he said. "Get in the Toyota. Stay away from your car."

I used the remote control on my key chain to lock the doors to my Audi and dropped the keys into the pocket of my sports jacket. I slid behind the wheel of the Toyota. "Now what?" I said again.

"The keys are under the floor mat."

I found them there.

"Start driving," Scottie said.

"Where?" I asked.

"I don't care. Just drive. And don't forget—I can see you."

He hung up. I started the car; the engine roared to life immediately. The Toyota might have been thirty years old, yet it was well preserved. I put it in gear and drove out of the parking lot. I spoke into my chest.

"I'm driving a 1977 Toyota Corolla." I recited the license plate number. I explained what had happened, emphasizing that when I left the Audi, I lost the car's microphone and its GPS system, just as Harry had predicted. "I have no idea what Scottie is planning next. He might be running me around the Twin Cities to make sure I'm not being followed. He might be off to check on another location, take up a position where he can watch, and when he's ready send me there. What do I know?"

I maneuvered the Toyota onto Hennepin Avenue and headed toward Uptown. Along the way I told the agents that the car had not been hot-wired; if the Toyota was stolen, it had been stolen with the keys in the ignition. "You should check to see if there have been any recent car-jackings," I said. I knew that the FBI and certainly Bobby Dunston didn't need my advice. It made me feel better to give it just the same.

It was twenty minutes later and I was circling Lake Calhoun for the third time, wondering once again if something had gone terribly wrong, when the cell rang.

The Franklin Avenue Bridge connecting Minneapolis and St. Paul was officially named the Cappelen Memorial Bridge after the man who designed it, only no one ever called it that. It opened in 1923, and at one time it was one of the largest bridges to span the Mississippi River, but its four lanes didn't carry as much traffic as they once did; the freeway bridge farther up the river now took most of it. Still, there were plenty of irate drivers stacked up behind me when I stopped the Toyota in the center of the bridge, put it in park, and activated the flashing emergency lights.

"I did what you told me," I said into the cell phone. "Now what?"

"Get out."

I did, but first I shut off the engine and removed the key just in case Scottie was planning a fast one—get me out of the way so he or his partner could boost the Toyota with the money in the back seat. He could have been concealed in one of the cars behind me. Why not?

A man was standing on the sidewalk and staring at me with angry eyes when I exited the car. He was wearing long brown hair in a ponytail and carrying a heavy backpack, yet he looked at least a decade too old for college. I wondered if he was a veteran who had paid for his University of Minnesota tuition by serving in the military; there was plenty of off-campus housing nearby. Or maybe he was a professional student who was studying everything at nearby Augsburg College except how to live in the real world. If he was a professor, I feared for the future of higher education.

"You can't park here," he said. I rounded the car and stepped on the sidewalk. "Did you hear me? I said you can't park here."

"Who is it?" Scottie asked. The cell was pressed hard against my ear.

"Some guy, don't worry about it."

"Get rid of him."

"Just tell me what you want me to do."

"Hey," said the student. "I'm talking to you."

"Walk to the railing," Scottie said.

I moved forward. The student attempted to block my path. I brushed past him.

"Excuse me," I said.

"What?" Scottie said.

"Don't push me," the student said. He grabbed my arm. I nearly dropped the cell pulling it free.

"Get out of my way," I told him.

"You can't park here. Lookit." He pointed at the avenue with his thumb. "Traffic is backing up."

He was right. The few cars behind the Toyota had become a long line; they were shifting into the second lane whenever an opening appeared.

"This is an emergency," I said.

I reached the bridge railing and looked down at the Mississippi River below. The bridge was only fifty-five feet above the water, but it might as well have been as high as Mount McKinley. My acrophobia kicked in, and I took two anxious steps backward. I've been afraid of heights since I was a kid. It doesn't bother me much when I'm in a tall building looking out a window, or even when I'm on a plane. Yet in the open on, say, I don't know, a bridge, it causes my heart to pound and my breath to grow short and gives me a feeling in my stomach that says I'm about to get hit by a really big meteor. My friends theorize my fear was triggered by some repressed childhood experience. They're mistaken. The reason I'm afraid of falling from a great height is that I can't fly.

"What emergency?" the student wanted to know.

"What's going on?" Scottie said.

"I don't see any emergency," said the student.

"What do you want me to do?" I said into the phone.

"Get your car off the bridge," said the student.

"Throw your cell phone into the river," said Scottie.

"What?" I asked.

"You heard me," the student said.

"You heard me," Scottie said.

"I can't do that," I said.

"Do you think you're something special?" the student asked.

"Throw it in," Scottie said.

"How are we going to stay in touch?" I asked.

"I have it covered. Now throw the damn phone into the river. Let me see you do it."

I glanced up and down the bridge. On the west side there were a number of fashionable homes. On the east I could see an auto repair shop and a store where you could get your furniture reupholstered. I didn't see anyone speaking on a phone; I didn't see anyone waving from a parked car.

"I'm waiting," Scottie said.

I held the cell phone above my head for a few beats, then flung it as far as I could. It seemed to hover in the air for a moment, then arch down toward the river. I didn't watch it fall.

"What are you doing?" the student said. "You can't pollute the river with your junk."

"Would you please shut the hell up?" I said. I pivoted away from the railing and moved toward the car. I took two steps before the student grabbed my arm again, taking hold of my elbow.

"I'm reporting you," he said.

I pulled my elbow free and jabbed him in the face with it, catching him just below his nose. His head snapped back, and his hand quickly covered his mouth; blood trickled through his fingers. At the same time, I stepped toward him, swung my left leg around, hooking my foot behind his right knee, and swept upward. That, plus the weight of his backpack, was enough to put him down. The student hit the sidewalk with a dull thud, coming to rest on top of the backpack. He flailed his arms like a turtle on its back. His upper lip had been torn, and blood flowed down his chin. Some of it got into his mouth when he shouted at me.

"What's wrong with you?"

"I'm sorry." I was shouting, too, and pointing my finger. "I'm sorry I hit you, but I haven't got time to be a nice guy." I retreated to the Toyota. The drivers queued up behind me seemed relieved when I put it into gear and drove off. I was off the bridge and going east on Franklin when I heard a cell phone ring. It took a few confusing moments before I found it in the glove compartment.

"Yes," I said.

"I saw you hit the kid," the voice said. "You must really be pissed off."

"What now?"

"Getting a little frustrated, McKenzie?"

"What now?"

"Just drive. I'll tell you where in a minute."

Scottie rang off. I dropped the phone on the seat next to me and spoke into my chest.

"I don't know where I'm going," I said. "He just wants me to drive again. He's probably setting up the next rendezvous." I liked that word so much I repeated it. "Rendezvous." What else would you call it?

"You probably heard what happened on the bridge. I'm sorry about that. I hope I didn't hurt that guy too much. Some people just don't know when to mind their own business. I'm concerned, though. Not about the guy on the bridge, the kidnappers. I think they have a plan. What I mean by plan, I think Scottie's trying to strip me of all my wires. First we lose the GPS and microphone in my car. Now my cell phone. It makes me nervous about what we have left."

Franklin Avenue continued east to the freeway. I hung a left and then a right and followed University Avenue into St. Paul. I began to feel the way I had on the bridge looking down—the escalating heartbeat, the shortness of breath, the anxiety.

"Driving around like this is starting to get on my nerves," I said aloud. "Do I dare risk stopping? I don't have a tail, I'm sure of that. Maybe I should stop. There's Porky's Drive-In up a ways on University. I could pull in, sit in the car, have a Cherry Coke, wait for Scottie to call. Do you think I could risk that?"

Porky's loomed up on my right. I drove past it.

"Maybe not."

After Labor Day, the county pulls the lifeguards off the wooden towers at the various lakes it supervises. The rule was you swam at your own risk, but that didn't stop a half-dozen teenagers from frolicking on the beach at McCarrons Lake. Why they weren't in school, I couldn't say. There were also a couple of young women sprawled on blankets and jumbo-sized towels intent on catching what was left of the summer's rays. A middle-aged jogger leaned against the now-closed snack shack and stretched. He was wearing headphones; sweat stained the front and back of his shirt, and I thought he might be one of Honsa's agents. There was another man parked in an SUV near the entrance of the asphalt parking lot. He sat behind his steering wheel while reading a newspaper and eating a Dairy Queen sundae. I figured he might be an agent, too.

I was sitting in the Toyota in the parking lot where Scottie had told me to park, in the row nearest the beach and facing the water. Twisting in my seat I could see several other cars in the lot, but whom they belonged to I couldn't say. There were empty picnic tables scattered through the park and unused playground equipment near the beach. Traffic moved incessantly on Rice Street. There were two strip malls up near Larpenteur Avenue, plus a fast-food joint, a car wash, a pawnshop, a bank, a school bus depot, and a Dairy Queen that had not yet closed for the season. Modest houses ringed the lake. Scottie could have been anywhere, and after a while I stopped searching for him.

As before, I waited.

Finally the cell rang.

"Yeah," I said.

"There's a Plymouth Reliant in the row behind you and off to your right," Scottie said.

I found it easily enough. Tan, with plenty of rust, one of Plymouth's highly touted K-cars.

"I see it," I said.

"Boxers or briefs?"

"Excuse me?"

"Do you wear boxers or briefs?"

"Getting a little personal, aren't we?"

Scottie chuckled. "You're gonna love this, McKenzie," he said.

"Love what?"

"I want you to get out of your car and walk to the lake and jump in."

"Jump in?"

"First you're going to strip down to your skivvies, then jump in."

While I hesitated, Honsa's words came back to me: *Whatever Thomforde tells you to do, you do. No arguments. No discussion. If he tells you to jump in a lake, you jump. Understand?*

"You hear me, McKenzie?" Scottie asked.

"I hear you."

I stepped out of the Toyota and walked to the water's edge. The beach seemed more stone than sand, and the tiny rocks crunched under my feet. The teenagers didn't seem to notice me. I figured that was going to change in a hurry.

"Start stripping," Scottie said.

I set the cell on the sand next to me. It was about seventy-three degrees, a comfortable temperature, I thought until I removed my shoes and socks and stood barefoot. Next came my sports coat. My polo shirt was going to be tricky. While facing the open water, I pulled the back of the shirt up and over my head so that it covered my chest. With my right hand I gripped the body wire through the material of the shirt and yanked quickly. The wire, tape, and a fistful of chest hair came off, leaving a red blotch between my nipples that I hoped Scottie couldn't detect at a distance. I tried not to wince as I dropped the shirt and wire on top of my jacket. Next came my jeans. I peeled them off carefully. The plastic box containing the GPS transmitter peeked out from under the hem of my blue boxers. The way the tape holding it was wrapped around my inner thigh, there was no way I could remove it without Scottie noticing. And if I could have, what then? I dropped the jeans on top of my other clothes, retrieved the cell phone, and stood with my legs close together.

"You're not embarrassed, are you, McKenzie?" Scottie asked.

"Do you care?"

Scottie thought that was funny. "Take off your watch, too," he said. I did, dropping it on top of my jeans. He hadn't noticed the slight bulge in my shorts.

"All right," he told me. "You know what to do. Jump in the lake."

I set the phone on my clothes and walked into the water. You would have thought that the lake would have retained some of its summer heat. It hadn't. Goose bumps formed all over my body, and I began to shiver. I was convinced my feet were turning blue. I plowed into the lake until the water was covering my knees. Half the teenagers had stopped what they were doing to watch me, probably wondering what that old man was doing. I dove in. The shock to my system was so great that for a panicky moment I convinced myself I was having a heart attack. Still, I stayed underwater as long as I could. I came up gasping; the cold had knocked the breath out of me. I turned and pushed through the icy lake toward the beach. The water had pasted the boxers to my skin, and you could easily discern the outline of the plastic box if you looked hard. I moved quickly to the cell phone and turned sideways so Scottie wouldn't look.

"What now?" I said.

"Cold, was it, McKenzie?"

"Invigorating," I said. "What now?"

"Leave your clothes. Take nothing. Walk to the Toyota. I'm watching you."

I did what Scottie said while holding the phone to my ear. I was shivering, and my teeth began to chatter. The teenagers had found something else to occupy their attention. The jogger near the snack shack had disappeared; the driver parked at the entrance to the parking lot had moved on. *So much for Honsa's agents,* my inner voice said.

When I reached the car, Scottie told me to remove the aluminum cases and transfer them to the Reliant. I carried a case in each hand and the third tucked under my arm. I walked so that one of the cases was in front of my boxers. The cell was in my mouth. The cases were heavy and the going was awkward, yet the effort seemed to warm me. I set the cases next to the car and returned the cell phone to my ear.

"This is where it pays for you to be real smart, McKenzie, cuz if you fuck up I'll kill both you and the girl."

"What do you want me to do?"

"Open the cases, remove the money one packet at a time, and set them inside the trunk of the Reliant. Listen to me, McKenzie. Are you listening?"

"I'm listening."

"We'll bring the girl to you when we make the exchange. But there's going to be a gun pointed at her head. Now, we're going to take that money out of the trunk, one packet at a time, and if we see a GPS or listening device or any kind of bug, she dies and then you die. Ain't gonna be no discussion about it, neither."

"I understand."

"Be smart, McKenzie."

The trunk wasn't locked; the lid was resting on top of the latch, and it came up easily. I got the impression that Scottie was positioned so that he could see into the trunk, which put him across Rice Street at a bar called the Chalet, or someplace near it. I made an effort not to look.

I worked the combination on the cases and unlocked them one at a time. I had forgotten which one contained the GPS transmitter, and I was careful when I handled each packet of money so that I wouldn't put it into the trunk by accident. I found it in the second case. I used my body to block Scottie's view while I unwrapped a packet of twenties from around the device. I put the money in the trunk and slid the box under the car. I was putting all of my trust into the GPS transmitter taped between my legs. I thought, *This damn thing had better be waterproof or I'm going to shoot Harry.*

I finished the job, tossing the empty cases aside, and slammed the trunk lid closed.

"What now?" I said into the cell.

"That's a lot of money," Scottie said.

"One million bucks."

"For some reason, I didn't think there'd be that many bills."

"What do you want me to do?"

"Get in the car."

I did as I was told. The sun had baked the Reliant while it sat in the parking lot, and I was grateful for the warmth I found inside. The keys were in the ignition. The engine started hard; it was a decade younger than the Toyota, but the Reliant had not aged nearly as gracefully. The engine ran rough, and the exhaust was thick.

"Start driving," Scottie said.

The address the kidnapper gave me was for a shotgun house located in the Badlands, not too far from Scottie's halfway house—not far from the St. Paul Police Department, either, for that matter. The house had once been yellow, but over time the paint had faded to the color of urine; the white trim was now gray. There was a FOR SALE sign in front of it. From where I was parked, I could see a half-dozen brightly colored Realtors' signs in front of structures up and down the street. Some of the houses were old with crumbling concrete sidewalks and frayed shingles. Others were new, freshly painted multi-family units. A white sixteen-foot moving truck, its huge doors open and its ramp down, was parked in front of a pristine duplex on the next block. I didn't see any movers, but I was willing to bet they were going, not coming. Despite attempts to revive the Badlands over the decades, the ancient neighborhood had been unable to shake off the distinctive aura of rust.

I rolled down the windows of the Reliant and waited. I listened to the engine ticking off its heat and the rumble of freeway traffic in the distance; I smelled the exhaust and burning oil that could have come from the freeway or the Plymouth or both; I watched the street. There were a half-dozen cars parked on both sides in front of me and a few more behind, yet I saw no one. Still, that didn't mean there weren't people watching intently from their windows. The possibility made me wonder if this was the end of the line or just another brief stop in the kidnappers' circuitous route. Yes, the location was handy to several freeways. It was also wide open to witnesses.

I waited.

And waited some more.

Nothing moved until a dirty red, late-model Pontiac Vibe station wagon approached from the opposite direction. It swept past and swung down on the wrong side of the street behind me. I watched in my rearview mirror as it backed along the curb until there was only a short space between my bumper and its tailgate. The Vibe was a small vehicle with a wimpy four-cylinder engine that had about as much pickup as a road grader, and I thought, *They're going to try to get away in this? Kids on skateboards could outrace a Vibe.*

I stared at the back of the driver's head with such intensity that I didn't hear or see anyone approach the Reliant until the kidnapper spoke.

"Put both hands on the steering wheel," he said.

His words startled me. I turned to look out the passenger window. A man dressed in white coveralls and a black ski mask was squatting on the cracked sidewalk about a yard away; I didn't know if he came from the yellow house or not. He had one arm wrapped around Victoria Dunston's shoulder and neck and another carelessly gripping a nine-millimeter automatic. He was pointing the gun at the girl's ear, yet she did not respond to it at all. She stood stoically, her jaw set, her eyes glittering.

"I said put both hands on the steering wheel."

I did what the kidnapper told me while staring into Victoria's eyes. I found there exactly what I prayed I'd find—rage, pure and untempered by humiliation or embarrassment or disorientation or shock or fear. She was angry, but she wasn't hurt. The sight of her nearly made me smile. *She's all right,* my inner voice told me. *She's going to be fine.*

"Here she is all safe and sound." The kidnapper spoke as if he had cotton in his mouth. He was still trying to hide his identity, yet it was Scottie—I knew it.

"This is how it's gonna work, you listening, McKenzie?"

"I'm listening."

"How 'bout you?" Scottie nudged Victoria. She didn't answer. "Now you're quiet. I gotta tell ya, McKenzie. This girl, she's got some mouth on her. The things she said to me—I thought you had to be married to hear girls talk like that."

"Possibly she was upset," I said.

"Oh, she's upset. Ain't that the truth, huh, honey?"

Victoria didn't reply.

"This is how it's going to work," Scottie said. "I'm going to stand here with the girl and you're going to sit there with your hands on the steering wheel. My partner is going to transfer the money from your trunk to the back of the wagon, one packet at a time, like we said. He had better not see any kind of GPS or listening device. If he does, you're both dead." I flashed on the device taped to my thigh. I squeezed my legs together, forced myself not to look down for fear of attracting Scottie's attention to it. "If it's cool, if we're satisfied, the girl, she goes into your car and the both of you drive away. We do the same. No harm, no foul. Okay?"

"Okay."

"Pop the trunk. There's a lever between the seat and the door."

I did what I was told. Afterward, I gripped the steering wheel in the ten and two positions and worked to control my anger.

"This won't take long," Scottie said.

I heard Scottie's partner get out of the Vibe and open the rear hatch of the station wagon, but I couldn't see him—the trunk lid of the Reliant blocked my view. I spent most of my time watching Scottie and Victoria. Scottie should have kept his eyes on me. Instead, he was watching his partner. Victoria stared straight ahead.

"Are you all right?" I asked.

Scottie answered for her. "I said so, didn't I?"

Victoria remained silent.

I wanted her to speak. I wanted her to smile. I wanted her to tell me how lame I looked sitting there in my wet shorts. Maybe if I made a joke. Only nothing came to me. I sat in the car, watching Victoria's face, my hands gripping the steering wheel tighter and tighter until the knuckles were white. After a couple of minutes, I heard the hatch of the station wagon close.

"We ready?" Scottie asked.

I didn't hear an answer, but Scottie must have been satisfied.

"A deal's a deal," he said. He took his arm away and pushed Victoria forward. "Get in the car," he said. Victoria opened the door, slid in next to me, and closed the door. She still didn't speak.

"Buckle your seat belt, honey," I told her.

She glared at me and shook her head as if she thought I were seriously deranged, but she buckled her belt.

"Okay," said Scottie. "You can go."

He put his gun in his pocket.

I started up the car, put it in gear.

"You're an asshole, Scottie," I said and hit the accelerator. "I'll be seeing you real soon." I glanced at him in the rearview as I sped down the street. From his body language, he looked like he had just been zapped with a Taser. I liked the look.

It bothered me that I didn't see any police vehicles as I maneuvered the Reliant through the Badlands and onto I-94. *Don't let them get away, don't let them get away,* my inner voice chanted.

Victoria stifled a sob next to me. It was the first sound she'd made since I found her.

"Are you all right?" I asked.

She nodded.

"You're safe now," I said. "You'll be home soon."

"I expected Daddy to come and get me," she said. Her voice was low, almost a whisper.

"Your father wanted to be here, sweetie. The kidnappers wouldn't let him. They were afraid of what he might have done."

"They were afraid of Daddy?"

"Big-time."

"Because they thought he might kill them?"

"Yep."

"Would he have?"

"Once he knew you were safe? Yeah, there was a real good chance."

"I'm glad, then, glad Daddy isn't here. I don't want them dead. I want them arrested so I can testify in court, so I can tell them that I wasn't afraid, tell them that they didn't make me afraid."

She was crying now. I reached across the seat and rested my hand on her shoulder.

"I don't want to cry," she said.

"It's okay, Tory. Cry all you want."

She brushed my hand away. "I don't want to cry!" A moment later, she said, "I wasn't afraid."

"I know."

"I hate those fuckers."

"I don't blame you."

We drove the rest of the way in silence until we reached the block where Victoria lived.

"McKenzie," Victoria said.

"Yes, sweetie."

"Please don't tell Mom and Dad that I used the F-word."

13

I had to grab Victoria's elbow to keep her from flying out of the car before it stopped. She already had the door open and her seat belt unfastened before I eased to the curb in front of her house. Shelby was standing at the front door. She started running the moment she saw us. Victoria sprinted to meet her. They had a splendid collision on the front lawn. Bobby and Katie were there a moment later to pile on. I stood next to the Reliant and watched, not even remotely embarrassed by how I looked until Honsa sidled up to me. He glanced down at the boxers and then up at me.

"Nice color," he said. "Brings out your eyes."

"You think?" I said.

Honsa was carrying the clothes I had left on the beach at McCarrons Lake. They were neatly folded.

"We thought you might want these," he said.

"When I left the ransom drop, they were loading the money into the back of a red late-model Pontiac Vibe station wagon," I said. "I didn't get a plate." I recited the address of the yellow house. "They might have been using it. I can't be sure."

"I'll alert Special Agent Wilson. The SWAT teams moved in just moments after your signal cleared the area. We haven't heard anything yet."

I thanked him for his consideration and made my way into Shelby's Place, taking my time as I passed the joyous pile, wishing I had the right to join in. I went into the bathroom and dressed myself. The tape fixing the GPS transmitter to my leg was painful coming off, but I didn't mind. I gave it to the tech agent when I emerged from the house. "You guys were right," I said. "It is waterproof."

The Dunston clan was now in a small tight circle in the center of the front lawn. Victoria was talking hard and fast, telling her family what had happened to her, the words spilling out in a gush. Honsa was listening from a respectful distance. He came over when he saw me.

"Agent Wilson wants you to return to the scene," he said. "Can you do that?"

"Sure."

"Leave the Plymouth here for our forensics people." He gestured at the tech agent. "We'll drive you."

"What happened?" I asked.

"Agent Wilson will explain." Honsa smiled a smile entirely unlike the professional smile he had continuously flashed during the past few days. This one was filled with glee. "You did good, McKenzie," he said.

"Yeah, how 'bout that?"

Honsa returned to the Dunstons to listen to Victoria's story; I had no doubt he would debrief her more formally later. I followed the tech agent across the lawn to his car. I caught Bobby Dunston's attention as I passed. He looked at me, just looked, his eyes filled with words he did not speak, that he didn't need to speak. He tilted his chin in a brief nod. I nodded back, and for a moment I felt like King Kong astride the

Empire State Building, thinking I was the biggest thing there was. Until the planes came.

Scottie Thomforde was dead.

He was lying on his back on the sidewalk in front of the yellow house, the black ski mask clutched in his right hand. Someone had pumped a single round into his face and another into his chest. By the lack of blood on his white coveralls, I was willing to bet that he had died instantly. I said his name out loud.

"That's what his ID said," Harry told me. "I just wanted to make it official."

Shakespeare wrote that "the evil that men do lives after them, the good is oft interred with their bones," but I think he's wrong. Staring down at Scottie I didn't dwell on what he had done to Victoria and the Dunston family, or any of his other crimes. I remembered that he was a sure-handed shortstop with plenty of range; I remembered listening to him playing the drums at the mixer at Merriam Park, trying hard to be Ginger Baker or Keith Moon.

"I'm sorry he's dead," I said.

"Me, too," Harry said.

"No, you're sorry because he can't lead you to his partner. I'm sorry because it shouldn't have ended this way. He had been a good guy once. God! What is his mother going to think, I wonder? Damn, Scottie. Dammit."

"This is bad. This is very, very bad."

Harry was standing outside the ominous yellow tape surrounding the crime scene. He was leaning against a dark-colored van; his arms were folded, his chin resting against his chest. The street had been closed, and various law enforcement vehicles were parked every which way along it. A group of men milled about on the far side of the van talking to themselves. Others, most of them wearing windbreakers with the white letters FBI on the back, a few dressed in the uniforms of the St. Paul Police Department, were scattered up and down the street; a few were inside the yellow house. They were all probably searching for clues, but you couldn't have proven it by me.

The yellow tape was held up by the SPPD uniform who carried the attendance log noting the names of everyone who had visited the crime scene. I ducked under it and joined Harry at the van. "No sign of the money, I suppose," I said.

"Nope."

"How the hell did you let him get away, Harry? You had two SWAT teams in position, for chrissake."

"We had to wait to make sure you were clear before we moved in. And now it looks like they knew we were coming."

"Well, duh."

"Look, McKenzie. We're going to get a lot of shit over this as it is. We don't need to hear it from you, too."

"We? There's no we." I pointed my finger at him. "I'm blaming you personally."

I would have said more except for the expression on Harry's face. I have no compunction about kicking a man while his back is turned, but never when he's down. Still, it was my money!

I glanced up the street. The cars I had seen earlier were still parked where they had been, except for the big white moving truck. Agents were progressing from house to house, searching for witnesses, maybe hoping the kidnappers were still holed up in the area. From their expressions and the way they went about their business, I don't think anyone liked their chances.

"You might want to have your agents check the duplex down the street," I told Harry. "There was a moving van parked in front of it before. Maybe the movers saw something—" Then it hit me. There were no movers, only the truck. "Oh, crap."

"What?"

"There was a sixteen-foot moving van parked across the street, its doors open, the ramp down. A truck that size, I bet the interior is at least ninety inches wide and a hundred eighty inches long."

"So?"

"The kidnappers loaded the money into the back of a Vibe. Did Honsa tell you?"

"Yes."

"A Vibe is about seventy inches wide and one hundred seventy inches long."

"Oh, you gotta be kidding me."

"I remember thinking at the time that it was a poor excuse for a getaway car—it's so small, such a weak engine. Only they didn't get away in the Vibe. I bet the kidnappers drove it into the back of the truck and got away in that."

"Tell me you got a license plate."

"No."

"A name painted on the side of the truck?"

"I didn't notice."

Harry went inside the van. While he was there, the FBI's forensic pathologist arrived, ducked under the yellow tape, and began examining the body. I turned my back to him. Harry exited the van and said, "Do you have anything else you'd like to share, McKenzie?"

"Sorry," I said.

"Look at the bright side. Victoria is safe and sound. Now we can conduct a proper investigation. We'll start by interviewing everyone you spoke to the day before yesterday. I'm convinced that one of them must have tipped off Scottie that we were looking for him and he subsequently told his partner. That's probably why the partner killed him, to protect himself."

"Umm."

Harry spun toward me. "Umm?" he said. "What does umm mean?"

"I umm . . ."

"You umm?"

"I might have made a mistake."

"Tell me?"

"After we made the exchange, and Victoria was safely in the car, and the car was in gear, and we were driving off, I might have said something."

"What might you have said?"

"I might have said something about seeing him real soon."

"You used Scottie's name, didn't you?"

"Yeah."

Harry grabbed the top of his head with both hands as if he were afraid it might fly off. "Yeah, I'd call that a mistake," he said.

"I wasn't thinking."

Yes, you were, my inner voice told me. *You were thinking how clever you were.*

"I'm sorry," I said, only I wasn't sure whom I was apologizing to—Harry, Scottie, or Scottie's mother.

"We all make mistakes," Harry said, which I thought was very generous of him. "If there's nothing else, you can go. In fact, I wish you would."

I agreed and asked for a ride to my car. Harry nodded his head at the tech agent, and the agent fished in his pocket for his keys. We started down the sidewalk toward his vehicle. Harry called after me.

"McKenzie."

"Yeah."

"Don't ever point your finger at me again."

The tech agent wanted to talk, but he seemed timid about it. I didn't give him an opening because I was still upset about Scottie. I was thinking that my careless remark might have cost him his life. While we were crossing the Mississippi River, going west on I-94 into Minneapolis, the agent finally said, "Your friends, Bobby and Shelby. I like them."

"So do I."

"They were very cool through all of this. Bobby got a little excited about Thomforde, I know, but other than that—I've been in on double-oh-sevens before."

"Double-oh-sevens?" I said.

"All of the FBI's files relating to kidnappings begin with the numbers zero, zero, seven."

You learn something new every day, my inner voice said.

"Anyway, I've been on some cases where the family, the husband and wife, they blame each other, accuse each other. You can't imagine some of the things they say to each other. I appreciate that they're under a great deal of stress and emotions are near the surface, but you would think, you would hope, that it would bring them closer together instead of tearing them apart. The way they behave—it always reminds me of something that my father used to say when I was playing football. 'Sports doesn't build character, it reveals character.'"

"My father used to say the same thing," I told him.

"Families facing a tragedy like this, a missing child, you learn about them in a hurry. What we learned about Bobby and Shelby, they're all right, they're going to be all right. I can only hope my wife and I, if something should happen to us, that we'll be"—he searched for a word, found one—"together."

"How long have you been married?"

"Eighteen months."

After that, he had plenty to say, mostly about his bride. He had fallen in love with her at first sight—apparently she was a combination of Joan of Arc, Madame Curie, and Scarlett Johansson. I didn't mind him going on about her. I liked that he was in love with his wife. Going by the divorce rates these days, it seems so few men are.

We took the Lyndale Avenue exit off I-94, drove west on Vineland Place, and eased onto Kenwood Parkway. The tech agent entered the

Parade Stadium parking lot, swung his car in a wide arc, and parked directly in front of my Audi. I thanked him for the ride and got out. He waited until I could prove that I was good to go, which I thought was nice of him. I was opening my door when a desperate squeal of tires made me look toward the street. A dark blue Chevy Impala was entering the parking lot at high speed. It accelerated straight toward us, then turned abruptly, moving parallel to where we were parked, like a man-o'-war about to deliver a broadside. The cannon—a handgun I couldn't identify—was held at arm's length outside the driver's side window.

"Down," I shouted and crouched next to my Audi, the car between me and the Impala. Bullets were already flying. I heard two of them slam into the body of my car. Fortunately, they didn't go all the way through. Anyone who thinks a car will protect you in a gunfight watches too much television—they're mostly tin and fiberglass, after all. At least eight shots were fired before the Impala turned again and sped toward the parking lot exit, hit the street, and drove west at high speed.

I rose slowly from cover. My senses were supercharged with adrenaline—my eyes and ears were processing too much data, and I was having trouble sorting through it all. I continued to search for the car, to listen for its engine, but it was gone. Finally I pivoted toward the tech agent's vehicle. "Did you see that?" I asked.

The tech agent was sitting behind the steering wheel and speaking calmly into his handheld radio. "Officer down," he said, not excited at all—he could have been ordering takeout.

Still, *officer down?*

I rushed to his car. There was a bullet hole in the driver's side door. The agent was giving his position and status when I yanked the door open. His left hand was pressed hard against his upper thigh. Blood was spilling from between his fingers and soaking his trousers and the car seat. I gently lifted his hand off his thigh to examine the wound, only I couldn't see the bullet hole for the stream of blood that was pumping out of it. I returned his hand, knelt on the asphalt, and began removing the laces from my Nikes to use as a tourniquet. The agent didn't miss a beat, still speaking calmly as he described the car. "Late-model dark blue Chevrolet Impala, Minnesota plates, first two digits *G* as in George, *P* as in Peter, heading west on Kenwood Parkway when last seen." I slid the shoelace around his leg and tied it above the wound. "We cannot pursue. Repeat, we cannot pursue. Dammit," he added after he set the handheld on the seat next to him.

"You got a pen?" I asked.

"A pen?" The agent searched his inside jacket pocket and produced a Paper Mate. I used it to twist the shoelace until it was tight around his thigh and the flow of blood ceased. I held it tight with both hands. Several sirens wailed in the distance. When a member of the law enforcement community goes down, people move fast. The tech agent leaned back against the seat and brought his hand to his forehead. He smeared himself with blood, realized what he was doing, took his hand away, and stared at the stained fingers.

"Oh, man," he said. "My wife is going to kill me."

"How's your agent?" I asked.

"He'll live," Harry said.

"Gosh, that's funny," I told him, but I really didn't think so, and Harry knew it.

"Bullet nicked an artery," he said. "He lost some blood; he's okay now. I doubt he'll be out more than a couple of days."

"How's his wife taking it?"

"She's upset."

"Your agent thought she might be."

"Yeah, but I think she'll get over it. They locked the door behind me when I left the hospital room."

"Bullet wounds as an aphrodisiac—we should try that."

"You first. Listen, McKenzie, I appreciate you taking care of my agent."

"Least I could do," I said. "It had to be the second kidnapper, you know. Who else knew where my car was parked?"

"Are you sure about the shooter's vehicle?"

"Blue Chevy Impala. Your agent got the digits *G* and *P*, but I can't confirm it. I was too busy crawling on my belly."

"Not a Vibe?"

"Not even close."

"The Walker has security cameras aimed at the front of their building and the Sculpture Garden. We're examining the tapes to see if they'll give us a lead. There are a lot of cameras in apartment buildings and businesses near the ransom drop. We're looking at those, too. Did you sign your statement?"

"I did."

"We'll ask you to take a gander at some pictures later if we generate any, but for now, you can take off."

"Where's my Audi?"

"Let me make a quick call." After Harry hung up the phone, he said, "It'll be out front in a few minutes. Sorry about the damage. I hope your insurance company will cover it."

"They didn't the last time someone shot it up. They did raise my rates, though. I now pay high-risk insurance."

"This sort of thing doesn't happen very often, you know."

"Really? It happens to me all the time."

"I mean kidnappers trying to kill the mark after the ransom is delivered, after the victim is freed. Usually they're either too busy counting their money or running like hell. Honsa thinks that mentioning Scottie's name the way you did might have spooked him. He thinks the kidnapper ambushed you because he's afraid you can identify him somehow."

"If I could, I would."

"Think about it. If you come up with anything, you'll let us know?"

"Sure."

"Please, McKenzie. Let us deal with this. Don't go out and play detective."

"Who? Me?"

"I don't blame your insurance company. You are high risk."

14

There was nothing about her appearance that I didn't like—riveting silver-blue eyes, short black hair, gentle curves that she refused to diet away. She looked like twenty million bucks. No, more. Enough to buy the Minnesota Vikings a decent backfield. I had known Nina Truhler for over two years. Yet there were still moments when I would look at her and feel my heart somersaulting in my chest as if I were seeing her for the first time. I liked to watch her; I was watching her now as she swirled and whirled behind the stick. To say she moved like a dancer would be a mere cliché and not a particularly accurate one. Her movements were more improvised than a dancer's yet remained fluid and assured, as if they were infused with an unshakable confidence, as if she couldn't imagine the possibility of stumbling or overreaching. Other men watched her as well. Nina was used to being stared at. It began when she was fifteen, and the only time it waned was during the third trimester of her pregnancy with Erica. I wasn't used to it, though. The two guys at the end of the bar drinking beer, they were beginning to annoy me. I told Nina so when she found time to chat. "That's sweet," she said. Which annoyed me even more.

She planted her elbows on the bar and leaned forward. I thought she wanted a kiss. Instead, she asked, "Well? What happened?"

I told her the entire story. She interrupted only to say how deeply relieved she was to hear that Victoria was now safely home with her parents. Nina was smiling when I finished.

"You had a pleasant day, didn't you?" she said.

"Did I?"

"Everything that happened, even getting shot at, you enjoyed it, you know you did."

"That's crazy."

"The way you told the story, the way your face lit up while telling the story, it's like customers that I've served who get a thrill out of reliving how they won the big game, or who want to buy rounds because they closed a big deal."

"I didn't enjoy it."

"Then why did you do it?"

"I couldn't refuse to help Victoria and the Dunstons."

"Of course not. You know Victoria and care for her. But what about all the others?"

"What others?"

"The other people you've done favors for."

I tried to explain; Nina cut me off.

"You're always quick with an explanation, and it always makes sense—nearly always," she said. "Still, you could just as easily find an excuse for *not* getting involved in other people's problems. Couldn't you?"

I took a sip of my drink.

"I've come to a conclusion," Nina said. "You're committed to lost and hopeless causes, not because you're an idealist or a humanitarian or anything like that. It's about pride; it's about self-esteem. This Wild West–gunfighter, white-knight, Scarlet Pimpernel life that you've chosen, it allows you to prove that you matter."

"Good try. Your Psych 101 professor would be proud. Except I don't agree."

"Explain it to me, then."

"I just like to be useful."

"Isn't that what I just said?"

"You make it sound like it's an ego thing."

Nina laughed at me. "Oh, honey," she said. "Of course it is."

"No, it isn't. I help people the way I do because it gives me a sense of accomplishment. It makes me feel that I haven't wasted my day. Not because it makes me a superior being or something."

"If that's true, why not go back to the cops?"

"I've been too long going where I want, doing what I want, unaccountable to anyone. I'm not sure I'd be very good at taking orders, now."

"Like you ever were."

"Or doing things by the book. Besides, the other kids resent me for being so damn good-looking, not to mention rich. I doubt they'd let me play with them."

Nina sighed like a stage actress playing to the upper balcony.

"Anyway," I told her, "I don't think you'd love me if I had a real job, if I worked eight-to-five."

"Of course, I would."

"Uh-huh."

"You know I would."

"Do you remember the first time we met?"

"You came into my place because you were following a woman who was involved in a gunrunning operation."

"If I recall, you were very excited by it. You went all Sam Spade on me, explaining how you knew she was cheating on her husband."

"Well, she was."

"What I'm asking, would you have spent time with me, would you have even spoken to me, if I had told you I was an accountant?" She didn't answer, so I asked, "Remember the second time we met, at the Minnesota Club?"

"That was the third time, but who's counting?" Nina said.

"You pushed a guy down a flight of stairs."

"He was reaching for a gun. He was going to shoot you."

"Probably he wasn't, but that's not the point."

"What is the point?"

"You smiled while he bounced on every step until he hit the bottom."

"Well . . ."

"You were having fun."

"Nah-uh."

"Last summer, we were attacked while you were driving down 94," I said. "The guy smashed the back of your Lexus and threw a couple of shots at us. You told the story for months afterward, told anyone who would listen."

"Did I mention how angry I was?"

"At the time, yes, very angry. Not so much later while you were telling the story."

"You're saying that I find it all as much fun as you do," Nina said.

"I never said it was fun."

She took my hand and spent a few moments twisting it in hers. "What you do is dangerous. Maybe it's more interesting than working eight-to-five, and maybe that makes you more interesting. It's still dangerous, and I can't help feeling . . . You know what my greatest fear is? That one day Bobby Dunston is going to come knocking on my door . . ."

"That's not going to happen."

"McKenzie, I look terrible in black."

Actually, Nina looked terrific in black, but I knew what she meant.

I kissed her cheek. I said, "I'm not a cop, I'm not a licensed PI. If things get dicey, I can always walk away."

"Except you never do. Ahh, nuts. I knew what I was getting into when I visited you in the hospital. Remember the cracked skull?"

"Epidural hematoma."

"Whatever," Nina said. She frowned at me, then she smiled, and then she kissed me, softly, without haste, on the mouth. It was a message kiss. It said, "You and me, kid. You and me." At least, that's what I heard.

"We'll be closing soon," Nina said. "Afterward, I'll be going to your house, and I'll be hungry."

The end to a perfect day, I thought.

The best egg rolls in the Twin Cities were served by a Vietnamese restaurant on Johnson Street in northeast Minneapolis. The beef lo mein was pretty good, too, so I called in an order for both, plus some cream cheese puffs. There were two Asian kids hanging in the lobby when I arrived to pick it up. One of them was wearing a Minnesota Timberwolves jersey, 21, Kevin Garnett's old number. They were studying the fish in a large, colorful tank with such intensity that I half expected them to announce, "We'll take that one."

The cashier asked my name, and I said, "McKenzie."

At the sound of it, Number 21 pivoted toward me. There was an expression on his face that said he knew me. I didn't know him, so I blew it off. A moment later, he pulled his pal out of the restaurant. That should have told me something. It didn't.

The cashier filled my order; I paid and left. Stepping through the door, I noticed that the kids were standing next to a battered Chevy Malibu across the street and down the block. Neither was looking at me. I went to the Audi, started it up, checked for traffic, and pulled into Johnson Street. As I accelerated away I heard two soft pops that reminded me of a small-caliber pistol. I glanced in my rearview and saw Number 21 standing in the middle of the street and gesturing wildly.

Was he shooting at you? my inner voice wanted to know.

Of course not, I told myself. *You're just paranoid after everything that's happened today.*

I was checking the scores on ESPN—the Twins were making yet another run at the Central Division championship, and normally I would have taken time to watch or at least listen to the game, except hey, I'd been busy. My house phone rang. Usually that meant that someone wanted me to donate money to one worthy cause or another; my friends nearly always call me on my cell. Then I realized that my cell was on the bottom of the Mississippi River.

I answered. Bobby Dunston was on the other end. "I've just seen the ballistics report," he said. "The FBI's been very good about sharing."

"What in the hell are you doing reading ballistics reports?"

"The bullet the FBI dug out of your upholstery was a nine-millimeter. It matched the slug they removed from Scottie Thomforde's chest. Which means it was the second kidnapper who came after you at Parade."

"Should you be working, Bobby?"

"I want to find the man who kidnapped my daughter. How 'bout you?"

"Bobby . . ."

"I'm not working. Jeannie Shipman dropped by to give me an update."

"Your young, beautiful, smart-as-hell partner?"

"That's the one. McKenzie, I want you to know that I don't think this is over. Watch your back, man."

"Screw my back, Bobby. Watch your own. Take Victoria and the rest of your family and go to my lake home for a few days. You have keys. Tory could use the vacation. I bet everyone else could, too."

"Tory is tough."

"No, she's not. She's terrified and putting up a front to hide it, mostly from herself."

"I already spoke with the department's psychologist. We'll be getting her therapy, getting her help. The rest of us, too."

"That's later. Right now, get out of here. Go up north. Teach Victoria how to fight. Teach her how to shoot a gun. Teach her to chop down a damn tree. That clump of birch behind the shed can go. Give her a chance to regain her confidence, her self-esteem."

"You just want us to do your yard work."

"There's that, too."

"For your information, I'm taking the girls to see their grandparents in Wisconsin tomorrow morning. Hopefully, the media won't find us there. Once Victoria was back, I guess people decided it was safe to talk about the kidnapping. The phone started ringing thirty minutes after Victoria came home and hasn't stopped. There are TV trucks parked in front of the house right now. I've been directing reporters to the PR guy at the department, but they're not satisfied with that. They want to interview Tory, and I won't let them."

"I wouldn't, either."

"The Feds want to debrief Victoria one more time; then we're leaving. In a couple of days maybe the media'll move on to something else and we can get back to normal."

I didn't think that was likely, but didn't say so. "Did she tell the FBI anything they can use?" I asked.

"Not much. Only two men were with her. She never saw their faces; they always wore masks. She remembers hearing the name T-Man, but no others. The one called T-Man received several calls on his cell phone. Victoria thinks the caller might have been a woman because the T-Man said 'babe.' You know, McKenzie, she did everything right."

"I know."

"The way she looked out for her sister, that took courage. God, I'm proud of her."

"Did you tell her that?"

"Several times."

"Tell her again."

"What makes you think you know anything about raising children?"

"Because I don't have any of my own."

"I want the bastards who hurt my daughter."

"I know."

"Remember what we talked about in the kitchen?"

"I remember."

Bobby paused for a moment; I heard him sigh. He said, "I want to thank you, McKenzie. For everything."

"I thought you already did."

A moment later, he hung up the phone. A funny thing happened when he did. I began to weep. My hands shook, and my body trembled uncontrollably. I couldn't stop. I understood the cause of it. The release of tension and all that. Only it seemed to go on and on, right up until Nina arrived. And then it was smiles the rest of the night and into the morning.

15

My auto-body man laughed when I said I wanted to bring the Audi in for an estimate. Apparently he got a kick out of repairing bullet holes— he actually seemed disappointed that there were only two this time. I told him that since my business brought him such mirth and merriment, he should give me a break on the price. He told me he'd give me a magnetic calendar for my refrigerator. I figured he might sweeten the offer, though, when I discovered a third bullet hole, this one lodged in the back of the car between the trunk lid and bumper. Funny I had missed it before, I told myself. The body shop was backed up and couldn't service me for a couple of days, so I left the Audi in the garage and drove to the Rosedale Center in my old Jeep Cherokee.

Joley called later that morning.

I had just replaced my drowned cell phone. The aggressive young lady staffing the kiosk at Rosedale had attempted to sell me a device with enough features to manage the space program. It had e-mail, text messaging, Internet search engines, a music and video player, a camera, maps and a step-by-step navigation system, games, an address book, a calendar, a memo pad, and voice-activated dialing. I asked if it also made and received phone calls, and she looked like at me as if I were Robinson Crusoe, just rescued from a deserted island after a couple of decades. Eventually I settled on a sturdy flip-phone, even though it came with several features that I expected never to use, like the camera, and she helped me program it to accept my cell number. I designated the Johnny Mercer–Jo Stafford cover of "Blues in the Night" as the ringtone, only the first time I heard it on the tinny speaker, I decided to change it.

"Hi, Joley," I said.

"McKenzie," she said. Enough time passed that I thought the cell phone had already failed me, but there was a muffled sound as if she had covered the mouthpiece of her phone, followed by, "Oh, McKenzie."

She must have heard about Scottie, my inner voice told me. I said, "Are you all right, Joley?"

"I'm . . . Yes, I'm fine. Could you come over? Could you come over to my house? Please?" Her voice seemed stilted and artificial; it held none of its usual seductive charm. *She's in mourning,* my inner voice said.

"I can come over," I said.

"Please hurry."

It wasn't a conversation I wanted to have, talking about Scottie, yet I hurried as promised, parking the Cherokee in front of her place. *Maybe you should get her out of the house,* I told myself. *Take her to an early lunch someplace crowded, where she'd be less likely to break down.* I was considering a few spots as I walked up her sidewalk. I was halfway to the door when it opened abruptly. I expected to see her standing there, grieving for her lost love. Instead, I saw a man dressed in white coveralls and a black ski mask. That's not what started me running, though. It was the handgun that I could clearly see when he pushed open the screen door.

I heard a single gunshot as I dodged to my left. I was accelerating quickly, pumping my arms the way I had been taught during my junior year in high school when I tried running track and playing baseball at the same time. I crossed Joley's yard and her neighbor's yard and the yard next to that. I had been a sprinter and proud of it, yet when I reached the hundred-meter mark I started doing the same thing I had done in school—I slowed down. A quick glance over my shoulder showed me that the man in the coveralls was still in pursuit. I couldn't tell if he was gaining or not. He was carrying the handgun in his right hand. He brought the hand up as if he were going to try for a running shot. By then I had reached the street, and I cut hard to my right. If he fired the gun, I didn't hear it.

I had no idea where I was going. I was just running, pumping my arms because Coach told me you can run only as fast as you can pump your arms. I was pumping them slower and slower. I had been slacking off for months now. Walking through my martial arts classes, watching TV instead of hitting the exercise equipment in my basement, finding something else to do other than Rollerblade five miles a day while carrying weights in each hand, like I used to. I told myself I'd get back in shape when I started playing hockey again. *Well, good luck with that if you can't even run a lousy half mile from a killer with a gun in his hand,* my inner voice said.

I glanced behind me again. At least the shooter was struggling, too. He slowed, then stopped altogether, resting his hands on his knees and gulping oxygen. I took refuge behind a parked car and watched him, ready to begin running when he did. Only he didn't, lucky me. He brought his gun up and sighted down the barrel. We were about a hundred yards apart. Even so, I ducked behind the car, although to hit me from that range with a handgun would have been miraculous. He must have thought so, too, because he didn't fire. Instead, he spun around and half walked, half jogged in the direction he had come.

I hadn't considered Joley until the shooter turned away, hadn't given her safety any thought at all. It was me I was concerned about, which, I decided, made me some kind of a jerk. I felt the guilt as I went to my pocket for the cell phone and fumbled it—my hands were shaking. Fatigue, I told myself. The cell phone was unlike the one I had dropped into the Mississippi River, the buttons were in different places, and it took me a few moments to activate it. Eventually I called 911. "Shots fired," I said, even though there had only been the one. I gave the operator Joley's address as well as my name. She asked for my location. I had to walk up the street a bit to read the signs. She told me that the police were on the way. I told her that I would meet them at the house. She said that was unwise, and I agreed with her.

The St. Paul cops were already on the scene when I reached Joley's house. 'Course, I had given them a big head start while I cautiously retraced my steps, leery that the attacker would jump out at me again at any moment.

Joley's front door was open. I saw two uniforms inside, along with Detective Jean Shipman, Bobby Dunston's young, beautiful, smart-as-hell partner. I opened the screen and stepped across the threshold. Joley was sitting in one of her immaculate chairs; Jeannie was interviewing her. The cops didn't see me until Joley sprang from the chair and crossed the room.

"I'm sorry, I'm sorry," she chanted as she wrapped her arms around me. "He made me call you, he made me. I'm sorry."

"It's okay," I said. I was glad she was apologizing to me. It meant I didn't have to apologize to her.

Jeannie was standing directly behind her. She was a tall woman and attractive, with freckles the same color as her hair. When she was a kid, everyone told her how cute the freckles were and she liked to hear it; not so much now that she was passing for an adult. She flashed a two-second smile at me.

"There you are, McKenzie," she said. "I thought we'd have to send the dogs out after you."

I told her that would have been nice, especially if one of the dogs had been carrying a keg of brandy around his neck.

"I couldn't help it, McKenzie," Joley said. "You have to believe me."

I brushed the hair out of her eyes; they were tearless, bright, and clear. "Of course I believe you," I said. With a voice like hers, how could I not? I led her back to the chair.

"I don't know how he got into the house," Joley said. "I turned around and there he was. At first I thought he was a thief. Then I thought he might be a client who somehow discovered my true identity. He touched me, McKenzie. He did things with his hands. I was so frightened. Then he pushed me into a chair and said, 'Maybe later.'"

"Did you recognize his voice?" Jeannie asked.

"No."

"Could it have been one of your customers?"

"I don't think so. I can't really be sure. He didn't speak much. He said, 'Maybe later,' and then he told me to call McKenzie. He said I was to call him and tell him to come over to the house—that was about all." Joley looked into my eyes. "He didn't say anything about you or why he wanted you. After I called, he waited by the door. When you drove up, he went outside and started shooting. That's the last I saw of him."

"Did you search the house?" I said.

Jeannie grimaced as if I had insulted her, then let it go. "Tell me about the shooter," she said.

"He was dressed like the men who kidnapped Bobby Dunston's daughter," I said. "He was dressed like the man who killed Scottie Thomforde."

"He must really hate you."

"It worked in my favor. If he hated me just a little less, he might have waited until I rang the doorbell. I wouldn't have had a chance."

"You didn't recognize him, Ms. Waddell?" Jeannie said. "You didn't recognize his voice?"

"No."

A question came from behind us. "Do you know Thomas Thomforde?" We spun toward it. Harry was standing just inside the doorway. He held his ID in front of him like a shield.

Jeannie shouted at her uniforms. "Can I get someone to secure the goddamned door? It's a crime scene, for chrissake."

Harry smiled at her. "Good afternoon, Detective Shipman," he said.

Jeannie smiled back. "Good afternoon, Special Agent Wilson. To what do we owe the pleasure?"

"There is an excellent chance that the case you are currently working is connected to a federal kidnapping case that I am working. I would be grateful, Detective Shipman, if you allowed me to sit in on your interview, perhaps share any evidence you might have uncovered."

"May I ask who called you?"

"I did," I said.

Jeannie gave me a look that could have melted asphalt. "Certainly, if McKenzie says it's all right, I'll be happy to cooperate with the FBI," she said, although the tone of her voice suggested otherwise.

"You're most kind, Detective Shipman," Harry said.

"Think nothing of it, Special Agent Wilson."

"Hmm."

"Ahh."

"What's going on?" Joley said.

"Mating dance," I said. Both Harry and Jeannie gave me a look. Forget melted asphalt. Think about what's in a deep, dark hole beneath the asphalt.

"Do you know Thomas Thomforde?" Harry repeated.

"Tommy? Sure I do," said Joley. "I knew him when we were kids. I haven't seen him for a couple of years, though."

"Was he the man who terrorized you?"

"No. Why are you asking about Tommy?"

Harry gestured with his head, and he, Jeannie, and I moved away from Joley. "Tommy Thomforde is missing," he told us.

"Missing or hiding?" I said.

"We pulled our men off him to back up McKenzie when he delivered the ransom," Harry told Jeannie. "No one has seen him since."

"His mother?" I asked.

"She says she hasn't seen Tommy since he left for work yesterday morning. Beyond that, she's not being very cooperative."

"I can't imagine why," Jeannie said. "One son dead."

Harry smiled at her.

Jeannie smiled back.

I brushed past both of them and went to where Joley was sitting. I knelt in front of her chair and took her hands in mine. "Joley, listen to me very carefully. This is important."

"What?"

"Was Scottie Thomforde really here the night before last, the night Karen Studder and I spoke to you?"

"Yes."

"Are you sure?"

Joley pulled her hands out of mine. "Yes, I'm sure," she said.

"He knew I was looking for him."

"He was in the bedroom upstairs. He was listening. I'm sorry I lied, McKenzie. I didn't know what else to do. Scottie and I . . . I didn't want you to know that we were, that we were . . . I was embarrassed." Maybe she could read my mind. Maybe the expression on my face told her that my brain was screaming at the contradiction, because she added, "The person I am on the phone isn't the person I really am."

Probably it was cruel; I said it anyway. "Considering what you do for a living, Joley, I doubt anyone would have cared."

"I thought you might have cared."

You can be such a jerk, my inner voice told me.

No one spoke for a few moments, and I was working myself up to apologizing when Harry broke the silence. "Ms. Waddell, when did Scottie arrive?" he asked.

"It was early."

"How early?"

"Right after lunch. About one thirty."

"Did he make any phone calls?"

"No, we spent the entire afternoon . . . He didn't make any phone calls."

"At what time did he leave?"

"About ten."

"Thank you, Ms. Waddell."

There was more talking to be done, mostly about the intruder who tried to pop me, and Jean Shipman did most of it. Afterward, Harry and I went outside and walked slowly to his car.

"Where's Honsa?" I asked.

"It's my case now," Harry said. "He does his thing, the NOC stuff. This is my thing. Listen, McKenzie. We know that Thomforde made three phone calls to Bobby Dunston's home. The last one was at six-oh-five, and he made the call while on the move."

"Which means Joley was lying," I said.

"Unless it was someone else on the phone."

"No."

"It could have been Tommy. The voice was disguised."

"No."

"Then how do you explain the discrepancies?"

"I told you, Joley is lying. Think about it. If she was telling the truth, then logic would suggest that the moment Karen and I left her house she would have hurried upstairs to tell Scottie that we were looking for him. Scottie would have immediately contacted the halfway house and reported in. He didn't. Instead, Scottie arrived at the halfway house at least two hours later. Is that logical?"

"It is if he figured he was already screwed so he might as well get in one more good one before he was violated."

"How 'bout this: Mrs. Thomforde tells Scottie that Karen and I are looking for him. To protect himself, Scottie comes over here and convinces Joley to alibi him for the entire day."

"Why would she still be sticking to the story? Scottie's dead."

"Two possibilities," I said. "One, she's frightened by the man who put a gun to her head and told her to call me. Two, she's in on it."

"Three," said Harry. "She's not in on it, but having lied for Scottie the first time, she's now afraid that if she tells the truth she'll be implicated."

"Victoria Dunston said that the T-Man spoke to someone on the phone. Someone he called 'babe.' "

"Do you think Joley Waddell is the babe?" Harry said.

"Beauty is in the eye of the beholder."

"Still, he could have been speaking to a man. Babe Ruth. Babe Winkelman. Babe the Blue Ox."

"I'm just telling you what I heard."

"We'll pull Joley's phone records and canvass the neighborhood, see if we can find a witness who saw Scottie Thomforde. It doesn't make sense, though. Kidnapper has a million untraceable, why hang around to kill you?"

"I don't know."

"Why risk revealing himself by trying to kill you?"

"I don't know."

"If he wanted both the money and you dead, why not take you off the board at the ransom drop?"

"You keep asking the same question," I said.

"Whoever the second kidnapper is, this isn't about being afraid that you might identify him," Harry said. "He has a grudge. A big one. Big enough that taking a million off you won't satisfy. Tell me, McKenzie. Who doesn't like you?"

"You want a list?"

Harry took a notebook and a pen out of his pocket and gave it to me.

"Seriously?" I said.

He opened the passenger door of his car. "Sit. Write."

I sat, I wrote, jotting down names as they came to me, names of people who might want to kill me. It took nearly an hour. I was distressed by the length of the list and depressed by its quality. They were punks, all punks, even my upper-middle-class enemies. No one smart or audacious enough for a caper like this.

I gave the list to Harry. He said, "Maybe you should lie low for a few day till we can sort all this out."

"I could do that," I said. At the same time, I was staring across the street at nothing in particular, contemplating my next move. Harry hit me hard on the shoulder with the back of his hand.

"Go home," he said. "Lock the doors. Stay away from the windows."

"Sure."

I didn't go home; I doubted Harry believed that I would. Instead, I drove to the Thomforde residence. On the way, I took the time to call Nina on her cell phone. She was at Rickie's. I told her that I was coming over and she shouldn't leave until I arrived, and she said okay. I didn't tell her that she might be in danger. I figured it was one of those conversations best had in person.

Mrs. Thomforde answered the door when I knocked. I was a bit surprised when she hugged me and asked me to come inside.

"Some of my friends are coming over in a few minutes," she said. "I have to go to the funeral parlor to start making arrangements. The police said they would release Scottie's body in a couple of days."

"I am so, so sorry," I told her.

She thanked me for my concern and offered coffee, which I accepted. I watched as she poured. Mrs. Thomforde was old-school, like my father. Time and experience had draped a cloak about her shoulders, the same cloak worn by many of her generation. She wore it to keep the hurt to herself, so as not to burden others with it. Any tears she had for her youngest son were shed in private. At the same time, there was a great tenderness to go with the reserve. I saw it in her eyes when I mentioned Scottie's name.

"I wish," she said, stopped, started again. "I think when you look back on your life, you'll find that there are one or two moments that change everything, that set you down a path that you just can't get off of. You don't recognize these moments at the time they take place. Sometimes you won't even know that they took place at all until years and years later. Like with Scottie. I should never have bought him that drum kit. If he hadn't played the drums, he would have kept playing hockey and baseball with you. He wouldn't have met Dale Fulbright. He wouldn't have gone to prison. He wouldn't have . . . I don't want to believe it, McKenzie. I know it's true what they say about Scottie. That poor little girl and Bobby Dunston—I never liked him, but for this to happen, for Scottie to be involved. I just don't want to believe it."

"I don't want to believe it, either."

"People keep asking questions. The police. The FBI. Who were Scottie's friends? What did he do? Where did he go? I don't know the answers, McKenzie. I don't know anything. He wasn't staying with me. He was at the damn halfway house. They should be asking questions over there. The person who runs it. Roger something . . ."

"Roger Colfax?"

"Even he was here asking questions about where Scottie went and who he knew. If he doesn't know the answers, how am I supposed to? If Scottie had been staying here, if he had been with me, maybe, maybe . . . I don't know."

Mrs. Thomforde didn't say anything for a few moments, just stared into her coffee mug. Finally I spoke. "They can't find Tommy." I said "they," not "we"—I wanted to maintain the illusion that I was merely a family friend offering my condolences. "Do you know where he is?"

"No."

"Do you think maybe Tommy was involved in the kidnapping?"

"I don't know what to think."

"Mrs. Thomforde, when we were at the Silver Bucket the other day, Karen Studder said that Scottie went out to a bar the Saturday night he was supposed to be at your house. You said it wasn't true. It was true, though, wasn't it?"

She nodded.

"Do you know who he went with?"

"Tommy," she said. "He went with Tommy. I thought it would be all right, two brothers having a beer together. I thought Tommy would take care of him. I thought . . ."

"That night at the Silver Bucket, right after Karen and I left, you made a call on your cell phone."

"How did you know that?"

"Who did you call?"

"Tommy. Why?"

I didn't say. Mrs. Thomforde closed her eyes. When she opened them again, she said, "You never know when those moments will sneak up on you, McKenzie. You never know when a decision will change your life."

I called Harry as soon as I left Mrs. Thomforde and repeated what she had told me. Turned out she had already confessed pretty much the same thing to him earlier. Still, he thanked me for the information. Then he told me to go home. "You're interfering with an ongoing criminal investigation," he said.

Like I haven't heard that before.

16

I found Nina in her office at Rickie's, sitting behind her desk, her elbow planted on the blotter, her chin resting in her hand, a pair of readers perched on her nose as she tapped a pen on top of the intimidating sheaf of papers in front of her. She looked up when I entered, grinned, dropped the pen, and slid the glasses off and into her top desk drawer so deftly that only a semiprofessional investigator might have noticed it.

Nina came around the desk and gave me a soft, moist kiss. "Hey," she said. "What's the surprise?"

"Surprise?"

"You said not to leave until you arrived." Nina raised and lowered her eyebrows Groucho Marx style. "You have something in mind, big boy?"

"Yeah, about that. I was thinking that you're due for a nice vacation. You've been working much too hard lately."

"Hmmm." Nina raised her eyebrows again and smiled brightly. "You know, Erica is going off on her band trip tomorrow. Toronto. Five days."

"You should go with, listen to her play."

Nina's smile was replaced by a frown. "Are we talking about the same thing?" she said.

I asked her to sit down. She sat. I explained what had happened at Joley's house. I told her that the FBI now believed that Victoria's kidnapping and the two subsequent attempts on my life might have been perpetrated by someone who was trying to settle a grudge against me. She wondered what that had to do with her.

"If the FBI is right—and I'm not convinced they are—this person is using people I care about to get to me. First Victoria Dunston, then Joley Waddell. I'm afraid next he'll go after you and Erica."

"Why would he do that?"

"Because I love you."

Nina gave it half a dozen beats before she replied. "You can be such a jerk, McKenzie."

"What did I say?"

"I love you."

"Nina—"

"You can't say that while we're walking around a lake or holding hands in front of a fireplace or standing on the damn street corner. No, I have to be in danger before I hear it."

"I've said I love you before."

"When?"

"Dozens of times."

"Name one."

"It's not like I keep track."

"Well, I do."

"Nina, you're missing the point."

"The point is that one of your crusades has gotten you into trouble and now you're bringing it into my place. I don't want you to do that. You need to keep your business out of my place."

"That's not the point."

"McKenzie, I am not going into hiding just because you're in trouble.

No way. If I did that, I'd spend the rest of my life on the lam—is that what you call it, on the lam?—because let's face it, you're always in trouble. If we were talking about Erica, that'd be different. Fortunately. Erica is leaving the country tomorrow at about ten o'clock with a dozen chaperones and about a hundred of her closest friends, so she'll be all right. As for me, I have a business to run, and since we are fast approaching the dinner hour, I suggest you get out of here and let me run it."

The conversation had not gone the way I had expected. I decided to try again. I reached across the desk and took both of Nina's hands in mine. I squeezed them gently.

"Sweetie," I said. "I need you to be safe. I understand that you're reluctant to go into hiding, but we can hire bodyguards—"

"No."

"Nina, be reasonable."

"Look down," she said.

I glanced at the sheaf of papers our hands were resting on.

"That's an insurance policy," she said. "It covers my business. Why do I have a feeling that hanging around with you is going to raise my premiums?"

"Nina—"

"Forget it. I am not going to have guys with guns around my place." She pulled her hands out of mine. "It seems to me that this is your problem, McKenzie, not mine."

She has you there, my inner voice said.

"Okay," I said aloud.

"McKenzie, I'll be fine. Now go away, will you?"

Schroeder Private Investigations was a cop shop. Every man who had ever worked there had been an investigator for one law enforcement agency or another—sheriff's office, police department, even the FBI. They all acted like it, too, answering calls in white shirtsleeves and shoulder holsters, sitting behind gray metal desks with cigarettes dangling from their mouths. It was located on the third floor of an outdated office building in downtown Minneapolis. The directory listing the building's occupants was hand-written. So were the legends identifying each office; they were painted in gold and red on a ten-inch-wide, floor-to-ceiling glass panel next to the doors. A heavy curtain kept everyone from seeing inside. I walked in without knocking.

A woman intercepted me in a reception area just inside the door. "I'm here to see Greg Schroeder," I said. "My name is McKenzie."

She led me halfway across the large, busy room until a voice boomed out. "Rushmore McKenzie," the voice said. "I'll be a sonuvabitch." She abandoned me as Schroeder approached.

Schroeder's fortunes had ebbed and flowed over the years. At one time, he had had as many as a dozen investigators working for him, yet when I first met him he was alone. Now there were five investigators in the office and I couldn't say how many more on the street.

"Last time I saw you was down in Victoria, Minnesota," Schroeder said. "Seems to me I saved your ass."

"So you did. Difficult shot, if I recall."

"Come." Schroeder led me to a metal desk against the far wall. "Sit."
I sat in front of the desk.

"So, to what do I owe the pleasure?" Schroeder said.

I told him I wanted to hire a few bodyguards.

"To protect whose body?"

I opened my wallet and retrieved a photograph of Nina. Schroeder took one glance and said, "That's a body worth protecting. Who is she?"

"Nina Truhler."

"Your girl?"

"Yes."

"Tell me about her."

I gave him every detail I could think of, including the license plate number of her Lexus.

"What are we protecting her from?"

I explained that as well.

"No specific individual to watch for," Schroeder said. "Makes it tougher. Where is the lady now?"

"Rickie's."

"Okay. I'll pull in a couple of guys. We'll go over there. You can introduce us. We'll give her a couple of rules to follow—"

"Umm."

"Umm, what?"

"You can't let her know that you're watching her."

Schroeder studied me for a few beats. "That'll cost you extra," he said.

"Price is no object."

"People say that, yet they rarely mean it."

"I mean it."

"What about you? Want a couple guys watching your back?"

I shook my head. "Nah," I said. "I'm a big boy. I can take care of myself."

"Famous last words," Schroeder said.

I decided to take Harry's advice—finally—and go home. In fact, that was the plan after I stopped for a meal at a pretty good deli I knew on Como Avenue. Only my cell phone rang—I still hadn't changed the damn ringtone. A voice from my sordid past told me I should drive to a club in downtown Minneapolis.

"You really want to meet me," Chopper said. "You really want to meet me right now. It's what you call a matter of life and death."

Stroll along Block E in downtown Minneapolis these days and you'll hear opera—*La Bohème, Tosca, Madame Butterfly, Don Giovanni, La*

Traviata. They were playing Bellini's *Norma* from a speaker on the corner of Seventh and Hennepin when I crossed the street. It was meant to drive off the riffraff that were now congregating in the area between Hennepin and First avenues and Sixth and Seventh streets. I suppose it might work. Opera, after all, is a complex art form that uses a different style of voice than we're accustomed to, and that makes some people uncomfortable. On the other hand, I didn't care for the music at all until an ex-girlfriend exposed me to it, and now I like it, so who knows? Instead of ridding the streets of the less desirable among us, it might turn them into opera fans.

Still, you can't blame the local merchants for trying. There was a time not too long ago when a tourist couldn't swing a commemorative shopping bag on Block E without hitting a prostitute, john, pimp, drug dealer, drug addict, mugger, pickpocket, panhandler, or loitering teenager. It was the most notorious chunk of real estate in Minneapolis, a place of disreputable businesses, rough-and-tumble bars, peep shows, sex-oriented bookstores, and triple-X movie theaters that accounted for 25 percent of all the arrests in the city. The city council's response to this blight on their fair community was to invoke eminent domain, seize all the businesses, and bulldoze them, literally turning Block E into an asphalt parking lot, thereby impelling the sinners to locate elsewhere.

A decade later, a few enterprising entrepreneurs decided that *E* stood for "Entertainment" and subsequently transformed the block into the crown jewel of Minneapolis's thriving club and theater scene. A movie house, a pizza joint, an ice cream parlor, a game center, a Hard Rock Cafe, and other attractions were brought in, and the area was lit up like the inside of the Hubert H. Humphrey Metrodome during a ball game. Only, along with the tourists and suburbanites, the bright lights also attracted a criminal element, and Block E was once again becoming known for its casual shootings and what the cops euphemistically referred to as "disturbances." Thus the experiment with opera. I almost felt guilty for humming along.

I found Chopper in an upscale club near Block E. He was drinking tap beer at a small table with a thin, twitchy white dude who had felon written all over him. The pair had demanded the attention of customers and the waitstaff alike, if not for their scruffy appearance, then certainly for their voices, which were loud and annoying—I heard them from six tables away. Not even the club bouncer dared try to do anything about them. I suppose it was fear. Chopper was sitting in a wheelchair, and nobody wanted to be accused of insensitivity toward the handicapped.

"Hey, hey, hey," Chopper called loudly as I approached, doing his best Fat Albert impersonation. "Long time, man."

I caught the eye of an alarmed waitress and made a circular motion with my finger as I sat, and she went off to fetch a round of drinks.

"So you're fuckin' McKenzie," the felon said.

"Lower your voice or I'll kick your teeth in," I said.

His face tried to turn red with anger, but he was so pale all he could manage was pink.

"Hey, hey, hey," said Chopper.

I pointed a finger at him. "You, too."

"I don't need this shit," the felon said. Quietly.

"It's cool," said Chopper. His voice didn't carry beyond the table, either. "McKenzie's cool. You gots t' know the man has reason to be hostile."

The waitress came with our beers. "These guys running a tab?" I asked as she distributed the glasses.

"Yes, sir."

"I have it." I dropped a fifty on her tray. "Keep the change."

"Yes, sir, thank you, sir," she said and hurried away.

"That's real white of ya, McKenzie," Chopper said.

"It's not hard to make people happy," I said. "Just speak softly and pay your bills."

"Yeah?" said the felon. "How happy you gonna make me?"

I turned to Chopper. "Who is this?"

Chopper downed what was left of his first beer and started working on his second. In between sips, he said, "This here is—"

"Ain't no need for names," the felon said.

"This here is a friend of mine," Chopper said. "And a friend of yours."

"Is he?" I said.

Chopper gestured at the felon with his glass. "Tell 'im what you told me," he said.

"We ain't talked about whatchacallit, recompense, yet."

"No money gonna change hands. What you doin' is a favor to me."

"Fuck that."

Chopper's eyes grew wide and menacing. Hell, I was frightened and he wasn't even looking at me. But then, I knew his history. When I was in harness, I found Chopper sprawled in a parking lot in St. Paul with two slugs in his back. Apparently he had run afoul of a rival dope dealer. I saved his life that night (ask Chopper about it, he loves to tell the story), though the damage to his spine put him in a wheelchair permanently. Six weeks later, he wheeled himself out of the hospital. Two days after that, we found the dealer and his two bodyguards under the swings at a park near the St. Paul Vo-Tech. Someone had nined all three of them from a sitting position. The murders were never solved. Of course, that was before Bobby Dunston took over the homicide unit. Shortly after the killings, Chopper moved to Minneapolis. He now made his living operating a surprisingly lucrative ticket-scalping operation; he even had a Web site. What else he was involved in I didn't know, nor did I care to know.

"You owe me, man," Chopper said.

The felon gave him the mad-dog, only his heart wasn't in it. After a few seconds—just enough time to satisfy his manhood—he said, "Aww, fuck it," and drank more beer.

"Tell 'im," Chopper said.

"Tell me what?" I asked.

"There's a price on your ass," the felon said.

"A price?"

"A contract."

"A contract?"

"What I'm sayin'."

"What are you saying?"

"McKenzie," Chopper said. "Watch my lips. Man put a hit on you. Open contract. Pays fifty large."

"Fifty thousand dollars?"

"What I'm sayin'," the felon said.

"That's ridiculous," I said.

"I agree," Chopper said. "I know guys who'd do it for five."

"I know guys who'd do it for the cost of a Happy Meal," the felon said. "Less if they're crackheads."

"What are you guys, crazy?" I said. "A contract? On me?"

"You are McKenzie," the felon said.

"Yes, I'm McKenzie."

"Well, then."

"A fifty-thousand-dollar contract on me?"

"You fuckin' quick on the uptake."

"Listen—"

"I'm just sayin' what I heard."

"Where?"

"Where what?"

"Where did you hear this?"

"Around."

"Around where?"

"Around. Just around. It's in the fuckin' wind."

I couldn't believe I was hearing it right. I turned back to Chopper for confirmation.

"Fifty grand, every douchebag in the world be gunnin' for you," he said. "That kinda change, it's gonna attract your high-priced talent, too. Your serious professionals."

I had no idea what to say to that.

"Man must really want you dead," the felon said.

"What man?"

"Dunno."

"Who's shopping the contract?"

"Dunno."

"How are you going to collect if you don't know who's buying the hit?"

"I wasn't lookin' to collect."

"Do you think you could find out?"

"Fuck no, man. I did my civic duty."

"I'll pay."

"Not enough, man. Not enough." The felon stood. He looked down at Chopper. "We good?" he asked.

"Yeah."

"I'm outta here," the felon said. "That fuckin' music they playin' drives me nuts."

We sat quietly at the table after he left, nursing our beers. After a few moments, I said, "Chopper?"

"I'll ask around, but there are people know we're tight," he said. "Could be hard to get the intel, know what I'm sayin'? Then there's that guilt by association thing. I ain't sure I even want to know you for a while."

I certainly couldn't blame him for that.

"I appreciate you calling me," I said.

He nodded.

"What do I owe you?" I asked. Chopper was nothing if not entrepreneurial.

He surprised me when he said, "Nothin', man. Gratis."

"My God, Chopper. Next thing you know, you'll be voting Democrat."

They were playing Handel's *Rinaldo* when I stepped out of the bar and started walking up the street, only it barely registered. My head was down, my shoulders were hunched, and my hands were in my pockets—the perfect vic. I should have been more attentive, more aware. Still, if you had just been told that a person or persons unknown was paying fifty thousand dollars to see you dead, I bet it would throw you for a loop, too.

The kids outside the Vietnamese restaurant the night before now made sense to me, and so did the extra bullet hole in my Audi. Jeezus, they were shooting at me, trying to kill me, and I didn't even notice. How dumb was that? On the other hand, I just couldn't imagine what I had done—or to whom—to deserve such attention. I skimmed in my head the list of enemies I had given Harry. Nothing popped out at me. Probably the hit had something to do with Victoria Dunston's kidnapping, only that was just a guess, and it seemed even goofier to me than the hit itself. If I had just collected a million-dollar ransom, I'd take the money and run. Wouldn't you? "Damn," I muttered. Then it occurred to me that if the kidnapper was behind the contract, he was using my money to pay for it.

"Damn!"

My head came up when I shouted the profanity. There were plenty of people on the street hopping from club to club and theater to theater. Most of them looked my way. Out of the corner of my eye, I saw two young black men in satin Chicago Bulls warm-up jackets that didn't. Instead, they glanced down and away.

My Cherokee was parked at a meter on Eighth and Marquette. I knew I'd never make it. Instead, I turned north on Hennepin and joined the river of pedestrians, going with the flow, seeking safety under the blazing streetlamps. Only they didn't make me feel safe. Last week a gangbanger had attempted to shoot a rival with a .44 Magnum, missed, and killed an innocent bystander who had stepped out of a bar not ten feet from where I was now walking. There were plenty of pedestrians and bright lights then, too.

I thought of my own guns locked in my safe at home. *What are you doing walking around unarmed?* my inner voice wanted to know. *People are trying to kill you.* On the other hand, what would I have done with my weapons if I had thought to bring them along? Start a running gun battle on crowded Hennepin Avenue? *You should have listened to Schroeder; you should have hired someone to watch your back.*

I kept walking. Traffic moved incessantly along the avenue. I tried to hail a cab. One stopped, but before I could reach it, it was seized by a young woman decked out in little more than a faux fur jacket and a belt.

One of the things they teach you about surveillance is to never reveal that you're aware you are being followed until you can use the information to your advantage. While trying for the cab, I looked behind me. A mistake. The two black men saw me seeing them. They began gathering speed. I gave up on a cab and increased my own pace. They started running. I started running, weaving in and out of the foot traffic, crossing Sixth against the light. I had no idea where I was running to until I reached the parking lot on Fifth Street. The state had built a light rail train system connecting downtown Minneapolis with the Minneapolis–St. Paul International Airport and the Mall of America. The Hennepin Avenue Station loomed in front of me. I cut across the parking lot at a gallop, juking and jiving around parked cars to reach it. I was dragging by the time I jumped the tracks—it was the second time that day I had run for my life and the second time I realized how badly I had let myself go. *Never again,* I told myself as I crossed the platform and headed toward the train. I figured I was home free until the transit cop standing in the doorway blocked my path.

"Do you have a pass?" he asked. He was smiling when he said, "You can't buy a pass on the train. You have to buy them—" He pointed at a vending machine on the platform.

Oh, for chrissake, my inner voice shouted. I was too out of breath to say it aloud.

I dashed across the platform. I found two one-dollar bills in my pocket and was fumbling with them when my pursuers arrived, moving confidently, looking no worse for chasing me. *Bet they work out,* I told myself as I fed the bills into the vending machine.

One of them slid a hand under his Bulls jacket. The other reached behind his back.

"Hey," I shouted.

They halted.

I pointed at the light pole. There was a security camera mounted there, and it was pointed right at the platform.

"Smile," I said.

They looked at the camera and then at me. They didn't smile. I pointed at the transit cop standing in the doorway to the train and looking out. They didn't smile some more.

By then the machine had spat out a pass. I carried it just as casually as I could across the platform to the train. I stepped aboard and showed my pass to the transit cop.

The two black men stared at the cop. Possibilities flickered over their faces. The cop nodded at them. "The train's leaving in a few seconds," he said. "You guys better hurry."

The two men gave him a maybe-next-time shrug and turned away.

"Have a nice night," the cop called to them.

One of the black men gave him a wave.

Minnesota Nice. Gotta love it.

17

I had never actually ridden the Hiawatha Line before and was surprised by how smooth and efficient the trip was. The train took me past the Government Plaza, the Metrodome, the VA Medical Center, and on to the airport. Once there, I disembarked at the Lindbergh Terminal and made my way to the cabstand. A porter asked if I had any alcohol on my person. About three-quarters of the nine hundred airport cabdrivers are Somali, most of them Muslim, and some refuse fares that are traveling with duty-free booze—it's forbidden in Islam to carry alcohol. "I wish," I said. He hailed a blue-and-white, and I had the driver take me back to Eighth and Marquette in downtown Minneapolis. There was no one lurking in the shadows that I could see, so I paid off the driver, fired up the Cherokee, and drove to Falcon Heights.

I pulled into my driveway, triggering a sensor that set off a ribbon of light that led all the way to my garage in back of the house. Only I didn't park in the garage. Instead, I stopped parallel to my front door. My plan was to pack a bag and take the next stage out of Dodge. My address wasn't listed in the phone book, yet I knew it wouldn't be too difficult to learn where I lived. For fifty thousand dollars people would be willing to make the extra effort. I hadn't decided where to hide—certainly not Nina's. I'd call her, I decided, but not stay with her. Lead assassins to her doorstep? Not a chance, I don't care how many guards Schroeder put on duty.

I was pondering likely hideouts when I left the Jeep Cherokee and crossed my lawn to the porch. The porch stretched the length of the front of my house and was divided into two sections. One half was open and empty except for the wood and canvas chair that hung from thin chains attached to the ceiling. The other half was enclosed by a fine mesh screen to keep the mosquitoes at bay and was furnished with lounge chairs, wicker tables, and a sofa. I sometimes entertained there and on a couple of occasions spent the night. Which reminded me, I should bring the furniture in before the weather turned cold.

I climbed the concrete steps and crossed the porch to the front door. Mail, mostly credit card solicitations, was crammed into a black box. I removed it from the box and tucked it under my arm while I tried to fit my key into the lock. The key met with resistance. I examined the key in the light from the driveway and streetlamps beyond, thinking I had selected the wrong one by mistake or was holding it upside down. Only there was nothing wrong with it. I tried again and failed. *What the hell?* I rubbed my thumb over the lock. There was something there, a tiny sliver of wood protruding from the slot. Someone had jammed a toothpick into the lock and broken it off, and I thought, *Thieves do that.* It worked as a kind of burglar alarm for anyone inside the house, warning them if the owners came home early. Or perhaps the lock had been sabotaged to force me to go to my back door, where there was less chance of being observed by neighbors. Either way . . .

I dropped the mail, turned, leapt over the low wooden railing, and began fleeing across my lawn. A voice behind me shouted, "Stop."

I didn't listen.

"Stop." This time the word was punctuated by the sound of two gunshots.

I turned my head when I hit Hoyt. I was being chased by a man who looked an awful lot like the felon, Chopper's friend, the one who said he wasn't interested in collecting the fifty thousand dollars that was on my head. *Liar, liar, pants on fire,* my inner voice said. I kept running.

This makes three, I told myself. Three times I'd been forced to run for my life on the same day. It was getting tiresome. I thought about screaming for help, see if I could rouse a neighbor to action. Only I had caused a ruckus two years ago when I shot a guy off my front porch, and many of my neighbors had signed a petition asking me to move. I really didn't want to get them involved. *Not to worry,* I told myself. This time I had a plan. I wasn't running from, I was running to.

I raced along Hoyt, north up Coffman Street, across Folwell, and over someone's sprawling lawn. All the homes in this area belonged to the University Grove Association. Each was unique, designed by committee-approved architects to house bigwigs from the University of Minnesota—professors, administrators, regents—including at one time famed football coach Bernie Bierman. Behind the houses was a rocky and heavily wooded ravine that stretched all the way from the water culvert under Cleveland Avenue to the Lauderdale Nature Preserve. It was quite narrow; at one time it had been a streetcar line, and you could still see abandoned railroad ties and a concrete platform with steps leading to it. Yet it gave homeowners the illusion that they were living on the edge of a wilderness. It was there that I decided to make my stand.

The felon was gaining on me when I plunged over the edge of the ravine—I couldn't believe he was in better shape than I was. I tripped over something and tumbled headfirst over jagged stones, tree roots, and brush. I recognized them solely by the way they tore up my body; I couldn't see a thing. I came to an abrupt halt at the bottom of the gully, stretched across a hard-packed walking path. I waited for a moment to catch my breath and shake my head to get the chimes to stop; I might even have moaned once or twice. At the rim of the ravine I heard the felon. I couldn't see him, yet I knew he was being more cautious than I had been, easing himself into the ravine, moving slowly. Of course, he could afford to be cautious. He had the gun.

I went to my knees, still trying to control my breathing. It took about thirty seconds to gain my night eyes; shapes and shadows began to fill in. For the first time I noticed that the moon was full. The crazies always came out during a full moon. Crazies and werewolves. I rubbed my hands together. My fingernails weren't growing and hair wasn't sprouting from my knuckles, so I concluded I must be one of the former.

Beyond the ravine were the University of Minnesota intramural soccer fields, and next to that was a complex of well-lit condos. To make a run for either would be like carrying a neon sign on my back that said FIRE AT WILL. I gained my feet and scampered forward along the worn footpath, dodging rocks and low-hanging tree branches. I knew I couldn't remain on the path for long; footsteps on loose rocks told me the felon was close. I searched for a place to hide. There were several trees and high bushes off to my right that cast a shadow darker than the night that surrounded me. I crawled into it.

The felon had moved to the bottom of the ravine. Moonlight flickered off his clothing, his gun, his hands, his pale face, and I was able to follow his progress. He paused when he reached the narrow footpath and searched the ground all around him. He went a few steps in one direction, a few in another, while listening hard. Long moments passed. He picked up a large stone and threw it far to the left of me. It made a crashing sound as it hit the wall of the gully and rolled against a tree. The felon pointed his gun with both hands toward the noise, yet only silence followed. He turned slowly, moving the gun in an arc in front of him. He seemed to hesitate when he spied the trees and high bushes. He peered deep into the shadow where I was hidden.

I had hunted with my father when I was a kid—pheasant on farmland near the Iowa border, grouse and deer up north. He would talk about the animals' natural camouflage. The trick, he said, was to make them move. You could look right at an animal without seeing it, unless it moved. The felon was looking at me now. I didn't move, and he didn't see me.

The felon hesitated, then began creeping in the opposite direction. Each step took him farther away from me. Five yards, ten, fifteen, twenty. He halted, brought his gun up, and aimed at something in the darkness. "McKenzie," he hissed. I crouched low against my tree, reaching out to maintain my balance. My fingers closed around a thick tree branch. I picked it up and determined that it was about two feet long. At the same time, the felon straightened up, letting his gun rest against his thigh. He turned and began following the path toward me.

He was moving casually now. I didn't know if he was continuing the chase or searching for a way out of the ravine. He stopped, stared at something, and continued walking. He stopped again when he reached my hiding place. Again he seemed to look straight at me. My fingers tightened on the tree branch. He kept walking, but only a few steps before he halted. He brought his gun up, aimed, and then lowered his gun.

"McKenzie," he shouted.

A desperate move, I thought. Did he really expect me to answer?

"McKenzie?"

Well, why not?

I stepped out of the shadow and moved to within striking distance.

"Here," I said and swung the tree branch. All my anger and frustration, all my fear was in the blow as I hit him at the point where his shoulder and neck merged.

I could feel his body give under the force of the blow.

I could hear the sickening snap as his collarbone splintered.

That'll teach him, my inner voice said.

He staggered forward and dropped to his knees. He brought both hands up to the injured area. He didn't start shrieking until his fingers felt the bloody tip of the bone protruding through the skin.

He had dropped his gun; I couldn't see where it had fallen, and that worried me. I grabbed a fistful of the felon's hair and yanked backward, pulling him well beyond reach of where the gun might be. He fell against his shattered shoulder and screamed even louder.

I was running short of time; surely the neighbors bordering the ravine would hear him and start debating over whether or not they wanted to get involved. The branch was still in my hand, and I jabbed the felon with it. "So you weren't looking to collect, huh?" I said.

Something resembling words choked out of his mouth. I could recognize only one—"Please."

I jabbed him again, and his groaning and moaning increased in volume. "What's your name?" He answered, but I couldn't understand what he said. I crouched next to him and tried again. "What's your name?"

He managed to spit out, "Pat Beulke."

"Who's shopping the hit on me?"

He said, "I, I, I—can't," or something that sounded like that.

I pressed down on his shoulder with the flat of my hand, and he howled like a dying animal.

"Tell me."

"Dog, Dog, Dog . . ."

"What?" I leaned closer so I could hear.

"Dogman-G."

"Who's Dogman-G?"

"Used to be . . . gang . . . North Side . . . Minneapolis."

"Don't ever let me see you again," I said. "If I were you, I'd hide from Chopper, too."

I tossed the branch away and followed the ravine to Cleveland Avenue. I climbed the hill to the sidewalk and followed it past the tennis courts, just a harmless homeowner taking a midnight stroll through the peaceful streets of Falcon Heights and St. Anthony Park, in case anyone stopped to ask. I probably should have felt guilty about what I had done to the felon, about leaving him unattended in the gully. I didn't. I didn't even feel guilty about not feeling guilty. I guess I'm becoming callous as I get older. People trying to kill you will do that.

I took the long way returning to my house, this time heading for the back door. The door was locked, and I took that to mean that the felon hadn't been inside. Still, I switched on all my lights and went from room to room searching for damage. It didn't take me long to find Tommy Thomforde. He was lying on his back in the middle of my empty living room. There was a bullet hole in the center of his forehead. I sat on the hardwood floor next to him. Going strictly by touch, it seemed to me that he had been dead for a long time.

"The neighbors aren't going to like this at all," I said.

"Don't you believe in furniture?" Harry asked. I get that question a lot. My father and I moved into the house right after I came into my money, yet I had managed to furnish only a few of the rooms in all that time. No sense rushing into anything, I figured.

"I bought a dining room set last month," I said.

Harry took a look at it: eight chairs, a table, and a matching buffet hand-carved from rich, dark wood in the 1930s. There was nothing else in the room, not even a painting on the wall. "Pathetic," he said.

He had me there.

"Just so you know, we found the big white moving van on the East Side," Harry said. "We found the small red Vibe station wagon inside the big white moving van on the East Side."

"Did you happen to find my million dollars inside the trunk of the small red Vibe station wagon inside the big white moving van on the East Side?"

"We didn't, but you know, McKenzie, money can't buy happiness."

"It sure hasn't so far."

The forensic pathologist announced that they were ready to move the body. "There is no question that he was killed somewhere else and dumped here," he said, confirming what the rest of us had concluded an hour before he arrived.

"So I've got that going for me," I said.

"Quiet, McKenzie," Harry said. To the pathologist he said, "Any idea about time of death?"

"Between twelve and twenty-four hours."

"Geez, Doc, I could have told you that."

"Do you have a medical degree, Agent Wilson?"

"No."

"I see. So you're just guessing."

"When will you have something more definite?"

"Call me later today. Much later."

When the pathologist moved away, I said, "I'll be curious to learn if Tommy was alive when I was being shot at this afternoon," I said.

"Did you think it was him at Joley's?" Harry said.

"I will if you will."

"We asked Scottie Thomforde's co-worker and the bartender at Lehane's to identify the T-Man from a photo array that included Tommy's picture. Neither of them could do it."

"Yet Mrs. Thomforde said he was at Lehane's with Scottie."

"No, she said Tommy and Scottie went out together. That's not the same thing."

"That's true, I suppose."

"If Tommy was the T-Man, who shot him?"

"The Babe."

"I hate nicknames."

"I don't blame you—Brian."

"I should invent a nickname for you," Harry said.

"If you must know, all the women call me Long John."

"No, they don't."

"Yeah, but they could if they wanted to."

"What I can't figure out is, why dump Tommy's body on your floor?"

"That confuses me, too."

"It has to be some kind of a message."

"Yes, well, I got the message. Take this."

"What?"

I gave Harry a set of keys for my front and back doors. "If you and your people need to return to the house, you have my permission to come and go as you please," I said. "Do whatever you want to do. Search the place. Drink my beer. Watch the ball game on my plasma TV. Whatever."

"What are you going to do?"

"Take off for a few days."

Harry eyed me suspiciously. "And do what?" he said.

"I thought I'd go hunting."

It was midmorning before the Feds and the other cops finally departed, giving my neighbors plenty of time to see them and their vehicles when they went out for their morning papers. Oh, well. As soon as they left, I dashed upstairs, showered, shaved, and dressed. Under my polo shirt and sports jacket I wore a white level II Kevlar vest with Velcro straps that was rated to withstand the blunt trauma of a .357 Magnum jacketed soft point. It had cost me six hundred dollars. I bought it on a whim, thinking I'd get about as much use out of it as the Belshaw Donut Robot Mark I mini-donut machine that I had purchased around the same time. I just wanted to own it.

Afterward, I packed a bag and carried it to my basement, where I unzipped it again. I rolled back a rug and removed four reinforced tiles to reveal a safe that was embedded in my floor. From the safe I removed my handguns: a Beretta nine-millimeter, a Beretta .380, and a Heckler & Koch nine-millimeter with a cocking lever built into the pistol grip. It was the same Heckler & Koch that I was carrying when I captured Thomas Teachwell in a cabin on Lower Red Lake. I holstered the nine just behind my right hip and the .380 to my ankle. I tossed the Heckler & Koch into the bag. I would have carried all three guns, but I only had two hands.

I also removed four packets of fifty-dollar bills from the safe, one hundred bills to a packet, twenty thousand dollars total. My father had called it "mad money" because he thought I was crazy for not putting it into a bank. Only time and experience had proved to me that it was always wise to have a little cash lying around. The safe also contained two sets of fake IDs. I took the best of them: a Wisconsin driver's license with my photo and the address of a mail drop in Hudson, five credit cards, a health insurance card, a library card, and a card that indicated I was a member of the National Rifle Association. All of the cards were legitimate, including the name on each. I had taken Keith Kahla off a gravestone in Eau Claire and subsequently secured his birth certificate. Eighteen months ago, one of Harry's less than ethical colleagues compelled me to hide underground for a few days. It wasn't a pleasant episode in my life. Afterward, I enlisted the aid of a woman I knew who produced fake IDs for illegal immigrants out of a photography studio in St. Paul. I've been prepared to run ever since.

18

It was only 10:30 A.M., yet Greg Schroeder looked as if he had been awake since June. I found him in his office sitting with his feet resting on top of his desk in front of the far wall. His hair was unruly, his face unshaved, his clothes wrinkled, and he was smoking. He smiled when he saw me.

"You look like shit," he said.

"If you say so, it must be true."

"I was up all night babysitting your girl. Just saw the young one off on her band trip. What's your excuse?"

I sat in the same chair as on the previous visit. Schroeder righted himself, crushed the cigarette in a crowded ashtray, opened the bottom drawer of his desk, and removed a half-filled bottle of Booker's and two glasses of doubtful cleanliness.

"You look like you could use a beverage," he said.

"I thought it was a cliché, private eyes sitting in their offices drinking bourbon."

"How do you think it got to be a cliché?" He poured us both a shot and slid my glass toward me. "Besides, it's good for you." He downed his shot in one gulp. I thought it was only polite to do the same. "Studies from several prominent medical institutions prove conclusively that two ounces of alcohol each day helps prevent heart disease."

"I wonder what it does for the liver."

"I didn't read that far ahead. So, McKenzie." Schroeder leaned back in his chair and returned his feet to their perch on his desktop. "I notice the Kevlar vest you're wearing."

So much for concealment, my inner voice said. I tapped my chest. "I'm starting a new fashion trend."

"Just out of curiosity, exactly how much trouble are you in?"

"There's a contract on my head. People have already tried to collect on it."

"So I've guessed. How much?"

"Fifty thousand dollars."

"Fifty—that's nuts. You can kill a president for fifty thousand."

"It's nice to know I'm highly valued."

"What do you want me to do about it?"

"I want you to keep me alive while I track down the man who issued it."

"How are you going to do that?"

"One punk at a time."

"Or we could stash you someplace safe and I'll do the looking."

"No."

"No?"

"What can I tell ya, Greg? I'm a manly man doing manly things in a manly way."

"Uh-huh. In that case"—Schroeder righted himself again and reached for the Booker's—"you had better get those two ounces in now. Who knows if you'll ever get another opportunity."

Schroeder poured, I drank. While I drank he pulled a contract out of the top drawer of his desk and pushed it across to me. "Sign this," he said.

As my dear old dad always advised, I read it first. "What the hell?" I said.

"Something wrong?"

"Five hundred a day plus expenses."

"That's standard."

"I know, still—one thousand dollars if you use your gun? Five thousand dollars if you actually kill someone?"

"It's not that I don't count that as part of the service," Schroeder said, "but there's a certain emotional jolt involved, as you know. Besides, they're your enemies. They should be cheap at twice that price. Also, if we get arrested, it's up to you to hire the best lawyer that money can buy. Remember, I get two fifty for every day I spend in jail up to one hundred thousand dollars. This is nonnegotiable."

I didn't know what to say to that, so I didn't say anything, just stared with my mouth hanging open and my eyes wide. Schroeder gestured at the paper in front of me. "It's my rich-guy-gone-bad contract. You are rich, aren't you, McKenzie?"

"Not as rich as I used to be," I said.

"Sign, sign."

I thought about leaving. Then I thought about the four slugs he put into a man who was *this* close to shooting me one cold and dark night. I signed.

"Now I get to watch you play private eye," Schroeder said.

"Something like that."

"Do you have a lead?"

"Dude calls himself Dogman-G."

"Really? Think he gets much street cred with a name like Dogman-G?"

"Who knows? Maybe it was a choice between that and Trevor."

"Personally, I think Trevor sounds scarier. What do you know about him?"

"He's a North Side gangbanger."

"That's it?"

"I have some contacts in St. Paul that might be able to help."

"I hate St. Paul."

"Who asked you?" Schroeder wasn't the first resident of Minneapolis who treated St. Paul with disdain, but at these prices I didn't want to hear it.

"Let me try something," Schroeder said. He picked up his phone, checked a number, punched it into the keypad, waited, and said, "Hi, Sarge," when someone answered. "It's Greg Schroeder . . . Not bad, not bad, you . . . ? It could be worse, Sarge. She could be a lesbian." I didn't know what Schroeder was talking about, but he and the Sarge thought it was awfully funny. "Say, Sarge, what do you have on a banger calls himself Dogman-G . . . ? That's it? Seriously, that's all you got . . . ? I appreciate it's hard to keep track. What is it they say, there's an asshole born every minute . . . ? Do you have his straight name . . . ? No, no, I appreciate the effort . . . Put it on my tab . . . You know it. Thanks a lot."

Schroeder hung up his phone. "I have some sources over at the MPD that I pay for information when I need it," he said. "This one, the sarge, he says that the gang unit suspects that this Dogman-G's been moving product in North Minneapolis. That's it. They don't have a sheet on him. They don't even know his real name. All they know for sure is that he's into dogs. Pit bulls."

"So we're back to St. Paul," I said.

"Bite your tongue."

A half-dozen years ago, Officer Willie Buckman was responsible for one of the most colossal animal-abuse cases in Minnesota history, resulting in four felony convictions and forty-seven misdemeanor citations. The way Buckman told the story, it had been an accident. He was patrolling for the Minneapolis Police Department when he caught a domestic. When he arrived at the scene, instead of abusive spouses going at it, he discovered nearly fifty suspects watching a dogfight inside a garage. He called for backup. Arrests were made. Dogs were seized.

If it had been a drug bust, not much would have been made of it. But, it's a curious characteristic of society today that citizens are more intensely outraged over the mistreatment of dogs, cats, horses, and other animals than they are of humans. The arrests made Buckman a hero to the viewers of every local TV news program in the Twin Cities. Not to mention CNN and *Good Morning America*. Soon after, he was offered a position as an investigator for the Minnesota Animal Humane Society. Now he wears a brown and tan uniform with a gold badge and a sidearm and investigates cruelty-to-animals complaints and conducts training and workshops for the humane enforcement industry.

"The thing is," he told us, "we never did learn who called in the domestic. I always thought it was someone's ex-wife or girlfriend. Maybe a neighbor who wanted to remain anonymous. Most of the complaints we get, there aren't any names attached to them."

"You get a lot of those?" Schroeder asked.

"Oh, yeah. That's where we get most of our intel. Someone's pissed at someone else and they're looking for payback, they call in. Doesn't do us much good, though. You need hard evidence, and that's difficult to come by. Professional dogfighting is a very secretive, very suspicious world. It's hard to get close. I know who's out there; I know what they're doing. Proving it in court—dogs aren't real good at giving testimony, if you know what I mean."

"You should have stayed with the MPD," Schroeder said. "Jacking up kids smoking dope on the street corner or giving college chicks a chance to work off their DWIs."

"Or I could've become a PI," Buckman said. "Shooting pictures through the windows of hot-sheet motel rooms with digital cameras, negotiating with the babes over what they'll give you for *not* showing the pictures to their husbands."

"Don't knock it," Schroeder said. "That's how I met my third wife."

"How did that work out for you?" Buckman asked.

"You know how that worked out," Schroeder said, and the two men slapped hands. Boys just being boys.

"Excuse me," I said. "Do you know anything about a banger who calls himself Dogman-G?"

Schroeder threw a thumb in my direction. "You'll have to forgive McKenzie," he said. "He's got a lot on his mind these days."

"Oh, I can tell he's a fun guy," Buckman said. "Must be the Kevlar. And the fact that you haven't slept in twenty-four hours, am I right?"

"What can I say? They were broadcasting a *Charlie's Angels* marathon on TV Land."

Schroeder and Buckman both thought that was funny. Finally Buckman said, "Dogman-G, huh? Yeah, I know him. A wannabe tough guy deals drugs in North Minneapolis. He's a dabbler. He wants to be a real dogman, breed pit bulls and fight them on the circuit. Except he also uses pits to intimidate his competition, to mark his territory. Instead of flashing a nine-millimeter, he'll use a nasty-looking dog on a leash to frighten off his rivals. The real dogmen, the professionals, they don't care for that kind of behavior."

"Sure."

"Gotta remember, real dogmen, they don't see what they're doing as a brutal, cruel activity. They view dogfighting as a legitimate sport—they trace its roots back to seventeenth-century England. They're very traditional. They have a code. Rules. Protocols. You break them . . . It's hard to get into the club if you break the rules, and Dogman-G breaks the rules."

"The other children won't play with him?" Schroeder asked.

"Nope."

"How sad."

"Brings tears to your eyes, doesn't it?" Buckman said.

"Where can we find Dogman-G?" I asked.

"I have no idea," Buckman said. "You might try . . . There's a dogman up in East Bethel. Dogman-G's been spending a lot of time with him these days. I think he's trying to rehab his rep, get in with the right crowd."

"Where in East Bethel?"

Buckman gave us directions to an isolated farmhouse that were obscure at best. "I've been trying to get enough for a search warrant. No luck so far," he said. "If you guys stumble upon anything interesting, you'll let me know?"

Schroeder promised that we would. "In the meantime, you can go back to rescuing frightened kittens from trees," he said.

"Hey, don't knock it," Buckman said. "A lot of those frightened kittens have grateful women as owners."

"I hear that," Schroeder said, and they slapped hands yet again.

Oh, brother, my inner voice said.

Like a lot of rural towns in Minnesota, East Bethel claimed a small population—about thirteen thousand—yet a lot of size, approximately forty-eight square miles of lakes, wetlands, farms, and prairies. We found it thirty minutes north of the Twin Cities along Highway 65. We hung a right on Viking Boulevard and followed Buckman's vague directions more or less northeast until we came upon a small farmhouse at the top of a gentle rise. The house was surrounded by acres of brush, sun-packed dirt, and prairie grass. Just beyond the house was a large pole barn, and beyond that was the beginning of a thick forest. There were no plowed fields anywhere that I could see, no pens or corrals for animals. But there was a suspiciously large group of cars parked along the narrow county blacktop, and even more cars that lined a quarter-mile dirt driveway leading to the farmhouse.

"Think we're in time for the show?" I asked.

"Try to blend in," Schroeder said. "Kick the dirt, spit a lot."

We parked on the blacktop at the end of the line of cars. Schroeder left the doors unlocked and the key in the ignition. He popped the trunk, found a weathered knee-length duster, and put it on. "Who are you supposed to be?" I asked. "Jesse James?" He didn't say. There was a leather gun case in the trunk. Schroeder unzipped it and pulled out a short, black, boxy, and extremely ugly Heckler & Koch MP7 submachine gun. It was about thirteen and a half inches long, weighed four and a half pounds, and fired a thirty-millimeter-long bullet. The Germans designed it to pierce high-quality body armor. Like mine. Aficionados classified it as a "personal defense weapon."

Schroeder checked the forty-round magazine and slapped it into the pistol grip. "Too bad you're not paying me by the bullet," he said. I didn't know if he was joking or not.

Schroeder hid the MP7 beneath the duster. "Give me a couple of minutes," he said.

I watched as Schroeder cut a diagonal path across the field to the top of the dirt driveway, then past the driveway toward the barn. I started following as soon as I lost sight of him.

Moving along the driveway, I passed a man with a wooden, wedge-shaped tool in his hand standing next to a battered pickup truck. He didn't see me at first because he was busy kicking a pit bull that he held by a leash with the other hand. A blanket had been draped over the animal's head. I stopped, and he grinned at me.

"Damn cur," he said. "Ain't got no fight in him. Gotta toughen him up."

I thought how much I would like to "toughen" him up, but my inner voice admonished me. *Keep your eyes on the prize,* it said.

I continued along the road until I came across three rottweilers chained to a stake in the ground between the house and the pole barn. They were agitated and angry. I circled them cautiously, well beyond their reach, and walked up to the entrance of the barn. I expected to be stopped—I remembered what Buckman had said about secrecy and suspicion, and besides, didn't they charge admission to these things? But there was no one at the door. Instead, I found forty, maybe fifty men—white, black, Hispanic, Asian. Many were dressed like guys who worked outdoors, others in suits and ties. I was surprised by how normal they all seemed.

Most of them were hovering around a twenty-foot ring deep inside the barn. The ring was empty; I didn't know if we were late or early for the fight. I went searching for Schroeder. I couldn't find him, and then I did. He was standing in a corner of the pole barn where someone had set up a half-dozen folding tables surrounded by folding chairs. There were two metal tubs filled with ice and beer behind a counter built from sawhorses and wooden planks; the planks supported a dozen bottles of hard liquor and a cash box. The man behind the cash box was doing good business. I moved toward the makeshift bar, and Schroeder moved away. As we passed each other he whispered, "The reader."

Sure enough, I found a young black man dressed in a dark blue hoodie sitting at one of the tables. He had a shaved head, a close-cropped beard and mustache, a silver hoop hanging from his left ear, and a silver tooth that he sucked while reading a paperback edition of *The World of the American Pit Bull Terrier* by Richard Stratton. There were several other black men in the bar area, and I wondered how many of them were on his side.

I sat at the table in front of him, my hands in my pockets. He looked up from his book. "Wan' sumpthin'?" he asked.

"Dogman-G?"

He sucked on his tooth, then closed his book, using his finger to hold his place. "I know you?" he asked.

"Word is that there's a contract on some pinhead named McKenzie."

As I was speaking, a black man took up position behind Dogman-G's left shoulder. Another black man took the seat at the table to my immediate left. Both of them looked like they weren't sure what to do with their hands.

"Wha' zat got to do wi' me?" Dogman-G said.

"I heard you were handling it," I said.

Dogman-G eyed me suspiciously. "You a cop, man? You soundin' like five-oh to me," he said.

"I'm not a cop."

He studied me some more. "Why you come to me?" he asked.

"I was given your name."

"By who?"

"Pat Beulke."

Dogman-G glanced over his shoulder at the man standing behind him. "We know that boy?" he asked.

The man said, "We know 'im."

"Well 'nuff he can drop my name careless like that?"

"I'll take care of it."

My inner voice said, *Tsk, tsk, tsk, poor Pat,* but I knew sarcasm when I heard it.

Dogman-G looked across the table at me. His face had the bemused expression of a man who made his living catering to the vices of others. "Wha' you wan' know?" he asked.

"Fifty large is a lot of money. I want to make sure I heard the price right."

"It's cool. Fifty is the number."

"Are you buying the hit?"

"Nah, man," Dogman said. "I jus' the messenger. I know who gots the presidents, though."

"Who would that be?"

"Why you wan' to know?"

"It's personal."

"Zat right? Who are you?"

"I'm McKenzie."

Suddenly the two black men knew what to do with their hands. They began reaching for weapons. Except I was quicker. My hands came out of my pockets. In my right was the nine-millimeter Beretta that I pointed at the dude standing behind Dogman's shoulder. In my left was the .380 that I leveled at the chest of the black man sitting between Dogman and me. They raised their empty hands without being told to, although I didn't think they were surrendering.

"Gentlemen," I said, "I do not want to die, but if I do I'm not dying first."

I spoke loudly enough to spook the spectators who were milling about, waiting for the dogfight to begin. When they saw my guns, most made a rush for the door. About a dozen crawled under a gap in the back of the pole barn and fled toward the woods.

"Are you crazy, man?" Dogman-G wanted to know.

"Let's just say I've thrown caution to the wind and let it go at that. So, what do they call you? Dogman, or G?"

"You are crazy."

"G—I'm going to call you G. Listen, G, I'm really pissed off. Now you are going to tell me what I want to know or I'm going to shoot all three of you."

"Fuck you are."

"What's going to stop me? Fear of dying? I've got a fifty-thousand-dollar contract on my head."

"Fuck you, man."

"Have it your own way. Which one of your pals do you like the least? Know what? I'll choose."

I sighted down the .380 at the black man on my left, gritting my teeth as if I were about to squeeze the trigger. He recoiled, his hands splayed in front of his face. "No, no, man," he said.

"Wait," Dogman said. "I said wait. I mean it. Wait. That's my brother you're lookin' to cap."

"Aren't we all brothers under the skin?" I said.

"My brother brother, you shithead."

"Talk to me, G."

"Ease off, now. I'll tell you what you wan' to know. Just ease off. Fuckin' crazy."

"Who bought the hit?"

"I'll say, but it ain't gonna do you no good. You be dead soon."

"You betcha." I couldn't believe I said that. God, I how I hate the Coen brothers.

"DuWayne. DuWayne Middleton. It was him who put out the contract."

"Who is DuWayne Middleton?"

"You don't know?"

The guns were getting heavy; my extended arms were beginning to ache, and my hands wavered just a little. The way Dogman-G's posse glanced at each other, I knew that they had seen it. I couldn't keep this up much longer.

"No," I said. "Why does he want me dead?"

"Didn't say. Just said to pass the word."

"Where can I find him?"

"I ain't his social secretary, man."

"This DuWayne Middleton. He ever go by the name T-Man?"

"Fuck if I know. Maybe when he was in stir. Only I ain't never heard him called that."

"You've been a real prince, G. Now stand up slowly. You, too," I told his brother. "Keep your hands up." When they were all standing, I told them to take four steps backward. Then I stood straight up, not an easy thing to do while pointing two guns at three men; the back of my legs pushed against the folding chair. Dogman-G and his posse watched it tip over and clatter against the concrete floor. I ignored the chair and started walking backward, never taking my eyes from the three men, wondering where Schroeder was. Dogman-G's brother started to lower his hands.

"Ah-ah," I said.

He raised them again. He didn't look particularly frightened, and the farther away I got, the less frightened he appeared. From the expression on his face, I knew he couldn't wait to put me in the ground.

I turned and started running. I had been doing a lot of that lately.

I sprinted through the open door of the pole barn.

Hung a left so I'd have a straight line to Schroeder's car.

And ran within reach of the three rottweilers.

One of the dogs leapt at my throat. I brought my hands up. The barrel of the nine-millimeter caught him on the snout and deflected his leap, but that was dumb luck. His weight and the suddenness of his attack knocked me off balance. I went down hard on my shoulder. The dog hit the ground at the same time. Only he was quickly on his feet. I didn't even have time to stop bouncing before he came at me again. This time I clubbed him on the skull with the hard muzzle of my gun on purpose. He didn't seem to mind. He went for my hand and caught the sleeve of my sports jacket instead. It took a lot of effort to shake the sleeve out of his mouth. By now the other dogs were on me, too. One became frustrated when his teeth clamped down on the Kevlar protecting my chest. The other happily took hold of my ankle as I rolled away. I kicked him three times in the head before he would let go. I kept rolling until the chains holding the rottweilers grew taut, their barking, snarling jaws only inches from my face.

They jumped back, startled, when the ground directly between us exploded, showering them with debris. A hole appeared, like a divot in a sand trap. I saw it before the sound of a gunshot registered in my head. I heard another as I rotated my prostrate body toward the door of the pole barn. Dogman-G's brother was shooting at me with a .40 automatic. He was holding it sideways like they do in the movies and shooting it with one hand, which helped explain why he missed at such close range. I brought both of my guns up and fired three rounds. Two shattered the door frame, and the third round seemed to disappear into the heart of the barn as the brother dove back inside.

I rolled some more, scrambled to my feet, and resumed running. I circled the dogs that kept barking and snarling and leaping at me and headed for the far side of the farmhouse. The pain in my ankle surged all the way to the top of my head and then recycled itself with each step, slowing me down. I heard another gunshot and felt a bullet skip off the Kevlar vest over my left shoulder. It felt as if I had been hit by a fastball. The blow knocked me off stride and nearly spun me around. Nausea rose up from my stomach to my throat, and my legs threatened to buckle. It seemed necessary to show no fear, to keep running. I had gained the side of the house when two more rounds thumped into my back. They seemed more powerful than the first, as if someone were hammering me with a baseball bat. I went down, sprawling face-first into the scrub brush. I managed to hold on to both of my guns. They did me no good. I couldn't move my arms or my legs. It was as if everything below my shoulders were paralyzed.

I turned my head and saw Dogman-G and the second black man running toward me, their guns leading the way. Dogman-G was smiling. He shouted something. I couldn't hear what he said over the sound of a machine gun. Both men halted abruptly. Half a dozen red volcanoes erupted across their chests and stomachs. They twisted and contorted and fell backward against the hard ground.

A hand grabbed the collars of my shirt and jacket and yanked upward.

"Get on your feet," a voice said. "Get up, dammit. Are you hurt? Can you walk? Go, go."

I was numb yet ambulatory. The hand pushed me forward, and I made for the car, stumbling, nearly falling, the pain in my ankle almost a delightful memory compared to the way the rest of my body now felt. Schroeder walked backward beside me, his MP7 sweeping the ground between farmhouse and pole barn, searching for a target that never materialized.

When we reached the car, Schroeder propped me against the front passenger door. He removed the guns that I was still grasping tightly in my hands, deactivated them, and tossed them into the backseat. He kept an eye on the farmhouse as he opened the door and shoved me into the front passenger seat. He circled the car, took one more look at the house and pole barn, tossed the submachine gun into the backseat, slid into the car, and drove off.

We went north and east, ending up near Pine City, about sixty miles from the Cities, before Schroeder was satisfied that we weren't being followed. I was doubled over and staring at the blood that oozed from my torn ankle onto my white socks and sneakers; only the safety belt kept me in the seat. I was still nauseous, but I managed to keep it to myself. I felt like crying and would have except I didn't want Schroeder to see.

"How you doin', McKenzie?"

"I've been better."

"Those slugs musta hurt like a sonuvabitch."

"Dog chomping on my ankle didn't help, either."

"We'll get you back to the office. Clean you up."

"What about . . . what about those guys?"

"Don't worry about it," Schroeder said. "Deal like this, I'd be surprised if it's even reported. More likely, the dogmen will tidy up, pretend it didn't happen—they don't want the cops looking into their business, and they already have a bad enough rep, you know? Just in case, I'll dump the MP7 first thing. Don't worry about Buckman. I'll talk to him. He'll be cool."

You can't do that, can you? my inner voice wanted to know. *Just leave them there, two dead men? Or is it three? The third man, at the entrance to the pole barn, did Schroeder get him? Did you? Where did that third shot go? You don't even know. What about their families? Their friends? Somebody must care about them. The cops, when they investigate, if they investigate— would they be Anoka cops or Isanti cops? Where the hell is East Bethel, anyway? What county? Christ, this is so wrong. You have to tell people what happened. You have to tell your story. Otherwise, Dogman-G and his brother, and the other one—nobody will know what happened to them. It will be like a ghost story. You have nothing to worry about. You won't get into trouble. After all, it was self-defense. Wasn't it? They were trying to kill you. For money. If not for the Kevlar vest, you'd be dead. They would have dumped you in a shallow grave and taken your driver's license to DuWayne Middleton to collect the price on your head. So they got what they deserved. No question. Anyone could see that. Still, you have to do something. Right? You can't just leave them there, can you?*

"Sure I can," I said aloud.

"What's that?" Schroeder asked.

"Nothing. Just talking to myself."

"We'll be home soon."

"Good."

"By the way, that's ten grand you owe me."

19

True to his word, Schroeder drove me to his office. He doused my ankle with antiseptic and bandaged it expertly. "You've done this before," I told him, in between shots of Booker's. Afterward, he brought my suitcase up from my car, and I changed clothes. I gave him five thousand in cash from my cache and told him I'd pay the balance later. I had the money. I just didn't want to run the risk of getting caught short—living on the run can get expensive. He said he would trust me for it. To protect his investment, he crossed the river into St. Paul, following my Jeep Cherokee to the St. Paul Hotel, where I registered under the name Keith Kahla.

Schroeder escorted me to the Ambassador Suite. It was the size of two regular rooms and had a king-sized four-poster bed complete with down covers and pillows, plus a luxurious, fully furnished seating area that was separated from the bedroom by French doors. From the window, I had a terrific view of Rice Park and the Ordway Center for the

Performing Arts, the St. Paul Public Library, and the Landmark Center beyond. I locked my weapons and cash in the room safe while Schroeder helped himself to the minibar.

"Is this your idea of hiding out?" he asked. He poured the contents of a tiny bottle of Scotch into a glass, regarded it carefully, and drank half. "You're a classy guy, McKenzie."

"Nothing but the best," I said.

"Do you need me for the rest of the day?"

"No."

"How 'bout dinner? I'll buy."

"No, thank you. I'm going to crawl into the shower, see if that'll loosen up my back." I could feel the bruises spreading even as I sat there. "Afterward, it's room service and bed."

"Good plan," Schroeder said. He finished his Scotch, moved toward the door, stopped, and turned to look at me. "Hey."

"Yeah?"

"Because of what happened before, you might feel depressed, you might feel lonely, you might feel a lot of things."

"Nothing I haven't felt before," I said.

"The thing is, call me if you decide to go wandering about. If you decide to check out a bar or something, if you decide you need to be around people. Okay?"

"I never did thank you."

"It's all part of the service."

"Thank you anyway."

Schroeder waved the words away and opened the door.

After he left, I took a business card out of my wallet and used my cell phone to call the number. Instead of "Hello," the voice said, "Karen Studder." As soon as I heard the voice, the depression and loneliness Schroeder predicted rolled over me like a rogue wave.

"Karen," I said.

"McKenzie? I'm so happy you called. How are you?"

"I'm okay. Tell me, are you one of those law enforcement scofflaws who pick and choose the ordinances they'll obey?"

"I occasionally drive over the speed limit. Why do you ask?"

"Have you been known to accept a bribe?"

She paused before answering. "What do you have in mind?"

"A hearty meal. Genial libations. A thousand dollars in cash."

"For what?"

"The current whereabouts of one DuWayne Middleton, lately a guest of the Minnesota Department of Corrections."

Another pause. "Keep your thousand dollars," she said. "I'll take the dinner and drinks, though."

"It's a deal."

"What about tonight?"

"Tonight's not good," I said.

"Just as well. I'm not at my desk. I won't be able to access the S3 until tomorrow morning."

"S3?"

"Statewide Supervision System. It's a centralized Web site that contains information on everyone under probation or supervised release in Minnesota."

"Tomorrow morning will be fine," I said.

"I'll phone."

"Please do."

"I'm really glad you called, McKenzie."

I told her I was glad that I did, too, only I had things to do and couldn't talk. She seemed disappointed by that. After I hung up, I felt a pang of guilt along with all my other aches and pains.

You should have told her that you have a girlfriend, my inner voice admonished me.

"I already did," I told myself.

Tell her again.

"I will. As soon as she gives me the information I need."

In the meantime . . .

"This is a first for me," Nina said.

"What is?"

"Spending the night in a hotel room with a man who is not my husband. What would my mother say, I wonder."

"Scandalous."

"Oh, I'm sure she'd use a lot more colorful adjective than that."

Nina snuggled closer to me and softly kissed the edge of my chin. The warmth of her breath on my skin was like an autumn breeze wafting up from the river; it gave me goose bumps even then, even after we had made love.

"Are you going to tell me now?" she asked.

"Tell you what?"

"Why you're so melancholy tonight."

"I'm not."

"If you don't want to talk about that, then tell me why we're in an expensive hotel instead of the perfectly good king-sized bed in your own bedroom."

I didn't say.

"Or why you suddenly have three bruises on your back and shoulder."

"You noticed that, huh?"

"Kind of hard to miss, McKenzie. They're the size of cantaloupes. Plus, your ankle is bandaged. And there was all that moaning when we were rolling about. Somehow, I don't think that was because of me."

So I told her.

I told her everything.

I felt her naked body stiffen against me as I spoke.

When I finished, she seemed as far away as Kuala Lumpur.

"Why do you do these things?" she said.

"Honey . . ."

"Honey, honey, honey," she said and rolled out of the bed. "Can't you find some other hobby? Something else to occupy your time besides what you do now?"

"Nina . . ."

"Don't talk to me."

A moment later she was in the bathroom, the door closed. I waited in bed for her to come out. She didn't. A lot of time passed. Finally I went to the bathroom, knocked softly on the door, and called her name. When she didn't answer, I opened the door. She was wrapped in the plush white robe provided by the hotel, sitting on the edge of the tub. Her eyes were red and swollen from tears, but she wasn't crying now.

Nina looked up at me. The glare from the bathroom light seemed to bother her, so I switched it off.

"I worry about you," she said.

"I know. I'm sorry."

She came off the tub and wrapped her arms around me. She rested her head against my shoulder—the sore one. I made an effort not to flinch. I caressed her hair and kissed the top of her head.

"You need a keeper," Nina said.

"Do you want the job?"

"Want it or not, I think I'm stuck with it."

"I love you."

"Dammit, McKenzie. There you go again."

A few moments later, we went back to bed.

20

Nina was gone when I woke. Considering how badly I slept, I was amazed she was able to slip away without my knowing it. I could only pray that Schroeder's people weren't also caught unawares. Nina left a note on my pillow: *I hope your back feels better. Call me when you can.* It was signed with three X's and an O.

You are one lucky sonuvabitch, my inner voice told me. And then I thought, *Luck has nothing to do with it. The credit all belongs to Nina.*

Thirty minutes later I was standing in the shower, letting hot water massage my aching back, wondering where I was going and how I was going to get there. Questions without answers. I had more money than I could ever spend and yet it didn't make me happy. It was just there. Maybe if I spent more of it, tried to adopt a playboy attitude. Or better yet, got a real job that would justify my existence. But, no. I had to be a cop. I had to sift through the emotional and physical debris of other people's lives, telling myself that it's a noble undertaking, insisting that I'm making the world a better place. It occurred to me, as I gingerly changed the bandage around my damaged ankle, that I wasn't doing a very good job of it.

A warm sun hung brightly in a cobalt sky and I thought it would be a good day to stay indoors, hang around the hotel, give my back and ankle a chance to mend. I didn't need anyone else shooting at me; I certainly didn't want to run for my life again—I wasn't sure I could. I switched on the TV and watched the *Cold Pizza* morning show on ESPN, except I was having trouble getting into it. My mind kept wandering in no particular direction. It was somewhere in Wisconsin with the Dunston family when my cell phone rang. Ten minutes later I was in my car.

Karen Studder wore her hair down around her shoulders and had given more time and effort to applying makeup than when I first met her. She was wearing a tight V-neck sweater—emphasis on the V—and a skirt that did more to exhibit her shapely legs than cover them, and I thought, *Is this for me? God, I hope not. I don't deal well with temptation.* I had wandered once before, with an enticing female cop in Victoria, Minnesota. That was eight months ago, and I had justified myself by insisting that I wasn't formally committed to Nina then. Now I was committed-committed, and there was a difference. I reminded myself of that when Karen held my hand for a couple of extra beats after shaking it. When she called earlier, I had asked her to meet me for brunch at the Copper Dome on Randolph near Hamline, not far from the Cretin–Derham Hall High School. I had hoped it would fulfill my pledge of a meal and drinks, except now I didn't think so.

Best keep your wits about you, my inner voice warned.

After we ordered and before our food arrived, Karen said, "Middleton, DuWayne H., has been in and out of prison most of his life, charged with major felonies that he pleaded down to minor felonies and minor felonies that became misdemeanors. He was released from the level four correctional facility in St. Cloud to his mother's custody three months ago."

"Any connection to Scottie Thomforde?" I asked.

"Not that I could see. I'm sorry I didn't think to download DuWayne's record for you. From what I read, it was always different crimes in different cities at different times, different prisons, different release dates, different parole units. Scottie was in Ramsey County; Middleton is in Hennepin."

"And never the twain shall meet?" I asked.

"Not through the system."

"Where can I find DuWayne?"

Karen gave me an address in North Minneapolis.

"Swell," I said. I knew plenty of horror stories about the East Side of St. Paul, only they were like Hans Christian Andersen fairy tales compared to the North Side of Minneapolis. I felt my back tightening in anticipation of a visit; it hurt with every deep breath.

Breakfast was served; I didn't give it much attention. Karen attacked her meal with fervor. *Good for her,* I thought. I hate picky eaters.

While we ate I reviewed my options. One of them was calling Greg Schroeder and the two of us busting in on DuWayne and putting a gun to his head. It worked with Dogman-G. Except I didn't want a reprise of what happened in East Bethel. Another option was knocking on his door and asking politely for information. Except what was keeping DuWayne from putting a gun to my head? One shot and he could earn fifty large.

"You say DuWayne is living with his mother?" I said.

Karen said that he was in between bites of hash browns.

"How does it work, probation officers?"

"What do you mean?"

"Can you visit someone else's . . . you call them offenders?"

"What do you have in mind, McKenzie?"

"I go over there alone, someone is going to get shot. Probably me. But if you go with me—"

"Wait a minute." From the expression on her face, Karen knew what I was thinking and the idea didn't appeal to her at all.

"We knock on the door all calm and peaceful, you flash your badge—why should there be any trouble? Especially if DuWayne's mama is there. I mean, you make home visits all the time, am I right?"

"Yes."

"How many of them end in bloodshed?"

"None so far, and I'd like to keep it that way."

"All I want to do is talk to the man. Besides, if he is running a contract on me, that's an illegal activity. Wouldn't you want to know about that?"

Karen paused, her fork halfway to her mouth. Slowly she lowered it to her plate and wiped her lips with a napkin.

"What contract?" she said.

I explained, making sure not to mention either Pat Beulke or Dogman-G.

When I finished, she pushed her plate away, folded her arms across her chest, and leaned back in the booth.

"I'm an officer of the court," she said.

"Exactly my point," I said.

Karen studied me for a long time. Finally she said, "If I do this, I expect a lot more in return than breakfast."

"Sure."

"Well," she said, "maybe my badge will keep us out of trouble."

'Course, it never worked that way when I carried one.

We drove to a neighborhood on the North Side known as Harrison. It used to be called "Finntown" in deference to the Finnish immigrants who originally settled there. Today it attracted a lot of working poor, including Hmong, Hispanics, and Somalis. Along the way, we passed dozens of abandoned houses with lawns that resembled wheat fields.

They were all victims of Minneapolis's "North Initiative," a program that was supposed to curtail the area's rising crime statistics by forcing homeowners to take better care of their property. Dozens of building inspectors had swarmed over the North Side citing residents for everything from flaking garage paint and missing storm windows to worn-out roofs and crumbling driveways. Over twenty thousand citations were issued in the first ten weeks alone—and the inspectors weren't even close to being finished. Homeowners were told that if they didn't correct the cited problems immediately, they would face escalating fines (which the politicians claimed only coincidentally added millions of dollars to the city's general fund). Except many of the residents were minimum-wage workers who couldn't afford the improvements. Which is why the North Side now had the highest foreclosure rate in the Upper Midwest.

As for crime—a group of teenagers was congregating on the corner when we turned onto DuWayne Middleton's street. A kid who was standing apart from the others flashed a signal when he spied the Jeep Cherokee, and the group casually scattered.

"Did you see that?" Karen said. "That was a drug deal."

"I saw it."

We drove another half block and parked in front of a house that was in need of fresh paint. The garage needed paint, too, and the asphalt driveway leading to it was crumbling badly; a few bare patches had been covered with plywood. Getting out of the car, I thought about the Kevlar vest in the back. There was just the one, though, and I didn't think it was fair for me to wear it while Karen went without, so I left it there. And they say chivalry is dead.

An old, small, thin black woman answered our knock. I said, "Mrs. Middleton—" She started in before I could speak another word.

"I got the money," she said.

"Ma'am . . ."

"I got the money, and I already talked to a contractor. Thirty-two hundred, he said. Thirty-two hundred to fix my driveway and the rest—eighteen hundred dollars is going to paint the house and the garage. I hired it done already. You can look at the estimates. I got written estimates, so you ain't got no business bein' here. You ain't got no call to give me no more fines."

"Ma'am—"

"You ain't turnin' me outta my house. This is my house. I'm going to live in this house and I'm going to die in this house and then I'm going to haunt whoever lives here next."

"Good for you," I said.

That slowed her down. She examined Karen and me more carefully.

"You ain't from the city," she said. "You ain't from Regulatory Services."

"No, ma'am," I said.

Karen flashed her identification. "I'm with the Minnesota Department of Corrections," she said.

"You here to check up on my boy?" Mrs. Middleton said.

"Yes, ma'am."

"Why didn't you say so?" She flung open the door and invited us in. "D'Wayneeee," she called. "Someone to see you." She pointed us toward a small living room. "He's watching the TV."

DuWayne didn't look any bigger than a small church; I was impressed that the sofa on which he sat could handle the weight. He was a hard-ass con with a broken nose and scars and prison tatts, eating from a bowl of Cocoa Puffs; the bowl and spoon looked like small and useless things in his hands. He was watching *The Price Is Right* when we entered the room. He seemed to take no notice of us.

"Mr. Middleton, I'm with the State Department of Corrections," Karen said.

DuWayne didn't reply.

"Sir, we would like you to answer a few questions."

He still refused to acknowledge our presence, just kept staring ahead, watching his program.

Screw this, my inner voice said. I stepped directly between DuWayne and his TV. He didn't seem to notice until I said something that made the lid on his right eye twitch just so: "My name is McKenzie."

DuWayne slowly ate a spoonful of cereal, dug into the bowl for another.

"For a guy who's paying fifty thousand to see me dead, you don't seem all that concerned that I'm here." 'Course, one look at his mother's house and I knew he wasn't buying the hit. "You're just another errand boy, aren't you?"

"Wha' you doin' here?" DuWayne asked before shoveling another spoonful of Puffs into his mouth.

"Dogman-G sent me."

DuWayne stopped chewing for a moment and his eyelid fluttered again. "Dogman," he muttered quietly.

He had nothing more to say, so I took the nine-millimeter from its holster, stepped forward, and pressed the muzzle against his knee. Karen hissed as if she were seeing something that alarmed her and said, "McKenzie, stop it." DuWayne didn't react at all. I could have been a character on TV for all I frightened him.

Well, this isn't going well at all, my inner voice said.

"Okay, DuWayne, I get it," I said aloud. "You're a stand-up guy. I should be embarrassed for even thinking that I could scare you." DuWayne smiled around a mouthful of Cocoa Puffs. "I was hoping we could do this without involving your mother. Guess I was wrong."

"What you talking about?" DuWayne said.

I spoke to Karen as I slowly backed away from him. "Better call Mrs. Middleton. Tell her to bring a coat. It's getting chilly outside." I kept the Beretta in my hand, and from the way DuWayne reacted, I was glad I did.

"You leave my mother be." He pointed the spoon at me. I had no doubt he could have dug a hole in my chest with it. In return, I pointed the gun at his chest.

"I'd love to, DuWayne," I said. "I really would."

"You makin' me angry. You don't want me to be angry."

I doubt the guy playing the Hulk in the movie could have said it better. Hell, change his complexion and DuWayne could have been the Hulk.

"Here's the thing," I said. "The money you gave your mother, the five thousand she's using to fix up her house, it's marked."

That caused both of DuWayne's eyelids to flutter. "Wha'? Marked?"

"I'm guessing the five K is a ten percent service fee that the contractor paid you to float the hit on me—ten percent of fifty thousand, that sounds right. It's part of a million-dollar ransom paid three days ago for the safe return of a twelve-year-old girl who was kidnapped—the daughter of the cop who runs the St. Paul Police Department's homicide unit, no less. Before the ransom was paid, the FBI marked every single bill. What did he pay you with? Twenties or fifties? I'm guessing the FBI will want to know how your mother got it. And if she says she got it from you . . ."

"D'Wayneee," Mrs. Middleton called from the hallway. I stepped farther away from DuWayne and hid the Beretta behind my back. DuWayne slipped his spoon into the bowl and resumed eating. Mrs. Middleton entered the room. "You want more cereal, hon?" she asked.

"No, thank you, Ma, I'm good," DuWayne said.

Mrs. Middleton looked both Karen and me up and down. She didn't offer us any Cocoa Puffs.

"You gonna be here long?" she asked.

"It's all right, Ma," DuWayne said. "We just talkin'. They be leavin' in a sec."

Mrs. Middleton nodded her head and left the room.

I brought the gun out from behind my back. I didn't trust DuWayne as far as I could throw him, which admittedly wasn't very far.

"You gonna leave my mama be," DuWayne said.

"Absolutely," I said. "I won't hassle you, either. All I want is a name. A location, too, if you have it."

"I don't got neither."

"That's not the answer I wanted to hear."

"Lookit. Man comes to me, white man. I ain't lookin' for him, he lookin' for me. He says a mutual friend, man we both know, says I could help 'im. I says help 'im what? He tells me. I says that's whacked, fifty large. He says he wants to make sure it gets done in a hurry. What am I gonna do, argue with him? He gives me five thousand. In fifties. A packet of fifties." *My fifties,* I thought but didn't say. "So I do what he ax, I spread the word."

"What's his name?"

"I told you, I don' know his name."

"How's he planning to pay off on the hit?"

"He hears you're dead, he contacts me. We work it out. Man's bein' real careful."

"You don't even know his name? Or where to find him?"

"No."

"You're doing all this on the honor system?"

"He don' pay off, it gets real unhealthy for him. He know that."

"But how can you find him?" Karen asked.

DuWayne shrugged. "There's ways," he said.

Yeah, there are, my inner voice reminded me.

"Who's your mutual friend?" I asked.

"Wha' about my mother?"

"The five thousand dollars that the contractor gave you, that was my money. If you give me a name, your mother can keep it, I don't care. We won't involve the FBI in her business, either. Does that work for you?"

"You trouble my mama, you die hard."

"I got a whole list of people who want to kill me," I said. "Your name isn't even close to the top."

DuWayne just stared.

"We're on the same page here, pal," I said. "I don't want trouble for your mother. Or you. What we're talking about, it's just business, am I right?"

"That's right," DuWayne said. "It's business."

"Give me a name and I'll give you another five thousand, in cash. Clean money this time."

"You got it on you?"

"I can get it in five minutes."

DuWayne shrugged his massive shoulders. I took that as a yes.

I led Karen out of the house and limped back to the Cherokee. I opened the driver's door. It hurt my back, but I leaned in and pulled a packet of one hundred fifty-dollar bills out from under the seat. I limped back to the house. This time when I knocked, DuWayne answered. He filled the doorframe with his bulk. I gave him the cash.

"Donny Orrick," he said.

"Where?"

"St. Cloud."

"The prison?"

"Why else anybody be in St. Cloud?"

"Good enough," I said. I turned away from the door, had a thought, and spun back again. "One more thing, the contractor. What does he look like?"

"White dude."

"Big?"

"He tryin' to be."

Visiting hours at the state prison in St. Cloud were between 3:30 and 9:30 P.M., yet it was wasn't even noon when I left DuWayne Middleton's house and drove Karen back to her car parked in the lot outside the Copper Dome. It took me about an hour driving north from the Twin Cities to reach St. Cloud, and that left nearly three hours to kill, eating, bumming around, trying not to think too much. It wasn't easy. You can see the huge water tower in the center of the prison yard from a long way off on Highway 10. It made me ponder some of the things that Karen Studder had told me about prison and what it does to people. I didn't want to agree with her; still, I was left with the certain knowledge that Scottie Thomforde had been a good guy before he went inside.

To reach the prison, I drove west on Minnesota Boulevard, crossing the two sets of Burlington Northern and Santa Fe railroad tracks that ran alongside the forbidding red-gray walls. The tracks reminded me of "Folsom Prison Blues" and Johnny Cash singing about that train a-rollin' 'round the bend.

The song kept repeating itself in my head, following me to an uncomfortable chair in the visitors' room. The room reminded me of the public lounges at the airport where passengers kill time while waiting for their flights to board. It was just as noisy, with children behaving the way children do when they're asked to sit and do nothing for long periods, impatient adults raising their voices at the indignity of unexpected delays, and a barely understood voice calling names and giving instructions over a scratchy speaker system. The seats were all bolted to the floor and to each other and arranged so that nearly everyone was looking at everyone else. I had to lean forward while I sat so as not to crack the skull of the woman sitting directly behind me. Even so, I was able to hear the instructions she gave her daughter. "Please, honey, tell him how well you're doing in school, tell him that you miss him, be sure to tell him that you love him."

"I don't love him," the daughter said. "I don't even know him."

When I hear that whistle blowin', I hang my head and cry.

I didn't want to feel compassion for anyone who was in prison—I had helped put some people there. I convinced myself that except for the extremely rare case of mistaken identity or judicial incompetence, everyone in the place was getting exactly what they deserved. Yet that damn song kept repeating itself. And I could imagine Scottie sitting in on drums.

Finally I was directed to a metal stool behind a partition that isolated the visiting booths from the rest of the waiting room. The stool was one of ten, all bolted to the wall. It faced a cinder-block chamber about the size of a dining room table that contained only a wooden chair and a telephone. Steel bars and reinforced glass kept convicts and visitors apart. I sat on a stool and waited. A heavy door opened at the back of the chamber, and a man with pale skin dodged in sideways, one shoulder at a time, like someone afraid of being noticed. The door was sealed behind him. He took one look at me and decided he didn't like what he saw. I reached for my telephone receiver and pressed it against my ear. Donny Orrick stepped forward. His prison threads hung on him like a label—this was a dangerous man.

He snatched his phone from its cradle. "Who you?" he asked.

"DuWayne Middleton sent me," I said. I had no leverage with Orrick. He was in prison, and all my money, guns, threats, and promises of favors joyfully returned weren't going to persuade him to answer my questions. So I decided to do the next best thing. Lie.

"What about?" Orrick said.

"He wants to know what you're trying to do to him."

"What are you talking about?"

"This man that you sent to him, he paid DuWayne in marked money, money that ties DuWayne to a kidnapping. Now the FBI is on his ass, and he wants to know why you're trying to jam him up."

"I ain't trying to—"

"You wanna know what's really got DuWayne pissed? He gave the money to his mother to fix her house. Now the FBI is trying to jam her up, too."

"Oh God."

"You know how much DuWayne cares about his momma?"

"Oh, God."

"God ain't gonna help you, pal."

"What can I do?"

"DuWayne wants to know who the man is. He wants to know the man's name, and he wants to know where to find him."

Orrick hesitated. "Who are you?" he asked. His voice was cautious and unsure, and I was afraid I might lose him.

"I'm the guy DuWayne sent because he couldn't come himself." I raised my voice just loud enough to attract the attention of the guard seated in a high wooden chair at the end of the corridor; then I deliberately lowered it. "He can't come because the Feds are watching him. He can't use the phone because it's probably tapped. He doesn't want to contact you in person anyway, you dumb fuck, because he's afraid of trading a kidnapping rap for a charge of conspiracy to commit murder. But you know what? You have every right to be cautious. You have every right to look out for yourself. I suggest that you send DuWayne a letter, because when I was in his mother's house in North Minneapolis this morning watching him eat his Cocoa Puffs, do you know what he said to me? 'That Donny, he doesn't call, he doesn't write. Maybe we ain't friends anymore.'"

"Thomas Teachwell."

"What?"

"Dude calls hi'self T-Man. That's his real name. Thomas Teachwell. He reached out the other day, said he needed someone dependable to handle something for him—something sensitive. I sent him to DuWayne. You gotta tell 'im, though. I didn't know nothin' about what Teachwell was doing . . ."

It went on like that for another minute or two, Orrick trying to clear himself with DuWayne without actually saying anything that could be used in a court of law. Only I wasn't listening. I felt as if I had been slapped upside the head with a two-by-four; the face reflected in the prison glass was ashen, the jaw slack, and all I could hear was Shelby Dunston's voice.

Is it because of you, McKenzie? Did they kidnap my baby to get back at you, to get back at you through us?

21

Sometimes I had the feeling that the Twin Cities produced the world's longest-running movable traffic jam just to slow me down. Lord knows it seemed to anticipate my every turn. It was late afternoon, and most of the traffic was moving out of the Twin Cities. Yet that didn't deter vehicles driving in from clogging every major artery I wanted to use. I tried not to let it rile me. It wasn't easy. I felt a rage so intense that I nearly choked on it.

Thomas Teachwell had targeted my friends, Bobby and Shelby and young Victoria and Katie—my family!—because I had arrested him. Because I had profited from arresting him—three million, one hundred twenty-eight thousand, five hundred eighty-four dollars and fifty cents—half of the money that I had recovered, half of what Teachwell had stolen. He killed Scottie Thomforde to get back at me, and probably Scottie's brother. He terrorized Joley Waddell. He put a price on my head that resulted in the death of two, maybe three other men.

Thomas Teachwell.

T-Man.

He wanted revenge.

I vowed to teach him all about it.

At the same time, I laughed at myself over the list I had given Harry, the one with all the names of people who might want to see me dead. It had never occurred to me to include Teachwell.

Both sides of I-394, from the Dunwoody Institute on the outskirts of downtown Minneapolis west to the Ridgedale shopping center, were nothing more than giant strip malls—six and a half miles of hotels, motels, restaurants, fast-food joints, clubs, bars, coffee shops, retail outlets, new and used car lots, gas stations, and office buildings. Yet once you got past the I-494 cloverleaf and the interstate became Highway 12, all of that disappeared. You were in God's country now, where the rich people lived, and they didn't allow the working class into their neighborhoods even to work. Instead, their highways, county roads, and streets were lined with pristine lawns, rolling hills, and unbroken forests. There wasn't even a Starbucks to blemish the countryside.

I took a county road and followed it around Lake Minnetonka into Orono. I was hoping for a bar to work off some of my rage; I'd even welcome one that sold bottled beer at ten bucks a throw. Unfortunately, the only businesses I encountered were marinas that serviced the yachts of those not wealthy enough to own estates actually located on the water. A few more turns and I was on a long, private blacktop that led to a huge house on the west arm of the lake.

To say the area was exclusive would be redundant. Lake Minnetonka was actually a collection of sixteen interconnected lakes and heaven knows how many bays and inlets, and it was *all* exclusive—all twenty-two and a half square miles of it—and the impression it radiated was that nothing bad could ever happen here. 'Course, Virginia Piper might disagree.

Before I reached the house, I stopped the Cherokee, opened the back, and pulled out my Kevlar vest. I put it on and checked my guns. The nine I holstered on my belt at my left hip, positioning it for a quick cross-draw. The .380 I slid between my belt and spine. Only then did I drive up to the house where Thomas Teachwell once lived.

I followed the circular drive in back of the house until the nose of the Cherokee was facing out in case I needed to make a quick getaway. There were no other vehicles in the driveway and no people. I knew there were neighbors, but not close—I couldn't see their houses through the trees that dotted the property. I stepped out of the vehicle. A gentle breeze floated up from the lake and stirred the leaves. It was so quiet I could hear my heartbeat. A splendid isolation.

There's a lot to be said for exclusivity, my inner voice said. *You could afford to live here.* Well, yeah, except the people on the lake weren't the kind that attended the Minnesota State Fair, and if they went to a ball game, they watched from the comfort of a luxury suite. I doubted I'd fit in. Besides—I pulled the nine from its holster and cautiously approached Teachwell's home—I wasn't house hunting.

I approached the house in a crouch that strained my back and caused my ankle to throb. I let the Beretta lead the way while I watched the doors, watched the windows, watched for movement of any kind from anywhere. It was still. It was quiet. I poked my nose above windowsills. Rooms were laid out like the photo spreads of *House Beautiful.* There was no one lounging on the sofa eating Cheetos and watching Oprah, no one sitting at the table cutting coupons. I took a chance and rang the front doorbell. It echoed through the house like a ship's bell over a calm and empty sea and went unanswered.

I moved cautiously around the house. A multi-tiered lawn, landscaped with stone walls and gardens, sloped for the length of a football field to the shore of the big lake. Jutting into the lake was a wide wooden dock; a bass boat, a speedboat, and a luxury yacht were tethered to its pilings. A stone boathouse about half the size, yet twice as opulent, as my own house was set a few yards back from the shore. A tall, slim, blond woman in an oversized white turtleneck stepped out of the boat-house. I watched her stroll the length of the shoreline to the dock and over it to the bass boat. She pulled out two life jackets and started back to the boathouse. I holstered the Beretta and marched across the lawn. The sight of me startled her. She dropped the life jackets and moved backward, nearly stepping into the lake. I called to her. She recognized me then, halted, and held her ground. Her jaw was set and her fists were clenched when I reached her.

"What do you want, McKenzie?"

"I'm looking for your husband."

She gestured at my hip. "With a gun?"

"Yes."

"You thought he would be here?"

"Where is your husband, Mrs. Teachwell?"

"Ex-husband."

"Ex-husband, then."

"I don't know."

"Be sure, Mrs. Teachwell. Be very sure you don't know."

She glared at me for a few moments. "I haven't seen him," she said.

I wondered briefly if she was the "babe" that Victoria had overheard the T-Man speaking to on his cell phone. "You can lie to me all you want, Mrs. Teachwell," I said. "Not to the FBI. They'll subpoena phone records, they'll confiscate your computer—"

"I haven't seen him since—oh, why are you here, McKenzie? Thomas and I are divorced. Do you understand? Divorced. I'm not a part of his life anymore. He doesn't want me to be part of his life. He's—he's changed."

I'll say, I thought. "I need to find him," I said aloud.

Mrs. Teachwell pressed her fists against her hips in defiance and shook her head.

"It's serious, Mrs. Teachwell."

"It wasn't before?"

"He kidnapped a twelve-year-old girl. He committed murder."

Mrs. Teachwell shook her head again, only this time it was as if she wanted to shake my words out of her ears.

"Mrs. Teachwell—"

"It isn't true." She turned and faced the lake. "He wouldn't do that."

Mrs. Teachwell folded her arms in front of her in self-defense and lowered her head. Her shoulders trembled for a few moments, and I thought she was going to weep. It wasn't the reaction I expected from a divorced woman who's had no contact with her ex.

I waited for a few beats, then asked again, "Where is your husband?"

She shook her head violently.

I could have comforted her, I suppose. Rested my hand on her shoulder and told her that it would be all right. I couldn't bring myself to do it. She had been in love with Thomas Teachwell. I had the impression that she still was. That made her my enemy. I listened to her make some throat sounds, but the tears I expected didn't come. She spoke to me over her shoulder.

"Mr. McKenzie," she said.

"Yes."

"I have coffee," she said.

She led me to the boathouse, which could have sheltered a family of four. It had a toilet and shower, a Murphy bed, cable TV, a stereo CD player, a PC, plenty of furniture, a bar with a refrigerator, a small stove, and a brick patio all around. Mrs. Teachwell filled two china cups from a gourmet coffeemaker that was far superior to the one I owned. "Sugar, cream?" she said. "Black," I told her. I was surprised and a little disappointed when she gave me the cup without a saucer.

"This is the only boathouse I've ever been in that didn't have boats," I said.

"There's a locker in the back for equipment," Mrs. Teachwell said. "I use the rest of it mostly for parties. Why did you come here,

Mr. McKenzie? Thomas and I are divorced. We were divorced before he was arrested. You know that. So why did you come here looking for him?"

"Because I never believed it, the divorce, I mean. You were always there for him. At the jail, at the hearings, later when he elocuted following the plea agreement. Ex-wives, as a rule, don't behave that way. Something else. When I found your husband in the cabin up north, he was waiting, had been waiting for a couple of days. He could have slipped across the Canadian border anytime. That was his plan—cross the border and escape to Rio de Janeiro. He had it all worked out. It was a good plan. The plan would have worked. Instead, he waited. I think he was waiting for you."

Mrs. Teachwell took a chair facing a pair of French doors and Lake Minnetonka beyond. I watched her from where I was standing near the mahogany bar. I would have liked to sit, too, and rest my back and ankle, but she didn't offer a chair, and I couldn't impose.

"I was devastated when we divorced," she said. "I never saw it coming; couldn't believe it when it did come. There was no explanation. Thomas simply said, 'I'm divorcing you,' and walked out. He was so generous with the settlement, too. Gave me nearly everything. The house. Cars. Savings. Investments. He didn't even take his golf clubs. I thought there must have been another woman. There wasn't. For a brief period, I actually thought there must have been another man. Not that, either. It made no sense to me. Then it did.

"Thomas had been embezzling money for years. Millions of dollars. I didn't know it. It was the only secret he ever kept from me. Later, he told me that he originally did it to demonstrate to the board that it needed to take safeguards. Then he did it because it was fun. Then he did it out of habit. That's what he said. Of course, it was more than that. I believe Thomas had a Walter Mitty–like view of the world. He was never satisfied being a CFO. He wanted to be a swashbuckler. A pirate. He wanted to be Errol Flynn in *Captain Blood*. He wanted to be Han Solo and Indiana Jones."

Don't we all? my inner voice said.

"It was a kind of daydream," Mrs. Teachwell said. "It became painfully real only after the financial scandals at Enron, Tyco, World-Com, and all those other companies. Thomas was a smart man. He knew what was coming long before it got here. I'm talking about the independent financial audits that many shareholders began demanding from their boards. He divorced me. He divorced me and gave me everything to protect me. Then he waited. When his firm finally hired an independent auditor to examine the books, he took what money he had accumulated and ran. He asked me to go with him."

"You said no."

"I said yes, Mr. McKenzie. I would have gone to Rio with Thomas. I would have gone anywhere. Only I couldn't get away. The police were watching me; I was being followed. I was terrified that I would lead them to Thomas. So I stayed put. Thomas could have left the country. Should have left the country. Contacted me once he was safely in Brazil. You were right. He waited for me. Because of that, you were able to catch him."

"And then?"

"And then prison. Prison for him and a sort of prison for me. It isn't easy being involved with a jailbird. That's what some of our friends—ex-friends—called him. Jailbird. I didn't mind. I still had the house, the money; I had what he had given me. I visited him in St. Cloud. I told him that it all would be there waiting for him—that I would be waiting for him—when he was released."

"And then?"

Mrs. Teachwell nursed her coffee, kept staring at some distant point on Lake Minnetonka.

"He changed," she said. "Both physically and emotionally. Physically—Thomas had never been an athlete . . ."

"Yes," I said, remembering the doughy, overweight man I had trapped in the cabin on Lower Red Lake.

"In prison he became lean and strong from working in the weight room. At first it was attractive. Afterward, he became so big—it is possible to have too many muscles, Mr. McKenzie. While his body was changing, so was his demeanor. Thomas had been a soft-spoken man, timid and shy. As he became stronger and harder, he became louder. The guards would make him quiet down during our visits because he would shout. On a couple of occasions they returned him to his cell because he wouldn't quiet down. Over the years he became very angry. It frightened me how angry he became. He was incensed with you, of course. Soon his anger included the entire world. Me as well. He decided that I had caused his downfall, that I had ruined his life. Because he stole for me, he said, and because he had waited for me and I didn't come. He told me to get out of his life. He told me this many times. Finally, I did.

"It was prison," she said. "Prison changed him. Jeffrey Skilling defrauded millions of people, hurt millions of people, while he was CEO of Enron and he received a comfortable life in a converted college dormitory in Waseca, no bars on the window, no locks on the door, good food. Thomas, all he hurt was an insurance company, and he was condemned to a maximum-security prison with the worst scum on earth. That would change anyone."

"You haven't seen him since he was released?" I asked.

"No."

"He hasn't tried to contact you in any way?"

"No."

"Not even to get his golf clubs back?"

"Not even for that."

"If he does contact you, will you tell me?"

"He won't."

"He might."

Mrs. Teachwell turned in her chair to face me. Tears had welled up in her eyes again, and she brushed them away with her knuckle. "Why would he?" she asked.

"He's in serious trouble," I said. "When I'm in trouble, I seek out the people who love me best."

She thought about it for a moment, then said, "He won't come here."

"Will you tell me if he does?"

"No."

"Your husband is a fool, Mrs. Teachwell."

"Ex-husband," she said.

I liked Mrs. Teachwell. I liked that she stood by her man even though he really wasn't her man anymore. Others might censure her as some kind of Tammy Wynette throwback, a relic from an era that existed before women were given the right to vote. Not me. I think we all pray for such loyalty from the people we love. I wondered briefly if Nina Truhler possessed that kind of loyalty. *Sure she does,* my inner voice told me. *She's proven it many times.*

I dumped my Kevlar vest and guns in the back of the Jeep Cherokee and drove away from Mrs. Teachwell's house. I stopped when the driveway intersected with the main drag and made a phone call. The new cell didn't have Harry's direct number on speed dial, and I was forced to go through the switchboard. "Special Agent Brian Wilson," Harry said.

"It's McKenzie."

"McKenzie," Harry said. "I've been wondering where you've been off to."

"Orono," I said.

"What's in Orono?"

"The residence of Mrs. Thomas Teachwell."

"Teachwell? The embezzler?"

"It's him, Harry. He's the T-Man. He was Scottie's partner. He was the one who put a hit out on me."

"Are you sure?"

I told him I was. I told him why.

"I'll be damned," Harry said.

I sniffed at the remark. It was a good opening for a joke, only I didn't have one in me. I was too tired; my whole body pulsed with pain. Maybe next time. I told Harry to put a team on Mrs. Teachwell's house, to tap her phone. He didn't need the advice.

"Watch," he said. "I bet I scoop him up in less than twenty-four hours."

I didn't take the wager, but I did ask Harry to call me when he had Teachwell in custody.

"What are you going to do?" he asked.

"Hide out until you find him."

"That's it? You're not going to try to hunt him down yourself, get a little payback for Bobby Dunston?"

I flashed on the faces of two dead men in East Bethel—maybe three—and of the felon, left battered and broken in the ravine near my home. An hour ago I would have happily added Teachwell to the pile. Now, after hearing what Mrs. Teachwell had to say, I wasn't so sure. The necessity of revenge had transformed Teachwell. It turned him from a fairly decent guy who made a mistake into a raging monster, a man who thought nothing of injuring innocent people, of hurting children, to gain the vengeance he felt was his due. I could argue that I was more than justified for going after him. I just didn't want to become him.

"I've done my bit for God and country," I said. "It's time you professionals stepped in."

"Goodness gracious, but that's a mature attitude to take. Keep it up, McKenzie, and you'll become a full-grown adult in no time at all."

"That's always been my goal, Harry. It's what I long for late at night."

22

The sun was only a rumor of light on the horizon, yet traffic was still heavy by the time I left Orono and got back onto I-394. I didn't want to deal with it. I was angry with Teachwell, I was upset that I had brought grief to the Dunston family, my back ached, my ankle throbbed, plus I had three loaded guns in my vehicle—and while I had never succumbed to road rage in the past, I figured all the components were there. Instead of taking the risk, I stopped at Shelley's Woodroast to have a drink and immediately felt guilty about it. Lately, whenever I caught myself having a good time in an establishment other than Rickie's, I felt like I was cheating. Certainly I would have preferred driving to Rickie's and letting Nina buy me a drink, and dinner, too, for that matter. Only I knew there could be assassins lurking in her parking lot, waiting for me to show myself. That wasn't going to change until Teachwell was in custody and I had another chat with DuWayne.

I decided to call Nina and ask her to join me, if not at Shelley's, then at any other restaurant she fancied. Perhaps I could convince her to return to the St. Paul Hotel with me. It had a great restaurant, not to mention room service—nudge, nudge, wink, wink. Unfortunately, I didn't remember the actual phone number for Rickie's—on my old cell it was number 5. I needed directory assistance to place the call. I asked for Nina. Jenness Crawford, her assistant manager, said that Nina had left to meet with her insurance agent and then she was going to make a quick stop at home.

"I expected her back by now," Jenness said.

I thanked her and hung up. Only then did I realize that I hadn't memorized Nina's home or cell numbers, either. For the past two years I had merely dialed 3 or 4. Directory assistance wasn't going to help; both numbers were unlisted. I was about to call Jenness again when my cell rang. The display screen identified the caller.

"Hey, Nina, I was just about to give you a shout," I said.

"McKenzie, this is Nina."

"Yes, I know."

"Nina Truhler. You remember."

"Of course I remember. Your voice sounds funny. What's wrong?"

"Can you meet me at my house?"

"Sure."

"Can you meet me right now?"

"Nina . . . ?"

"My house is in Mahtomedi. Do you have the address?"

"I'm coming, Nina."

I was speeding east on I-394, weaving through traffic with one hand on the wheel. My other hand was pressing my cell phone against my ear.

"Nina's in trouble," I told Schroeder. "Where the hell are your people?"

"Hang on."

A few moments later, Schroeder was back on the line.

"I can't reach my operative," he said. "Where are you?"

I told him.

"Pick me up."

From the redwood deck on the back of Nina's house, you could easily see the eastern shore of White Bear Lake, about twenty minutes northeast of St. Paul. During the day it's busy with every surface craft you can imagine, and at night lights from the homes along the shoreline and the few boats still prowling the water twinkle like stars. Except in Nina's house. Not a single light burned anywhere inside. Which was wrong. Nina always kept a light on.

I approached the house from behind, cutting through her neighbor's yard, slipping from one shadow into another. In the distance, I heard music that grew louder before stopping altogether, and a woman's laugh, and somewhere a dog barked. The sounds came and went, people settling in for the evening; it was cool enough that most of their windows were closed. I knew Nina's weren't. She kept at least one open even in the winter. I stood beneath the window in a pool of black, my back against the wall of her house, and listened and heard nothing.

Nina had played it smart on the phone—of course I knew who she was, of course I knew her address. She was warning me. Teachwell was there, just as he had been in Joley Waddell's house; he had forced her to call, just as he had forced Joley. I could hear it in her voice. Maybe I wouldn't have if it hadn't been for my experience in Highland Park, but there you go. Somebody should tell Teachwell that it's not wise to call the same play twice in a row. I decided that that somebody ought to be me.

I quietly crawled up the stairs to the top of Nina's deck, keeping my head below the floor until the last possible moment. There were sliding doors that led to the kitchen. They were locked. I was always telling

Nina and her daughter to keep them locked when they weren't actually on the deck. *Now they decide to listen to me.* Nina had offered me a key, offered it more than once, only it was to the front door and I had refused it on the grounds that I had no business being in her house when she wasn't there. I crawled back down the stairs.

Nina's house had been built on the side of a hill. The deck was level with the first-floor living room, dining room, and kitchen and the street beyond. The basement opened into the backyard. The basement door was tucked beneath the deck. It also was locked. But it was cheap; Nina had not replaced it as I had suggested and I was able to loid the lock with a credit card.

I whispered into a Bluetooth mini headset that was wrapped around my ear and paired with a cell phone that Greg Schroeder had taped to my chest.

"The house is dark. No sign of movement. I'm going in."

"Roger that," Schroeder said

Schroeder wanted to be the one to enter the house while I waited in the Cherokee for his signal, especially after we found his operative in a car about a half block from Nina's house, dead, a bullet in his head. Nina was my responsibility, though. Besides, he was so agitated I couldn't trust him not to shoot up the place.

I slipped inside the house and gently closed the door behind me—I didn't want a gust of wind to slam it. I removed my shoes and waited for my eyes to grow accustomed to the dark. I tried to control my breathing, tried to remain calm, even as I removed the nine-millimeter Beretta from its holster and thumbed off the safety.

After a few moments, I tapped the microphone on the headset twice.

"Roger," Schroeder said.

We had arranged signals beforehand. Once inside I wouldn't talk, only tap. Two taps meant I was on the move and Schroeder should stand by. Four taps meant I was in position and he should bring the car up. If I got into trouble I was to yell for help.

I padded across the basement to the stairs. I crept up the stairs to the closed door at the top and cautiously turned the knob. It gave without a sound, and I nudged it open, revealing Nina's kitchen. I lingered for a moment, listening with all my might, and heard nothing except the blood pumping through my veins and the thunder of drums that was my heartbeat.

I moved in a crouch past the door into the kitchen. I held the Beretta with both hands and swung it first to my right, then to my left. Appliances winked at me in the scant moonlight that streamed through the kitchen windows. To my left was a long corridor that led to the living room, as well as one of Nina's four bathrooms, the second-floor staircase, and the front door to her house. Straight ahead on the other side of the kitchen was an arched doorway leading to the dining room.

I skated forward, my stocking feet sliding on the floor tiles, the nine leading the way, until I reached the opening. I poked my head past the arch. A chair had been pulled away from the dining room table and was set facing the living room. A figure was sitting in the chair. I recognized Nina from the shape of her head and the tilt of her shoulders. A glint of light reflecting off a smooth, glossy surface told me that her arms and legs had been bound to the chair with duct tape.

I waited, afraid to move until I knew exactly where Teachwell was. Headlights from a passing car flickered through curtains and around drapes and briefly gave the room an eerie sense of movement. For a moment I discerned the silhouette of a man standing at the edge of the large bay window. I heard his voice.

"It's him," he said. And then, "No, not yet," as the headlights swept past.

I tapped the headset.

"Neighbor, four houses down," Schroeder said. "Are you ready?"

I had a clear shot, but Nina's chair was too close to the line of fire, and I wouldn't take the chance in case I missed and Teachwell returned fire. I retreated back into the kitchen, trying hard to ignore the throbbing pain in my back and ankle, until I reached the corridor. The corridor was carpeted, and I was sure Teachwell would hear the rasping sound my socks might make on the material as I moved along.

Now or never, my inner voice said.

I tapped the headset four times.

"Here we go," Schroeder said.

I waited in the kitchen until headlights appeared through the tiny windows.

"Wait," Teachwell said. "Yes. That's a Cherokee."

I moved down the corridor, staying well clear of the walls to eliminate any chance of bumping and thumping, until I reached the arched entrance to the living room. I rounded the corner. The silhouette had shifted position slightly. It was now hunched in front of the window and peeking through the crack between the drapes.

Headlights illuminated Teachwell's face as Schroeder swung the Cherokee into Nina's driveway. It was blank and stark, yet his eyes flashed with anger and injury. Or maybe it was just the light. I braced myself against the base of the arch and sighted on the center of the shadow. My finger was slick with sweat inside the trigger guard.

"Don't. Move."

He didn't.

"McKenzie," he said. There was resignation in his voice; he reminded me of a poker player who knew he had a losing hand yet bet his cards anyway. "How did you know?"

"Fool me once, shame on you; fool me twice, shame on me."

"That's very profound."

"Yeah, I got it off an episode of *Star Trek.*"

The room seemed to breathe; I could feel cool air moving in and out through half-open windows in the front and back of the house.

"What now?" Teachwell said.

"That's for you to decide."

"Is it?"

"Drop your gun. Let me see your hands."

"Fuck that," Schroeder screamed into the headset—of course, he had heard every word. "Kill him. Shoot the fucker."

Teachwell turned his head, but not his body, and tried to find me in the darkness. The gun that I knew he had was out of my sight. He tossed words in my general direction. "You think you're clever," he said. "But I got you back. I got you back for what you did to me."

"Why don't you act your age, Teachwell?"

"I got you back."

"Shoot him," Schroeder shouted.

"If you wanted to kill me so badly, why didn't you do it when I delivered the ransom?" I said.

Teachwell's shrug was nearly imperceptible in the darkness. "The little girl," he said. "I didn't want to pop you in front of her. That would have been . . ." He shook his head. "I tried to be respectful to the little girl. She never did anything to me."

"Thank you for that."

"'Sokay."

I heard a car door slam, and seconds later Schroeder was at the door.

"What about Scottie Thomforde?" I asked.

He shrugged again. "You made him. I knew he would lead you to me."

"And Tommy Thomforde?"

"Him I shot for fun."

"And dumped his body on my floor."

"That was fun, too. I wish I could have seen your face when you found him."

Schroeder tried the door, but it wouldn't give. "McKenzie, let me in. McKenzie."

"What the hell happened to you, Teachwell?" I asked. "You were a decent guy who took a step out of line. You should have been able to get past it. How did you get from there to here?"

"Prison," he said. "I'm not going back."

"Fuck it," Schroeder said. He left the door. I guessed he was going to enter the house the same way I had. Teachwell didn't have much time.

"Drop your gun," I told him. "Put your hands in the air."

"I'm not going back," Teachwell said.

"Don't say that."

"I can't go back."

"Don't."

"You know my wife. Tell her—"

"Please don't, Mr. Teachwell."

"Tell her . . ."

He never finished the sentence. I guess he decided he didn't have anything to say to her, after all. Instead, he spun toward me.

I fired three times.

Teachwell's shadow seemed to rise up and then fell backward hard against the window.

I heard glass shattering.

And the tearing of fabric.

And nothing.

I waited—one Mississippi, two Mississippi, three Mississippi—my gun at the ready, telling myself that the man who's healthy, wealthy, and wise never rises too early. Four Mississippi and I launched myself forward, hitting the light switch that I knew was on the wall near the front door. Floor lamps flooded the room with light. I forced myself to ignore Nina and concentrate on the body in front of me. Teachwell was slumped against the wall, his back to the room. The drape was torn at the top and hanging precariously, exposing half the bay window. The window was broken. Teachwell's arm was caught on the jagged edge of glass halfway up. It appeared almost as if he were trying to pull himself upright. His gun was still in his other hand, lodged between his body and the wall. Normally, I would have kicked it out of Teachwell's reach;

that's what I had been trained to do. Instead, I left it there for the police to find. It would bolster my story later. Besides, Teachwell no longer had any use for it. I confirmed the fact with two fingers pressed against his carotid artery.

I heard Schroeder bounding up the basement steps. A moment later he was crouched against the wall, his MP7 submachine gun at the ready.

"Is he dead?" he said.

"He better be."

"What the fuck were you doing talking to him like that?"

I didn't answer. Instead, I holstered the nine and went to Nina's side. I carefully removed the tape from her mouth. She spoke breathlessly. Her first words surprised me.

"Don't worry about the window," she said. "I'll take care of it before Erica gets home."

"Are you all right?"

"He didn't hurt me," Nina said.

"Good."

Nina managed a smile and didn't complain when I tore the rest of the duct tape from around her arms and ankles. Tension and fear had caused her to perspire; her shirt was glued to her body and her perfume had a sour smell. Yet she didn't seem frightened. Perhaps she was pretending. I do it all the time. When I finished with the tape, she slipped off the chair into my arms. We held each other tight. I could feel the heat of her body. It was as if she had just completed a marathon and hadn't had time to cool down.

Schroeder was on his cell, calling the police. "Take your time," he told the emergency operator. "Fucker ain't going anywhere." He saw me looking at him, and he moved toward the front door, giving Nina and me some space. I yanked the headset off and dropped it on the floor.

"I knew I would be all right," Nina told me. "I knew you would get me out of this."

That's more than I knew, I thought but didn't say.

"It was because of Erica," Nina said. "He threatened her. He said if I didn't call you, he would find Erica. He would kill her. I would have told him no, except for Erica. I'm sorry."

"Don't be. You did the best, perfect thing."

I held her face with both my hands. Nina was still smiling, but tears were running down her cheeks onto my fingers. "I don't know what to say," she told me.

"Don't say anything."

"It really isn't that much fun, what you do. Is it?"

I could hear the whining sound of distant sirens coming closer and closer as I kissed her and held her and told her how much I loved her and how sorry I was that she had been put in jeopardy and asked her to forgive me. She blew it off. I could have canceled a date because my car broke down for all the resentment she showed me.

"It's not your fault" was all she said. Yet it was my fault—I couldn't shake the truth of it—and I told her so.

"Everything's messed up," I said.

"You did what was necessary," she said. "I can see that. Anyone could see that. What he did, Teachwell, what he did to Victoria and to me and to all the others, no one should be allowed to do that."

I kissed her again. "I must have been a helluva a guy in a previous life to find you in this one," I said.

We held each other for a long time, even after the sirens were silenced and the house began to fill with serious men demanding answers to serious questions.

Finally Nina said, "How did Teachwell know about Erica and me, about us, that we were together?"

"Someone told him."

It was a small house and not as well kept up as it should have been. I rang the doorbell, and when nothing happened I rapped on the door.

Karen opened it slowly. She was wearing a clingy blue robe that looked good on her and nothing else that I could see. "McKenzie," she said. She tightened the cinch on her robe. At the same time, she threw a glance at the room behind her as if there were something she didn't want me to see.

"I'm happy to see you," she said, but I didn't believe her. "What brings you here?"

"Hi," I said. "I hope it's not too late."

"Not at all." She swung the door wide. "Come in. Please excuse the mess."

There didn't seem to be much of a mess. Only a large soft-sided suitcase standing alone in the living room.

"Going somewhere?" I asked.

Karen casually wheeled the suitcase against the wall. "No," she said. "I've been getting my winter clothes out of storage, my sweaters and long-sleeve blouses and other things, and packing away my summer clothes before the cold weather sets it. It's getting colder."

"So it is."

"I'm glad to see you." This time she smiled brightly when she said it. I still didn't believe her. "What have you been doing since we parted? Have you found the T-Man?"

"Yes. He's dead."

"Dead? What happened?"

"Another ambush. The same as with Joley Waddell. Only this time, he was holding Nina hostage. I got the drop on him and I killed him."

"Just like that? Jesus, McKenzie. You killed him just like that?"

"No, not just like that. We talked a bit first."

"You talked? About what?"

"About why I was killing him. About how things got to that point."

"Is everyone else okay? Are you okay? Nina?"

"Yes."

"That's good, anyway."

"Sure."

Karen folded her arms across her ample chest and looked me hard in the eye. "Why are you here, McKenzie?" she said. "I'm glad you're here. I really am. But I've been flirting with you since we met and you've resisted all my charms. So why are you here now? You could've called me."

Oh, my, she's good, my inner voice told me. I paused, trying to see the words in my head before I spoke them. I didn't want to be excused later of leading or confusing her.

"The T-Man," I said aloud. "His name was Thomas Teachwell. Did you know him?" She shook her head, but that wasn't good enough for my purposes. "Did you know him?" I repeated.

"No," she said.

"Ever hear the name?"

"No."

"Are you sure?"

"Yes, I'm sure. Why do you keep asking?"

"A lot of little things, they all make sense now. Scottie returning to the halfway house the evening we went looking for him. I think you called him. While I was in Lehane's shooting pool and you were outside, I think you called him."

"What are you saying?"

"The next day we didn't hear from the kidnappers at all. Yet the morning of the following day, when Scottie called, he didn't ask if we had the ransom money. He already knew. He knew because you told him, because I told you when you called me while I was at the remote vault."

"That's crazy."

"Teachwell knew he could ambush me at Joley's because you told him we were friends."

"I didn't tell him. Scottie must have told him."

"He knew he could ambush me at Nina's for the same reason—you told him. Neither Scottie nor Teachwell could have possibly known about Nina, but you knew about my relationship with her."

"That's crazy talk. How can you blame me for this? I tried to help you."

"No, you were helping them. Victoria said there was a woman involved, a woman T-Man called 'babe' when he spoke to her on the phone. You're a babe. You told me so yourself."

"Not me."

"It's all easy to deny. No proof. No evidence. Nothing. Except—when we first started looking for the T-Man, we reviewed all the names of convicts Scottie did time with at Stillwater and came up empty. That's because T-Man, Teachwell, did his time in St. Cloud. There's no way they should have known each other, you said so yourself. But they did. How? Why? Because you were their parole officer. Both of them. I looked it up on the S3 Web site. Which makes your insistence that you don't know Teachwell a little suspect, Karen. Which makes me think you planned it all, Karen."

Karen's bag stood open on a chair against the same wall where she deposited the suitcase. She shook her head as if she couldn't believe what she was hearing and edged toward the bag.

"What are you going to do?" I asked. That stopped her. "With the money, I mean."

"I don't have the money."

"Karen"—I made a big production out of sighing like the tiredest man on the planet—"I don't care anymore. Scottie's dead. Teachwell's dead. Victoria is safe and sound. Nina's safe. All I want is my money. I'll even give you a finder's fee. Ten percent."

"Not half?" Karen moved closer to the bag. "That's what the insurance company gave you when you caught Teachwell."

"How would you know that if the T-Man didn't tell you?"

"Didn't you tell me?"

"I don't think so."

"Hmm." She stopped. Smiled. Looked up to her right. Took a small step, then another. "It seems I do remember a Thomas Teachwell now.

A glorified accountant who thought he was some kind of urban thug, who gave himself the nickname T-Man. He's one of the hundred or so parolees I supervise. There are so many that sometimes I forget who's who."

"A very plausible defense," I said.

"He was always whining about a man named McKenzie, an ex-cop who took all of his money and ruined his life."

"What about Scottie Thomforde?"

Karen was very close to the bag now.

"Scottie," she said. "He was another whiner who blamed all of his problems on someone else, who never took responsibility for his own actions. He moaned and groaned about a man named Bobby Dunston, who later became a big-time cop. I didn't pay much attention. They all whine, my parolees. Then one day Scottie mentioned his rich friend McKenzie and wondered how he and the cop could be so close."

"You connected the dots."

"Something like that."

"Why did you do it, Karen? Why did you bring Teachwell and Scottie together? Why did you kidnap Victoria Dunston?"

"So I could have a car just like yours."

As simple as that, my inner voice said.

"Why didn't you just take the money, then? Take it and run. Why try to kill me?"

"That wasn't my idea, McKenzie. You have to believe me. That was all Teachwell. I didn't want to kill anybody. Least of all you. I liked you. I really did. I even thought we might be able to get together. Teachwell was desperate to kill you. That's what attracted him to the job in the first place, the chance of hurting you, and he had the money. He wouldn't give me my share unless I helped him."

I wanted to say something—winners never cheat and cheaters never win, something like that, only pithy. I didn't get the chance. Karen dove for the bag and the .380 Colt Mustang inside it, as I knew she would. I was quicker. My Beretta was in my hands and leveled at her chest and I was shouting, "Don't you do that," before she could get her fingers around the pocket gun. She froze for a moment, then slowly brought her hands out of the bag. They were empty.

"Please," Karen said. "Please."

"Where's the money?"

"You won't shoot me, will you, McKenzie? I like you, McKenzie. I told you. I wanted to go to bed with you. From the moment I met you I wanted to. I still do. I know you want me, too."

"I said, where's the money?"

"I'm not going to tell you if you're just going to shoot me anyway."

Another theatrical sigh, and I lowered my gun just so. "Don't worry about it, Karen." I was going for weary resignation, trying to make her feel that nothing bad was going to happen. "Too many people have died over this already."

"The money is in the suitcase."

"Yeah, that's what I figured. I just wanted to make sure."

"You said ten percent."

"To hell with that."

"You said—"

"You knew when DuWayne Middleton gave up Donny Orrick it was only a matter of time before I identified Teachwell. You told him that he had one last chance to get me. You offered him a trade, didn't you? You traded Nina's name for the money. Didn't you?"

"I had no choice."

"None at all," I said.

Karen glared at me. "Take it and go," she said.

I brought my gun back up and sighted between her breasts. "Just leave you here? I don't think so."

"You said—"

"People were hurt because of you, Karen. People died." I counted seven but only listed four. "Then there was Victoria. An innocent. A child. There's a separate hell for people like you, Karen. For people who hurt children. I'm going to send you there."

"You said you wouldn't shoot me!"

"You hurt my friend's daughter—a child I love as well as if she were my very own. Did you honestly think I was going to let you get away with that?"

"You promised."

"I made a promise to Bobby Dunston, too. Not in so many words, but a promise just the same."

"McKenzie, please."

"I promised to kill the bastards who terrorized his daughter."

"You like me. I know you do."

"Two are already dead."

"McKenzie."

"You're the only one left."

"Please."

"Say good-bye, Karen."

"No!"

I squeezed the trigger.

Click.

Karen's eyes were wide and unblinking, her breath a locomotive's chug. "You, you—you're insane!" she cried.

"You betcha."

Five minutes later I was standing in Karen's front yard. My shirt was unbuttoned, and Harry was pulling at the tape that held the body wire to my chest.

"On the count of three," he said. "One, two—" and he ripped off the tape.

I cried out in pain. "That was cold, man,"

"What were you thinking, pulling a gun on her, making her squirm like that?"

"She had it coming."

"Yeah, but a good defense attorney might be able to do something with it."

"She confessed before I pulled my gun, which was in self-defense, I might add. Besides, you have the money. Now that you know the rest of the story, it should be easy for you to put all the evidence together. You probably won't even need the tape."

"It's already happening. The gun we took off Teachwell's body, it was used to kill both Scottie and Tommy Thomforde. And Schroeder's operative. Guess who bought it?"

"Karen?"

"It's not as easy for ex-cons to get firearms as people believe."

"Why did Teachwell shoot Tommy, do you think?"

"We spoke to Tommy's ex. She said that he said that he was about to come into some serious cash. We think Scottie must have let something slip when he was drinking with Tommy at Lehane's. Tommy was probably using the information for blackmail. You said it yourself—he needed money."

"That's what it's always about, isn't it? Money."

"Tell me something."

"Hmm?"

"Just between us—you were wired, you knew we were listening in. But if we hadn't been here, would you have?"

"Would I have what?"

"Killed her, McKenzie. Would you have killed Karen?"

"If I had wanted to kill her, I wouldn't have called you."

"With us waiting outside, it gave you a good excuse for not killing her. I understand. I wonder if Bobby will."

Just So You Know

Contrary to popular opinion, victim impact statements don't usually affect sentencing. Most prison terms imposed are mainly the result of plea agreements or strict adherence to sentencing guidelines. So when Victoria Dunston rose in federal court to confront Karen Studder at her sentencing, we knew that it wasn't going to accomplish much except, possibly, to give her some emotional closure. Only she didn't address Karen. Victoria stared at her long enough for all of us to get nervous about it, but then turned to the judge and said, "I have nothing to say to her. I did, I mean, I thought I did. I had a nice speech I memorized, only I think I'd rather talk to you."

"Go ahead, young lady," said the judge.

"I thought that this was going to be okay, coming to court and everything. Only it's not what I expected. I don't feel any better. I feel—I kinda feel worse because nothing bad is gonna happen to her. Not really bad, you know? I wanted something bad to happen to her. I wanted her to die."

"I understand," the judge said. I was happy that he didn't give her a lecture about the pitfalls of capital punishment.

"Daddy says that she cut a deal so that she would get out of jail. He said she'd be in jail for a long time, but that she made a deal."

"Yes."

"I know there's not much we can do about that, the deal, I mean. But there's something you can do, though, as judge, so I don't have to worry about it, so I don't have to be afraid that I'll ever see her again."

"What can I do?"

"When she gets out of prison, can you make it so that she can't live here anymore?"

"Do you mean in your neighborhood?"

"I mean in the entire state of Minnesota."

"Yes," said the judge. "I can order that."

The defense attorney objected. In exchange for her guilty plea, the federal prosecutor had offered Karen twenty-seven years and agreed to drop twenty-three other felony charges including a RICO beef, and he expected the judge to honor the deal. Only the judge reminded him that it was well within his power to amend the agreement, and if the defendant didn't like it, she could withdraw her guilty plea and take her chances at trial. "Just think how effective this young lady will be telling her story to a jury," he said. Karen quickly accepted the conditions.

It made Victoria smile for the first time in weeks. She was still smiling when her mother drove her to see the therapist later that afternoon. I told Bobby that despite the ordeal, I thought Victoria was going to be fine. He agreed with me. I never asked if he forgave me for not shooting the woman who was responsible for kidnapping his daughter, and he never said.

The day after Teachwell was killed, I returned to DuWayne Middleton's mama's house and dropped five grand in cash in the big man's lap; it caused him to spill some of his Cocoa Puffs. I told him that his client was dead, that I killed him, that it was in the papers. I told him that the contract on me was closed. I told him to pass the word. I said, "If I hear any more about it, I'll put a hit on you. Maybe save a few bucks and do it myself." He was watching Regis and Kelly at the time, so I didn't know if he was paying attention until Chopper called me a couple of days later at the St. Paul Hotel and said that the contract had been lifted, "with prejudice," he said, although I doubt that's the term DuWayne used.

Nina wanted to go out and celebrate. So we did. I took my gun. It was a long time before I went anywhere without it.